"You're reasonably good-looking."

"That's so flattering."

"And you seem to make friends fine."

"How would you know that?"

The women. The staring. All that whispering. Come on. He had to know . . . right? "Women lined up to talk with you at the Lodge."

He frowned at her. "We were at the same Lodge?"

She might call him McHottiePants in her head but some of the things the women in the Lodge said out loud . . . wow. Married. Single. None of that seemed to matter. Connor sat in a room and the gazes zoomed in on him. She noticed. He *had* to notice.

"So, of all the choices to run after, why pick me?"

His eyes bulged. *"Run after?"*

"Enough with the self-deprecating crap. Answer the question."

He whistled. "If you insist, the answer is I'm not sure . . ."

Also by HelenKay Dimon

ATTENTION: ORGANIZATIONS AND CORPORATIONS
HarperCollins books may be purchased for educational, business, or sales promotional use. For information, please e-mail the Special Markets Department at SPsales@harpercollins.com.

HELENKAY DIMON

THE SECRET SHE KEEPS

A Novel

WITHDRAWN

AVONBOOKS

An Imprint of HarperCollinsPublishers

THE SECRET SHE KEEPS. Copyright © 2020 by HelenKay Dimon. All rights reserved. Printed in the United States of America. No part of this book may be used or reproduced in any manner whatsoever without written permission except in the case of brief quotations embodied in critical articles and reviews. For information, address HarperCollins Publishers, 195 Broadway, New York, NY 10007.

First Avon Books mass market printing: January 2020

Print Edition ISBN: 978-0-06-289279-9
Digital Edition ISBN: 978-0-06-289280-5

Cover design by Amy Halperin
Cover illustration © Anna Kmet
Cover photograph © Yasmeen Anderson Photography
Author photograph by James Miyazawa

Avon, Avon & logo, and Avon Books & logo are registered trademarks of HarperCollins Publishers in the United States of America and other countries.

HarperCollins is a registered trademark of HarperCollins Publishers in the United States of America and other countries.

FIRST EDITION

20 21 22 23 24   QGM   10 9 8 7 6 5 4 3 2 1

THE SECRET SHE KEEPS

Connor Rye arrived on Whitaker Island a little after eight on an unseasonably warm fall evening. He knew the temperature was not the norm because all eleven people he met in and around the marina where the ferry landed told him exactly that. Then they asked if he, by chance, had a brother who once stayed on the island. As soon as he answered yes, the conversation took a sharp left turn into a discussion about his older sibling.

Happened every single time. Connor grew up listening to his parents, teachers, friends, and many women talk about Hansen's general greatness. Not that Connor minded . . . that much. He'd counted himself as his big brother's number one fan, or at least he had until Hansen got engaged after a whirlwind romance that started right here on Whitaker.

If island legend was correct—and he'd gotten an earful about that, too—the romance blossomed in the same cabin where Connor now stood. Probably around the two-burner stove he was leaning against.

Connor shot up straight and wiped his palms on his jeans because thinking about his brother's love life was not a thing he did—ever—and he really didn't want a mental play-by-play now.

He traveled to Whitaker for a much-needed break. He'd been on a wild roller-coaster ride of work and grief for almost two years. Twenty-three months and seven days to be exact. But who was counting?

He'd buried himself in the day-to-day operations of the family business while straining to keep everyone around him moving forward and, damn, he was exhausted. Haunted and bone tired. Completely out of gas and aching for normal.

So tonight he craved quiet. He really hoped for a few weeks of relaxation, but relaxation wasn't exactly his area of expertise. He'd settle for anything that sounded close. Tomorrow he'd set out, meet people, buy groceries, and otherwise pretend to be friendly when he felt anything but. Tonight . . . nothing.

He unloaded the last of the few provisions he'd brought with him at Hansen's suggestion. The first of many hints and interruptions over the last few days because his big brother had an equally big control issue. He'd texted up until Connor's flight took off from Washington, D.C. to Seattle, and again as Connor stepped on the ferry from Seattle to Whitaker. A never-ending trail of texts filled with instructions and a few warnings about not messing up the place. One pointed out that the house was on sibling loan only and not to get too comfortable.

Uh-huh. Noted.

Connor decided to end the day of traveling the best way he knew how: with a cup of coffee in his hand, his ass on the couch, and his feet propped up on something. The living room area of the cabin, all cozy with the cushy sofa cushions, looked like the perfect spot. He sank down into a nest of stuff piled at one end and groaned. He'd been skeptical of the wall of pillows and blankets, but he was a believer now.

He kicked off his sneakers and reached for the television remote. He would have turned the thing on but the lure of a pre-bed nap, one where he could close his eyes and not think too hard, proved to be a strong lure. He dropped his head back in the tangle of fluffy accessories and let his eyes drift shut.

The wind rattled through the two-story cabin and swooped to the loft above. Inside stayed warm, but the temperature dropped outside. If he had more energy he'd get up and start a fire. But that would have to wait for another day, preferably after he'd fueled up on island hospitality and some homemade nonairport food.

Drifting in and out, he sensed time passing but he had no idea how much. Just as he started to fall under, something jolted him awake. Wide awake. Blame the strange stillness in the cabin, but his muscles no longer relaxed.

He opened his eyes to complete darkness. Fatigue had pulled at him when he sat down but he was pretty sure he'd left two lights on, the one across the room and the one over the sink in the kitchen. Neither was on now. The steady hum from the old refrigerator had also vanished.

He jackknifed into a sitting position, then froze, trying to take it all in. An unsettling sensation washed over him. The movement of the air in the room wasn't quite right, but he couldn't name how. The confusion set his inner alarm buzzing.

He forced his breathing to slow as he concentrated on picking up any clues. A second later, a scraping sound, barely above a whisper, echoed around him. Then he heard breathing, labored and a little rushed.

Just when he started to jump up, he heard the grunt. Pain slammed into his head a second later. The hit dropped him off the edge of the couch. His knees smacked into the hardwood floor with a *thwack*.

"Shit." He blinked as he landed on all fours and fought to keep his focus.

One thought tumbled around in his head . . . *Move*.

He shoved the ottoman to the side and crawled. He'd only been in the cabin a few hours and struggled to remember the layout. The front door waited a few feet in front of him and off a bit to his right. And his cell . . . where the hell had he put it?

Footsteps thudded against the old floorboards. The attacker didn't attempt to hide the noise now.

Connor shifted, but something—no, that was definitely a someone—landed on his back. Not too heavy or with enough strength to pin him down for long but the pressure slowed his movements. He reached around to grab an arm or any limb he could reach when the attacker pressed a hand against his new head wound. One touch and the room began to spin. His arms gave out and his chest and chin crashed into the floor. The force of his yell surprised even him.

Off balance now, he wrestled for control. Repeated bouts of dizziness made it tough to throw the person off him. Everything whirled and raced as he tried to shrug and move. He choked back the need to throw up but froze when the attacker started talking. Right in his ear. Low and deep.

"Leave Whitaker now."

The insistent sound didn't hide the person's attempt to use a fake gravelly tone. A woman? Maybe . . .

Nothing about the hit-and-threaten move made sense but the buzzing in his head had his arms shaking. His body listed to one side as he fought to keep from face-planting on the floor. "I . . . what the hell?"

The pressure against his body vanished in a flash. Then he heard the thump of footsteps as the person raced away. A rush of cold air swept through the cabin. Connor dragged in enough to revive some of his energy and lift his head. Even in the relative darkness he could see the cabin door standing wide open. The pain knocking inside his brain refused to subside. A haze blurred his vision and he tried to blink it away.

Help. He needed help. Get checked. Find the attacker.

But he didn't know one person on the island. A few by name, but that was it.

He stumbled to his feet. Bobbing and weaving, he made it to the front door and slammed into the wall.

His fingers found the light switch and clicked it on. Nothing happened. The cabin up through the loft remained plunged in darkness.

The whole thing had been weird but thorough—cut the power, sneak in, and attack. But that didn't explain what the person wanted or why.

A few more blinks and his eyes finally adjusted to the relative blackness. Lumps that looked like furniture formed in the shadows. Taking slow steps, he bumped his way back to the sofa. Careful not to shift his head too much, he leaned down and patted the floor and the couch cushion in a desperate search for his cell. His fingertips knocked against it on the ottoman and it slipped to the floor.

"Mother . . ." Even talking hurt his head, so he let the front half of the grumbled profanity be enough.

A few seconds later he found the cell and turned on the flashlight, making sure to aim it away from him. The last thing he needed was a blast into his eyes. His headache would never go away after that.

Scanning the area right around him with a minimum of movement didn't make things better. He spotted the blood streaked across the floor, on his hand. He wasn't so great with blood. Seeing it made the dizziness come roaring back. He fought to stay on his feet long enough to make a call.

As the phone rang, one simple thought kept replaying in his head. He'd only been on the island a few hours and someone already wanted him gone.

CHAPTER 2

Connor hated hospitals. Hated dealing with police and answering questions. When his sister was killed all those months ago, his life split wide open. There was the man he was before and the one he'd turned into after. He went from being the younger son, working his way up in the family business, to the only one in the right headspace to lead.

In the "before," he'd been naive. Dedicated but still grounded in the belief that a healthy person needed outlets and friends. Time away from his desk and responsibilities.

Everything changed on that one day. Alexis plunged over that cliff during a hike because the one person in the world who was supposed to love and cherish her threw her off. Her psychopath of a husband wanted money and another woman, and he made Alexis disposable.

Since then Connor had disappeared into his work. With his parents broken with grief and his brother obsessed with revenge, everything fell to him. That included identifying the body and handling the police, the lawyers, and the press.

Sitting there now, with his legs hanging over the side of the hospital bed in the Whitaker Clinic's emergency room, feeling the panic swirling through the halls and the grim sense of urgency on the staff's faces, brought it all back. The sight of nurses rushing around. The smell of cleaning supplies and disinfectant.

The sensation that he would never be okay again.

Before he could muster his scrambled thoughts, the curtains surrounding his bed parted. He tried not to jump at the clinking sound of metal against metal as hooks slid on the rod.

Ben Clifford, the island's version of law enforcement, stepped into the open space. He'd been the one Connor called because Hansen had given him Ben's contact info for a meet-up once he got settled on Whitaker. This was his big brother's friend and he came rushing, asking questions and making sure Connor got in to see a doctor right away.

Things were calmer now as Ben gave a nod hello. "There are better ways to meet."

"I was thinking dinner and a movie, but yeah." Connor touched his head and felt the bandage. At least the urge to projectile vomit had subsided, but he guessed it would return with a vengeance if he moved too fast or the wrong way.

Ben frowned as his gaze searched Connor's face. "You sure you don't have an enemy back home that might have followed you here to Whitaker?"

Connor stilled. "Are you serious?"

"Let's pretend I am."

"I want to make sure I get this theory of yours." Connor waited for Ben to nod before continuing. "You think the attacker was angry with me back in D.C., so they got on a plane, then a ferry to follow me here, in order to tell me to go the hell back home."

"Huh."

Exactly. Connor couldn't make that stretch work with any amount of mental gymnastics. "I'm struggling with the logic of that."

"I get that, but logic isn't always the right motivator in cases like this." Ben stepped up to the bed. He wore jeans and a zip-up hoodie. Not the usual police gear but it seemed to fit with the laid-back style of the island on display so far. "Still, you make a good point."

"Hansen said you were practical." Connor turned his head and . . . yep, there it was. A vicious rush of bile. That's all it took to convince him not to try that again. "Any chance this is left over from the mess with Hansen and the guy who killed my sister?"

For a few seconds Ben just stood there, not saying a word. "You don't even use his name."

Connor didn't pretend to be confused. He knew who Ben meant. His sister's killer. "He's taken up enough of my family's time and energy. He was a predator and deserved the end he got."

"Can't argue with that." Ben nodded as nurses passed behind him and a few crowded at the monitor directly across from Connor's bed. "It is hard to see how this could be connected to that since that's been over for months. That guy is dead. Your brother is back home. Things have been quiet around here since the end of summer and now we're heading into winter."

"Quiet until I got here."

"Well, it is hard to ignore the timing and your head wound." Ben shrugged. "At least tying the past to this injury would be an explanation."

Connor really couldn't come up with another one. Even a business competitor gone rogue wouldn't engage in this sort of thing. "I'm usually the nonproblematic brother."

"That's what I was told." Ben turned and greeted the woman who stepped into the space with them. "Good evening, doc."

Connor recognized her as the one who'd worked on his head. She'd used a minimum of words while she checked him over. She'd been efficient and called out orders that sent everyone scurrying. She might be petite—not much over five feet—in her fifties or so, but everyone in the clinic took her seriously, and so did Connor.

She held out her hand to him. "Lela Thomas. I introduced myself earlier but you weren't really in a position to know much of what was happening around you."

They shook hands. "Connor Rye."

She winked at him. "Let's hope you're less trouble than your brother."

Her mix of confident and comforting worked for him. It also put him at ease in a place guaranteed to make him twitchy. "An hour ago I would have said yes."

"Now?" she asked.

He shrugged and immediately regretted moving. "It's an open question."

Some of her amusement faded as she snapped into doc mode. "The good news is, no concussion, but you did get rattled. You have a few stitches, and I'd like you to come back in a few days. But for now, you should get some rest. I'd prefer for you not to be alone, so you can stay here—"

"No." Connor thought about apologizing for the cracking whip of his voice but decided to pretend it didn't happen because it wasn't personal, and the doc had to know that.

She eyed him for a few seconds before talking again. "Okay. But I'd prefer if someone checked in on you periodically."

That struck Connor as a problem. "I just got to Whitaker. I don't actually know anyone here except Ben, and I met him a half hour ago."

"I have some forensic work to do at your place tonight," Ben said. "I'll put you up at Berman's Lodge, let the owner, Sylvia, spoil you, and I'll check on you a few times."

"That's not necessary." It was too much attention. Connor sucked at being coddled. Like, *really* sucked at it. People tried to help him and he had to bite back the urge to scream for space.

"It's one night," Ben said, clearly not impressed with Connor's refusal. "Then you can come with me to the cabin tomorrow and let me know if anything is missing."

"How will I know? I've been in town for about ten seconds."

"Right." Ben winced. "We'll figure something out."

The doc winked at Connor. "See? All problems solved."

Maybe it was the island air. That was the only explanation Connor could come up with for why no one seemed that upset about an attacker whacking him in the head for no reason. "Uh-huh."

"Look at it this way. You've been on the island for less than a day and have already made new friends." Doc Lela, which was what everyone in the clinic called her, checked his bandage as she talked. "That's a good sign."

She'd missed an obvious bad sign when it came to his dangerous island welcoming committee, but Connor let it slide. "There are probably easier ways to meet people than being attacked."

She smiled as she worked. "No kidding."

Ben laughed. "Welcome to Whitaker."

One good thing was that it had to go up from here . . . At least, Connor hoped that was true.

CHAPTER 3

Maddie Rhine couldn't stop shaking. She sat at her kitchen table and opened and closed her hand as she looked out the floor-to-ceiling windows to the water in the distance. It had been more than twelve hours and the fine tremor running through her fingers refused to stop. She was starting to think it never would.

She'd been terrified and in hiding for most of the last two years. Never getting a decent night of sleep. Watching over her shoulder and wrapping herself in loneliness to avoid more pain. When the killings happened on Whitaker a few months back she seriously considered running again, but the stark desperation to finally build a new life kept her rooted here.

Still, exhaustion tugged at her. She didn't have the strength to do this alone. Not anymore.

She looked at the letter resting on her table. The one she'd barely touched, except to open the envelope. She'd been trained in this. She knew not to handle the paper too much.

I found you, bitch.

Nothing subtle about that message or the angry, scribbling scrawl.

The knock at the door made her jump. Warm tea spilled over her hand. A second later that familiar racing sensation revved up inside her. The need to bolt, or at least hunt for a weapon and hunker down . . . and wait.

"Maddie?"

Ben's voice reached her through the door.

This was Ben. Safe, dependable Ben. With that cute face, he turned heads all over the island. Attractive on any scale. Tall, dark, and handsome, but to her, brotherly with a background in ass-kicking, which was exactly how she preferred the men she knew. At a distance and lethal, protective without smothering.

The one time he'd asked her out, she'd panicked. She wanted him near her as her last line of defense. Ever since her life had blown up, the idea of dating, of trusting another person on any sort of intimate level, left her cold and shaking. She stayed away and totally out of the dating pool because it was easier, safer.

She mentally insisted keeping her life and her world separate from other people saved them from harm. Some days she wondered if her reclusive existence really only made it easier for her. No attachments meant no possibility someone could hurt or disappoint her.

At the second knock, she got up and headed for the door. She opened each lock, all four. A rush of relief hit her when she saw him standing there, tall and sure. "Hi."

His eyes narrowed. "You okay?"

That would teach her to think her fake smile worked. "It's been a long morning."

"Same here." He glanced into the empty room behind her. "What's going on?"

She'd called him and asked for his help, something she never did. She knew she *could*, but she hadn't, until now. She tried not to drag anyone into her messed-up life. "I have a problem."

"Okay." He glanced behind her again. "Which is . . . ?"

Right. Invite him in, like a non-messed-up person might do.

It took a lot for her to abandon her safety precautions, but it was either call him to come to her or go to his office, and the latter felt like a big step compared to her usual loner life.

"Sorry." She gestured for him to come inside.

"Maddie, we've known each other for almost two years."

She had no idea where he was going with this, so she cut him off. "We've barely seen each other."

"You're the town's answering service. You handle all the calls for my office."

Is he always this chatty? "I do that from here. Alone. Without anyone around."

He made a face that suggested he was weighing his words and trying to find the right ones. "That's my point. Not once—ever—have you asked for anything.

The fact you did today is a clue something is very wrong. Just tell me what it is so I can help."

She appreciated the straightforward attitude. He was known for it and it relaxed her now. Maybe that would make the next ten minutes easier, though she doubted it.

She walked over to the table and pointed at the handwritten note. "This."

He frowned as he followed her. Lines appeared across his forehead and the scowl deepened as he studied the piece of paper. "What the hell is this?"

"It was on my porch. Slipped under the mat." Peeking out as if to taunt her. Just like the last two. "I've been getting notes, on and off, for a few months."

His eyes widened. "And you waited until now to tell me?"

"It's complicated." She couldn't exactly start a conversation with, *Maddie isn't my real name and my whole life is a lie*, even if that would be the one true thing she ever said while on Whitaker.

"Maddie." His tone sounded half exasperated and half stunned.

"There are things you don't know about me." Things no one could know. Her past loomed right behind her. Things had changed and she should be safer now to venture out and meet people, but the notes suggested otherwise.

"Your former handler called me."

Handler.

"I . . . you can't . . ." That's all she had. A sputtering mess of words that made no sense as a sentence.

He reached out but didn't touch her. "Easy."

Memories of her former life smashed into her, stealing her breath. She stepped back, ramming her calf into her favorite chair. "What are you talking about?"

"Evan Williams." Ben nodded.

Anxiety jumbled and churned in her stomach. "I don't know who that is."

He stared at her for a few extra beats without saying a word. "Wildflower at night."

He knew the name. The right name. And the code.

"How?" She forced that question out as a whisper.

While she fumbled and shifted her weight and generally wanted to crawl under the house and hide, Ben stayed calm. He didn't fluster or panic. The evenness of his voice wrapped around her. "When everything unfolded a few months ago, and the killing, and you were, well, secretive. I thought . . . you know, maybe . . ."

The wince gave him away.

"Did you think I did it? You thought I killed some random guy who showed up on the island?" *Good lord*. Talk about a communication misfire.

He backed up that wince with a guilty shrug. "You disappeared for a few—"

"I was hiding!" And she was yelling now. It wasn't fair to Ben but the idea that he thought she could kill someone almost doubled her over.

"On the island?" Shock sounded in his voice. "Where?"

Was that really the point? "I'm not telling you that. A hiding place ceases to be a good hiding place when you announce where it is."

"Okay, look." He held up his hands in mock surrender. "I don't know details of what happened in your past. I got the call from Evan, pitched as an informal talk between law enforcement professionals, that digging into your identity was . . . I believe the phrase this Evan guy used was *frowned upon*."

"Sounds like him." She could almost hear Evan's deep voice, all commanding and half threatening. Technically he no longer protected her or worked on her behalf, but he called and checked in often. Offered his support and insisted she get back in the program, just in case. They'd known each other ever since her life changed, and had become friends of a sort. Or the only sort she had.

"Where are the other notes you received?" Ben asked.

"I sent them to Evan."

"I can call him but I think we both know you took photos."

She rushed forward, stopping right as her hand brushed his sleeve. Then she dropped it. "I don't want to do this."

Ben being Ben, he stayed focused. He didn't reach out for her. He wasn't the type to crowd or plow through boundaries. "What?"

"Live in hiding anymore."

His forehead wrinkled in what looked like confusion. "Okay. But I was talking about Evan and the photos."

"It's all mixed together."

Ben visibly took a long breath. "Slow down and tell me how."

"Do you know who Evan is?" She didn't see Ben as part of some big conspiracy against her, but her past life had been complicated and dangerous and she didn't recognize either of those things until she walked into a disaster.

"I know he's with the Marshals Service and I know what the people there do. I don't think you're a fugitive on the run or I'd have agents all over the island." He hesitated. "So I'm guessing you need protection of some sort . . . or did. It would explain the hiding and minimal contact with people on Whitaker, except for your voice through a telephone."

He understood enough to get what she was about to say. It was more of an explanation than she'd given anyone in years. "I can't go back into hiding again. Not back to the kind where my life isn't my own and I don't decide anything."

"I can appreciate wanting . . . I don't know the right word. Freedom? But this is a serious situation."

"Which is why I called you. You're the police. This is your job."

"I'm not even sure what I'm dealing with other than this one threat. Seeing the other notes won't answer that fully, but they might help." He glanced at the paper again. "So would a little bit of background on why you needed Evan in the first place."

That was asking too much. She didn't have the energy or will for a full show-and-tell. "Please don't make me regret calling you."

"Just the notes then."

It was a fair request but still she mentally debated it. After a few seconds when she was sure her fingers would refuse to move, she pressed a few buttons and sent the copies to Ben's phone. "There you go."

"Thanks." He let out another breath, this one louder and longer. "I hadn't planned on sharing this, and I don't know if it's related, but we had an attack on the island last night."

She froze. Everything inside her stopped. She even held her breath. "What?"

"Hansen Rye's brother is in town and staying at the cabin. He was—"

"Wait, who?"

"Connor."

"That's not right."

Ben's gaze narrowed. "Excuse me?"

"But . . ." Her breath whooshed out of her. "The cabin is empty."

"Was."

"Was?"

"As in *not now*. I get the impression him coming to Whitaker was a last-minute decision, but he's here."

Her mind spun. The facts she knew . . . *thought* she knew. Empty, as in no one there. Locked and off-limits to anyone. She had asked around. She made it her business to know who came on and off the island and why. How had she missed him?

She swallowed hard but it didn't help. Her voice still sounded rusty. "You said something about a brother?"

Ben shook his head a bit and continued to stare at her. "Yes. His name is Connor."

That would mean that she . . . She closed her eyes and reached for her last bit of control. Breaking down in front of Ben was not in her plans today.

"Is he okay?" She gulped in air now. She could feel it stuttering and rattling around in her chest. She was two seconds away from wheezing.

"Maddie, is there something I need to know here?"

She doubled over with her hands on her thighs and wondered if that blow-in-a-paper-bag thing she'd seen on television worked. "That Whitaker is about as safe as a medium-sized city right now," she said, trying to make a joke.

He helped her into the kitchen chair without commenting on her current condition. "We're not quite at that danger level yet."

"If you say so." She threw her head back and stared at her ceiling. After a slow ten-count, some of the nervous energy pinging around inside her vanished.

"Trust me."

"His brother." The words came out in a harsh whisper.

"Do you know what happened at the Rye brothers' cabin?" he asked, sounding half like he'd formed an answer but wanted to test her anyway. "Were you there?"

Silence screamed through her. "Hmm?"

He shook his head. "I think you heard me."

"Do you need to get back . . ." He never stopped shaking his head, so she figured she could not fake her way out of this. She pulled her scrambled thoughts together to form a sentence.

"Maddie."

"What? You just told me about the cabin. I'm surprised. That's all." Not the best avoidance tactic, but it was all she had at the moment.

When she looked at Ben again, she found him staring at her with a look somewhere between concern and complete confusion. Of course he was. He had eyes. He had to recognize stress-lying when it played out right in front of him.

"I'm thinking someone sneaked into the cabin, heard Connor there, and panicked."

She hated how close he was. "I'm sure it was a fluke thing."

"Uh-huh." He finally broke eye contact and glanced at the letter. "I'm going to bag this note up and get it analyzed."

That's not what she expected him to say, but she was grateful for the reprieve from questions. This part she knew by heart, unfortunately. "There won't be any fingerprints. There weren't on the others. No prints. Paper you can buy anywhere."

"With that kind of thorough assessment you could probably do my job."

Dealing with criminals all day sounded like the ultimate nightmare to her. "No thanks."

He leaned against the table, facing her. "Now that you're breathing better there are a few things we need to do."

"Like?"

"You should come into the office to work until we can get a handle on who is sending you these notes." When she started to protest, he kept talking. "The more you're around people, the harder it will be for anyone to get to you. Being out here, by yourself in this house all the time? Not good."

"It's my home." She rented it, but then, everyone on Whitaker rented. It was a private island owned by a mysterious person who didn't pipe up and identify themselves. But she loved the cottage. It was out of a fairy tale with the flower trellis around the door and a garden out back, just off the patio. She'd loved it from the second she saw it.

"You need security," he said.

"I have a gun." One that she might start carrying on her at all times.

He rolled his eyes. "So do I."

That news caught her off guard. "I thought the town board didn't let you carry one."

He crossed one ankle over the other. "Protocol changed. Do you know how to shoot?"

"I learned that when I learned about how to handle a threatening letter. It was all part of the protection training. I had a handbook and everything."

"Really?"

"Evan insisted." She'd logged in hours at the shooting range and in self-defense classes. She had no idea if either would help if danger really knocked on her door, but she could at least sleep an hour or two at a time now without waking up in a panicked sweat.

"Right." He stood up again. "Come to the office with me and we'll work out a plan."

She shouldn't ask because it was weird for her to show too much interest, but she needed to know. "I don't think you answered me. Is Hansen's brother okay?"

"Connor is fine." Ben was too busy bagging up the note to look at her.

"Good."

He looked at her with an expression that dared her to lie to him. "But you'll need to apologize and explain."

Her muscles stopped working. "What are you talking about?"

He glanced at her. "Really?"

She tried to deflect because how could he know? "About an accident or whatever? Probably kids. Or someone got confused. I've just been here . . . you know. Answering phones."

"That's a lot of rambling."

"You're intimidating." *Sort of.* He might be fair and listen and not be a jerk, but he still had a job to do and she may have tiptoed a wee bit over the line of what was appropriate when it came to welcoming the island's newest visitor.

He'd surprised her and she panicked. Ben got that part right. After fifteen minutes of debating how to get down from the cabin's loft and get by the guy, she'd been wound up and the breaker switch was right there, so . . .

"This isn't my first day on the job, Maddie."

Her mind raced with justifications and excuses. She blocked them all out and went with denial. "So?"

"I know guilt when I see it. You saw a guy and panicked, or you were in that cabin for a reason. Either way, Connor got hit." He nodded in the general direction of her front door. "Grab your coat and let's get this over with."

She refused to believe he was some sort of human lie detector. "I didn't do anything."

"You're really going to play it this way?"

Until the very end . . . or until she came up with a logical reason for what happened last night. "I think so. Yes."

"This is going to be interesting."

CHAPTER 4

A half hour later they pulled up to Whitaker's version of a police station. It was a small office attached to the far end of the building that housed the library. Maddie knew from her few previous trips in to pick up extra work assignments that it consisted of a small reception area, Ben's office, a conference room, and a jail. The old furniture and peeling green paint on the walls only added to the Whitaker-doesn't-have-much-crime ambiance.

Ben walked through the empty reception area, past the table piled with years-old magazines, and headed straight for his office. She joined him because she didn't think she had any other choice. With each step she followed Ben's lead and stripped off her winter coat. By the time they slipped into his office he had his off and was reaching for hers to hang them both on the coatrack in the corner.

Her hands froze in midair with the coat dangling off her fingers when she realized they weren't alone. He was in the chair in the corner. *Him*. The guy with the bandage on his head. The same one who was about to cause her a lot of trouble because she'd panicked. An uncharacteristic move that she would now pay for, and she deserved it, but that didn't mean she wasn't going to try to run from this like she did everything else in her messed-up life.

As they entered the room, he got up. She'd snuck a peek at him from her hiding position in the loft last night. Now the full impact hit her. Tall and lean with short black hair that fell in loose strands on his forehead, begging for someone—not her, of course—to brush it back.

He, who looked too good for her comfort.

He wore one of those thin, down coats that hugged his shoulders and highlighted his trim waist. The jeans dipped low on his hips, showing off a sexy torso . . . no, not sexy. Long. Lots of people were built like that, all perfect and angled with muscles popping out here and there. No big deal.

Not that she noticed, but *come on*. The body and that face. The pronounced nose and deep-set eyes. He could cut glass with that chiseled chin.

"Do you have news . . ." The man's gaze bounced to hers and those dark eyes widened. "Sorry. I didn't mean to ignore you."

Ben snagged her coat and hung it up with his before heading for his desk. "Connor Rye, this is Maddie Rhine. I just noticed your names sound alike."

She glared at Ben for that.

"Hi." Connor smiled at her as he held out a hand in greeting.

She hadn't figured out how to make any of her muscles move again. Lost in the buzz humming in her brain, she stared at Connor's long fingers. Since when were a guy's hands hot?

"Uh, okay." His eyebrow lifted as he started to drop his arm. "Not the handshake type?"

"Sorry." She grabbed for his hand and pretended not to notice the smile that came and went on his lips as she squashed his fingers in a death grip.

"No problem."

So much for playing it cool. "You look like Hansen."

She just blurted that out. Still held his hand in a clench that made him wince and came out with a brilliant gem like that. She finally let go of his fingers and stepped back. Rammed her butt right into the doorknob and gasped.

This was turning into a hell of a day.

Connor looked from her to Ben. "Just so I'm forewarned here. Are there any other Korean, or Asian people at all, on Whitaker or am I it?" When neither of them answered, the hottie nodded and started talking again. "I'm just trying to figure out if everyone is going to assume that I'm related to the last Asian guy who lived here because of some weird stereotype or for some other reason."

And now he thought she was an ass. Possibly a racist one. Maddie silently congratulated herself. This was going really well.

"First, you're one of three, though I'm not sure how good our residents are at telling Korean from Japanese or any other group because, you're right, they seem to think all local Asians are related." Ben slid into his leather chair and nodded for Connor to retake his seat.

Connor sighed. "That's bullshit."

Ben nodded. "Agreed. And, second, you actually are related to Hansen. I knew that when we met last night because you said it. Also, because your brother sent me a photo of you so that I could welcome you when you arrived on Whitaker. You are one of the few people on Earth who actually looks like their photo, by the way."

"Fair enough." Connor glanced over his shoulder at her. "And you?"

Lines of babble filled her brain. She had to wade through all the words and ridiculous verbal wrong turns to find something to say. "Ben told me you were here and had some trouble last night. I made the connection from there."

"Maddie answers phones for the police department and a bunch of businesses in town." Ben looked at her then stared at the empty chair next to Connor. Ben didn't say another word until she sat down in it. Then he glanced at Connor again. "The longer you stick around the island, the more likely you'll hear her voice on the other end of the line."

"Okay." Connor didn't sound angry or confused or . . . anything really. His deep voice rolled out of him with ease, all confident and sure.

That made her twitchy.

She shot up and out of her seat again. "I should get back to work."

Ben cleared his throat. "Maddie."

She got to the door in two steps. Nearly ran into it before turning around to face Ben again. "Hmm?"

"Is there anything you want to say to Connor?"

She glanced at Connor and the confused expression on his pretty face. She feared that every time she saw him from now on or heard his name the phrase *Connor McHottiePants* would run through her head.

Yeah, no. "Nope, I'm good."

"Maddie." Ben's voice sounded louder and more firm this time.

Her shoulders fell and she stopped fumbling with the doorknob that refused to turn. "Stop saying my name."

"I have all the fibers and prints. Sooner or later I'll—"

"No!" Not this way. She wanted to slide into it. Let some of Connor's anger burn off first.

Connor's frown took on a need-to-run tinge. She recognized the expression because she saw it in the mirror most mornings.

"Should I come back?" Connor started to stand up. Got halfway there. "This feels like a personal thing."

Wait, no. Not personal. She had an explanation. It was . . . a mistake. Being neighborly and she misfired. Very simple. "It's not."

Ben sighed. "It's about you."

Connor sat back down hard enough in the chair to make the wood creak and groan under what she was guessing was a pretty impressive butt.

His eyes narrowed as he stared at her. "What's going on?"

She thought about counting to ten or inhaling really deep to find some well of hidden courage inside her. She didn't have time for either because Ben opened his mouth, and she knew whatever tumbled out would not be good for her. She held up a hand to him. "Stop."

Ben sighed again. "Let's get to it."

She shifted a bit so she stood just off to the side of Connor's chair. "It was me."

Connor stared at her. "What was?"

"What happened. It was me." There, she said it. Now he could—

The staring gave way to a frown. "I'm lost."

This was Ben's fault. She glared at him. "I told you this was the wrong time."

"You never said that and you would be incorrect if you had." Ben tapped his pen against his desk blotter. "Do it now while you can still fix this, or I take over."

Connor cleared his throat. "Could someone—"

Maddie dove in, cutting Connor off midsentence. "I was walking by and thought someone was breaking into the cabin. You could have been dangerous, so I got out of there fast."

Okay, none of that was true. She'd gone to check out the cabin as a potential hiding place, in case she needed one in the future. With Hansen she'd watched the house for more than a week. Lately there was some activity when one of the town's two cleaning services stopped by.

It only took twenty dollars slipped to the cleaners' receptionist to find out the person who hired the service wasn't Hansen. That got her thinking. Notes. Someone possibly hiding on the island and watching her . . . and the idea for a cabin search took hold.

"I don't . . ." The sort-of smile vanished from Connor's face. "Wait . . ."

She really didn't want to. She wrapped her fingers around the doorknob instead. Pressed until her palm ached from all the clenching. "So, we good here?"

"No," Ben said.

Connor turned in his chair and faced her. "What are you telling me?"

She tightened her grip on the knob. "Nothing."

"I'm going to say your name again," Ben warned.

As if she needed two angry men staring at her right now. "This is why I don't like coming into the office."

Ben snorted. "Is it?"

"Hold up." Connor raised one finger. That was it. Just one. "Could we get back to the part where you admitted to breaking into my cabin?"

Just her luck that he was the type to have no problem keeping up with a purposely disjointed conversation.

"I saw movement and wanted to scare off whoever was inside your cabin, the same cabin I thought was empty and not really yours."

The words landed and sat there. No one said anything. Both men continued staring at her in silence. She had to fight to keep from shifting her weight around. Or bolting from the room.

"So, yeah. That happened." She cut off the words there, figuring less was better in this instance.

Connor leaned forward in his chair. "You were playing the role of informal neighborhood watch?"

"Sure. That sounds reasonable, right?" After years of pretending to be someone else she should be better at lying. She vowed to work on that skill to prevent scenes like this in the future.

Connor didn't blink. "You're the one who hit me?"

"I was trying to help." That wasn't even a little bit true. With the notes, she was on edge but he still deserved an explanation. Shame she didn't have a good one. Except panic. She lived in that state now.

No one had stepped off the ferry and stayed on Whitaker in more than a month. After all the press died down about the killings that happened here over the summer and the unexpected visit from a US Senator, gawkers came. She hid from all of them, not wanting her location to be exposed in the rush of interest about the people on Whitaker, who they were, and why they came here. She ignored every reporter and refused to read any of the special interest stories or the news about what happened.

Then he came—McHottiePants—right as she'd started to relax, and she hadn't been ready.

Connor hadn't stopped watching her since she made the semihonest, half-rambling admission of sorts. He leaned forward and balanced his elbows on his thighs. "I was napping on the couch."

And that was a good point. One she couldn't really get around without accidentally tripping up and spilling far too much about her past. "Yeah, well. Criminals are weird. We've all heard stories about them robbing banks and dropping their driver's licenses."

Connor looked at Ben. "Does that sort of thing happen a lot on Whitaker?"

He shook his head. "Never, actually."

She fiddled with the knob, turning it and ignoring the clicking sound it made. "I thought I was helping."

"By hitting me with . . ." Connor's eyebrow rose. "What was it?"

"A piece of firewood." From his yard, but she left that part out because they had enough facts floating around without adding more.

"Jesus," Ben whispered under his breath.

"Not a hard hit." She felt like that qualification should be out there.

"Lucky me." Connor didn't show any emotion. "And once I was on the floor you jumped on my back."

Ben whistled that time. "This story keeps getting better and better."

She tried not to be distracted. Breaking eye contact with Connor didn't prove to be that easy anyway.

Something about McHottiePants held her spellbound. "Self-defense classes."

"More like a wrestling class."

"As I said. It was an honest mistake." Time to go. She got the door halfway open. "Back to work."

"Wait a second." Connor's voice sounded flat but it still came with a punch of power behind it.

She sighed at him. All she wanted was to get out of there before guilt pushed her into babbling about her entire life story. Something she never did and didn't want to start now. "Any chance we could chalk this up to a terrible mistake and move on?"

His eyes widened. "I have four stitches."

That explained the bandage. The guilt thumped and kicked at her. It bubbled up inside her and had her looking at Ben. "You didn't tell me that."

"This is my fault now?" he asked.

Okay, no. But . . . She gnawed on her lip as she returned her attention to Connor. To that bandage. To the cute way his hair stuck up a bit around the edges. "Does it hurt?"

"Yes."

She really thought she'd grazed his shoulder. The room was dark and her nerves had been bouncing around and all that tension had her patience pulled tight and . . . man, she really did hurt him. The thought of that made her feel sick.

"The goal was to stun you so I could run out." Not that the explanation made his pain any better, but it was the truth.

"Well, that worked." He sat back in his chair again, not breaking his focus. "Did you come in when I was sleeping?"

That sounded better than the truth about her being there, lying in wait and searching the place for both hiding place potential and for answers on who paid the cleaning people. "Sure."

"Then how did you get in the door?"

Well, damn. She was hoping he'd skip over that part. "Hmm?"

"The cabin, Maddie." The calm returned to his voice.

Are we on a first-name basis? She guessed she couldn't really bark at him about that under the circumstances.

Her mind raced to fill in the blanks and make sense of her previous *really* bad choice. But that was the point. She'd messed up. Fear and panic fueled her actions and he'd paid the price. That sucked and her chest ached at the thought of hurting him.

There wasn't a reasonable way to explain the unreasonable. So she fell back on semitruths again. "I walked through the front door. Like people do."

"It was locked."

She thought she saw a flicker of a smile cross his face before he shot back that answer, but that couldn't be right . . . could it? "Are you sure?"

"I live in Washington, D.C. I lock my door like people who live in cities do."

Okay, yeah. She was out of her league. He didn't let things go. She needed to get out of the room now, think, and come up with . . . something. "That's very smart. Good for you."

Then she did what any woman in her place would do. She ran out of there, leaving her coat and most of her dignity behind.

CONNOR STARED AT Maddie's back as she raced out of the office, letting the door bounce against the far wall, and bolted through the reception area to the outside. As far as exits went, it was impressive.

A lot about the scene he just survived struck him as impressive. Like her. She was about five-foot-seven of pure fire. The dirty-blond hair, wavy and long, framing her face like a halo. Those big green eyes. That not-to-be-ignored ass.

And she had a swing that nearly knocked him out, which brought his mind back to his main concern. "She just walked out of here."

Ben made a humming sound as if he were trying to figure out what he just witnessed. "Yep."

"In the middle of the conversation." That was the part that had Connor stumped. Did she really think she could run and he would let this drop?

Ben nodded. "That did happen, yes."

"She didn't even apologize."

"It kind of sounded like she expected you to thank her for watching after the cabin, but I agree that part was fuzzy."

Right then Connor decided he liked Ben. He didn't play games or throw his weight around. He looked and sounded as stumped as Connor was. But none of that explained Maddie's actions. "What the hell is going on with her?"

"Admittedly, even for Whitaker that conversation was weird." Ben shuffled the folders around on his desk and took out some papers. "Look, you can press charges and—"

"I'm not doing that." Connor knew panic when he saw it. He'd failed his sister but he'd learned to look for the signs now. He had no plans on being the world's savior, but he had made a personal vow to step in when and if he could. There had been enough death on his watch.

"Because?"

"There's obviously something strange happening with her. Around her. I'm not sure." He sensed whatever drove her to attack him was bigger than what they could cover in a few minutes during this conversation. "And, not to be an asshole here, but I don't exactly trust the police."

"Subtle."

Connor shrugged. "It's a learned response."

He'd spent so much time after his sister's death trying to get someone, anyone, to believe she had been killed. Hansen had gone to extremes and gotten himself in trouble. Connor had tried to follow the rules. Back then he'd marched up the chain of command and told his story. Doing the right thing in the right way earned him nothing. Not a damn thing.

"I get you have a past, but I think you'll find I'm not a total dick," Ben said.

Connor guessed that was true but he wasn't ready to admit that yet. "Maybe."

"But about the charges. You have every right. Upset or not, what she did was not okay."

Connor waved the words off. There was no way he was putting a tough woman who was trying not to be scared in a jail cell. He refused to be that guy. "I just want to know why she went wild." A thought hit him and he froze. "Wait, did she and Hansen have some sort of problem?"

"I doubt they ever met."

That made absolutely no sense. "He lived here for a year. I've been here for about a day and have had two run-ins with her."

"She's . . . reclusive. People tend to say they just saw her but can't describe what she was wearing or what she was doing. She has a unique ability to blend in." Ben looked like he wanted to tell Connor more, as if he were waging some internal battle, but then shook his head.

"You know that's unusual, right? I mean, I get that Whitaker works differently from other places, but her level of self-protection and wariness is a bit much."

"There are things in her past, things that are none of our business, that make her very careful of people and promises. She's not the type to let people in."

Just as Connor suspected. "Join the club."

Ben nodded. "Then you get it."

"Her antipeople stance is fine with me so long as she doesn't come into my house and attack me with a stick again."

Some of the seriousness strangling the room eased away as Ben laughed. "Not an unreasonable requirement. But at least we know there's not some angry person out there, trying to hurt you."

"I should be able to sleep in the cabin tonight without a knife under my pillow."

Ben's smile grew. "Aren't you the risk taker?"

"One question."

Ben braced his hands on the armrests of his chair. "Shoot."

"Any other women on the island in the habit of breaking into a random stranger's house and attacking him?" Because even Connor had his limits.

"Excellent question. We'll see, won't we?"

CHAPTER 5

Connor liked Sylvia Sussex the second he met her. She owned Berman's Lodge, the combination historic hotel and favorite eating establishment in the middle of Whitaker's downtown. She was also the head of something called the Whitaker Board, but when he asked for details, she just rolled her eyes. And that made him like her even more.

From the way she nodded and waved to everyone who walked into the open dining room, she seemed to know the whole town. The details she whispered as each person passed their table suggested she knew a bit of gossip about everyone. Also a very useful trait.

When people got too close to him or failed to hide their attempts at listening in on their conversation, her protective instincts kicked in. She glared them into submission. He admired that skill.

His quick stop to grab the few things he'd left in his room last night turned into an early lunch. She insisted and he didn't argue. She might only be fortysomething but she had the same order-him-around skills as his mother. Maybe not to his mom's professional level of bossiness, but still impressive. Sylvia decided and he didn't get a choice. Since he was eating what might be the best lemon chicken of his life, he decided to agree to almost anything Sylvia said from here on out.

"Does Ben have any idea who might have broken into the cabin?" Sylvia asked as she motioned for the server to bring more water.

Connor hesitated, knowing his answer could drive them straight into awkward territory. "We know."

She set the knife down on the side of her plate. "Already?"

"The person admitted it . . ." He searched for the right words but quickly gave up. "Sort of."

"I'm confused."

He scanned the quiet room. The lingering stares stopped and a few heads turned. The sounds of clinking silverware and the mumble of chatter suddenly filled the room. This island had a quaint charm but no one could call the residents subtle. "That makes two of us."

The server appeared at the side of their table. Sylvia waited until the man refilled their glasses and set down a basket of what smelled like freshly baked bread. "Are you always so cryptic? Because people around here love mysterious things. You'll hear a lot about how people keep to themselves and don't gossip."

He couldn't help but smile at her sarcastic tone. "And?"

"None of that is true."

"How very charming." He'd traveled here from D.C., a town not exactly known for its ability to keep secrets. There was always some anonymous source ready to tattle on someone.

"Let me put it this way." Sylvia balanced her elbows on the edge of the table and leaned in. "You've been on Whitaker for one day and I've received over twenty texts about you, seen a few emails with your photo attached—"

"Uh . . ." Yeah, that didn't sound funny.

"—and answered about a hundred questions in this dining room, which is packed, and you'll notice no one seems to be eating."

He took a second to look around the room. The same heads that turned away from him before did it again. Forks rose in unison from each table. "What are they hoping will happen?"

"They're waiting for you to do something."

The topic made him squirm in his chair but the easygoing back-and-forth conversation with Sylvia relaxed him again. Her smile eased his growing discomfort. "Like?"

"I have no idea."

"I'm thinking I should have vacationed in the Bahamas." He'd thought about just that last night as his head pounded and he silently cursed Hansen for suggesting this was a good place to relax. He'd spent so much time focused over the last two years, not dating and not doing any of the usual hang-out-with-friends stuff he did before his life changed.

"Nah." She reached for the bread and tore off a piece. "Another island would be boring compared to here."

"I could use some calm." He was pretty sure that qualified as the biggest understatement of his life.

"Then you *are* in the wrong place."

Before he could shoot back a sarcastic response, a shadow fell over their table. The person came up from behind him, and he had no idea from where. He glanced up . . . and there she was. Again.

Maddie waited there, wearing jeans and what had to be the biggest coat ever made. It swamped her body. She frowned as she spoke. "Hello."

Sylvia lowered her bread to her plate. "Maddie?"

"I thought you never went out," he said because he really didn't know what else to say.

Maddie shifted until she stood right in front of their table, blocking their view of the rest of the room. "I know Sylvia."

"Wait." Sylvia looked from Connor to Maddie and back again. "Have you two met already?"

"Maddie has an unusual way of welcoming visitors to Whitaker."

She threw him an expression that suggested she wouldn't mind cracking another piece of wood over his head before turning and smiling at Sylvia. "May I get my mail, please?"

Sylvia looked like she was going to say something. Even opened her mouth and closed it again before finally nodding. "Sure."

She got up and walked out of the dining room. Connor watched her go before turning to Maddie again. "Do you live here?"

"On Whitaker?"

The clueless act had to be on purpose. There was no way she misunderstood that question. "You're killing me."

She frowned at him. "What?"

He honestly couldn't read her at all. The need to study her and learn more tugged at him, but he ignored the sensation. He had enough problems without taking on hers. But it wouldn't kill him to be friendly, so he tried again. "Do you live at the Lodge?"

"I have a house." And that was it. She didn't offer another detail. Hell, she barely looked at him.

"You're not big on polite conversation, are you?"

"No."

He conceded this round to her. "Then I'll finish my chicken."

He chewed and felt her staring. He refused to give her the satisfaction of looking up. If she wanted his attention, she could ask for it.

After a few seconds, she sighed at him. "You don't need to tell people about the . . . you know. The thing."

He glanced around and saw the entire room was looking at them, so why not give them a show by continuing the conversation? Let them guess the topic.

He lowered his knife and fork to the table and swallowed the last bite of chicken. "The thing?"

"What happened in the cabin." She lowered her voice to a whisper. "The misunderstanding."

Holding a conversation with her would take some practice. He couldn't lose focus for a second. "Is that what we're calling it?"

She hit him with a second sigh. This one telegraphed the clear message that she thought he was annoying. "I really don't want to be the subject of gossip."

"Me either."

"Then we're agreed."

He had no idea what understanding she thought they just reached. "I didn't—"

Sylvia walked back into the room, holding two letters and what looked like a magazine. "Here you go."

"Thanks." Maddie took the small bundle and pivoted around Sylvia. She was out of the room and out of sight a second later.

He didn't know where she'd skidded off to and didn't try to guess. But something about her . . . maybe her obvious dislike of him . . . had him thinking about her. "What's her story?"

"Some people have their mail sent here. She's one of them."

"Is that really what you thought I was asking?" Connor doubted it because he could see Sylvia's knowing smile.

"You've been here one day and already have a crush?"

Nope. He was not playing this game. "It was a question, not a proposal."

"Quiet. Loner, possibly lonely, but I don't know. She doesn't share."

That sounded familiar. The description fit him, too. "Did something happen to her?"

"Something happened to everyone, Connor."

He had to admit those were wise words. "Good point."

"If you're going to ask her out—"

"I'm not." He could be attracted. From a distance. Silently. That was as close to wading into Maddie's world as he intended to go.

"Okay, but just know that you didn't pick an easy road."

He tried to ignore the comment. He really did. Picked up the bread and took his time buttering it. But Sylvia let the words sit there, twisting in his head, and he finally snapped. "Meaning?"

"She's alone for a reason. Don't push. Whatever happened . . . I don't know. Just be careful. She's not fragile but she's wary."

He was well aware of what happened when someone pushed Maddie. Hell, he'd been sitting quietly in his house when she took offense and whacked him. He still couldn't make those pieces fit together in his head. No matter how much he wanted to drop it and walk away— far away—he worried that might not be possible.

But he didn't intend to share the truth about that weakness with anyone. "I don't have any intention of getting in Maddie's way or of getting to know her better."

Sylvia nodded. "Sure."

He hated that. "What?"

"I heard what you said."

He didn't love her tone. "But you don't believe me."

"Not even a little."

CHAPTER 6

The next day Maddie hovered on the small front porch of the cabin for close to ten minutes. She lifted her hand to knock but stopped. Tried and halted. Repeated the cycle three times until her indecision annoyed even her.

She debated dropping the box and running away. Thought about turning around and going back home without leaving the box because this whole thing had been a reckless and silly idea. Like, epically bad. She'd made it clear last night that whatever talking, meeting, seeing each other was going to happen while Connor was on Whitaker had ended. They were done.

That was the right answer. No more contact. She would treat him the same way she treated everyone else on Whitaker, as if he were invisible. She was not a make-new-friends type. She didn't see a need to change that lifelong characteristic now.

Just as she turned to make her great escape, the front door opened. A curse slipped out before she could choke it back.

No one could have luck this bad.

She shifted again, this time to face him. The *him* who seemed to haunt every minute of her life since he landed on this stupid island. The stark white bandage stood out against his skin. That part still made her cringe, but that was sort of why she'd showed up today.

Hovering in the doorway, Connor looked every inch of the McHottiePants label she'd tagged him with in her head. The faded jeans and gray long-sleeve T-shirt fit with the relaxed island surroundings. The ruffled hair and socks suggested he'd been doing something low-key before she arrived . . . and now she wondered what.

In truth, he made standing look sexy, which just ticked her off.

Confidence pounded off him . . . and that lopsided smile had her a little breathless. She blamed her lack of recent exercise for the last part. She refused to admit his cute face played any role in her raspy breathing thing.

He held her gaze for a few seconds, then looked down. Before he could say anything, she shoved the box into his midsection.

He grabbed on to it with a small grunt. "Uh."

"It's for you." She was pretty sure he knew that, but just in case.

He lifted the lid and his face lit up with a smile a second later. "Cake."

"It's a pie."

"Is this an *I'm sorry I hit you with a log* cake?" He sounded downright amused by the idea.

"It's still a pie." And it wasn't really a log, but she refused to debate that because no part of that story reflected well on her.

"Yes, I see that."

"Pumpkin." He could probably see that, too, but maybe if she pointed it out, he'd stop talking about cake.

"Right. The traditional apology pie flavor." He nodded before closing the lid again. "Much appreciated."

Right as she made up her mind to drop off the pie and bolt, he stepped back in the doorway and gestured for her to come inside. That struck her as friendly but unnecessary. They weren't friends. She really didn't have any of those. Had learned the hard way not to.

"Maddie?"

The sound of her name in his deep, rich voice made her blink. Yeah, she hadn't been expecting the low rumble or the way it made everything inside her tighten in anticipation.

She didn't move. Well, she didn't until he held the door open with his elbow while balancing the box in his hands and lifting his eyebrow in question at her. She took the no-handed move as a challenge.

Game on.

She slid just inside the door and stopped. Leaned her back against the wall and let her gaze roam over the room. From the overstuffed couch and leather ottoman in the center of the open room, to the kitchen area stretched along the far wall, to the ladder leading up to what she knew from her check of the place held a loft bedroom.

Last time she was in the cabin she'd had exactly three minutes to look around before he walked in and she hid. Now she noticed the place had a cozy, warm feel to it. Not updated but very lived-in with the frayed material on the couch's armrest and missing handle on one of the kitchen cabinet doors.

"I really was trying to watch over this house." The words slipped out before her brain cells kicked in.

"When you broke in?"

"We agreed it was my version of neighborhood watch."

"I think we both know that's not true." He walked past her to the kitchen and set the box down on the narrow island. He balanced his hands on the counter on either side of it, as if weighing whether he should dive in or not. "I remember what you said to me when you jumped on my back."

He stared at the box but she was pretty sure he was talking to her. "You misunderstood."

"Uh-huh." He didn't blink. "I haven't told you what I heard yet."

"Right." She really wished he would let the whole mess from last night go, but she doubted that was going to happen, so might as well sit down.

She took in the pillows spread out on the couch and the blanket rolled into a ball and shoved into the corner. That's where he'd been sitting when she . . . well, she didn't want to dwell on her bad choices and picked the ottoman instead.

Sitting there, her mind turned to the other night. The smell of pine and the light buzzing sound from the old refrigerator. Memories slammed into her, one after another. When he'd walked in, her heart pounded and her insides shook. Common sense ran out of her and she moved on surging emotion. Stupid, irrational panic.

She looked at the bandage on his head now and regretted every minute and every decision she'd made from flipping the switch to cut the power to hitting him.

"But the more I think about it, I'm convinced the whispered warning wasn't meant for me." He came around to the front of the island and leaned against it. "I think you want someone else—not sure who—to leave the island and leave you alone."

He was a lot cuter when he wasn't trying to analyze her. "Are you always difficult?"

"You think I'm the problem here?" He folded his arms in front of him. "Interesting."

He was and she hated that. She'd spent every minute of the last two years of her life trying to separate from other people. Not get involved or care. Not take a minute to stop and assess all she'd lost.

Something about him made her rethink everything from her need to be alone to the belief she could live without any sort of intimacy. Turned out that was a miscalculation. The more the days passed without touching or feeling anything, the more she yearned for both.

An hour after she learned his name, she researched him. Conducted her usual litany of online searches and collected information. Assembled a little file on him and everything. The next step usually involved categorizing him as a nonthreat, then forgetting him. But with him, she'd kept searching.

Finding photos of him proved easy. He was a big-time engineer turned businessman in Washington, D.C. Ran a family operation and won some sort of award last year for innovative thinking. Not bad for thirty-three.

But none of that explained why he popped up on an island where people went to start over or disappear completely. "Why are you on Whitaker?"

"I needed a break."

That seemed legitimate, but it didn't tell her much. "From what?"

"My life."

She stared at him, looking for any sign that he was messing with her. She recognized other tells. The little things that reached through that firm outer shell of confidence. A hint of exhaustion around his eyes. The subtle slump of his shoulders. The way he watched her with a mix of wariness and interest.

He lifted his chin in her direction. "Why are *you* on Whitaker?"

The steady flow of heat moving through her since she stepped inside his house shut off. That fast, the mental vault inside her slammed shut. "I live here."

"Huh."

She hated that sound. "What?"

"I think we just traveled in a tidy conversation circle that made sure I didn't learn a single thing about you." He dropped his arms to his sides and stood up straight. No more leaning. "That's an interesting skill you have."

"Ben told me you're not pressing charges. So . . ." She waved her hand at the box on the counter. "Hence the pie."

"I guess we're done talking about ourselves."

Good, he got it. She almost sighed in relief. "Yes."

He glanced over his shoulder at the box, then back to her. "And you brought this dessert because you're sorry."

She slipped her keys out of her pocket and passed them from one hand to the other. "I am."

The jingling sound echoed through the cabin and bounced off the high ceiling.

He looked at her hands before settling his gaze on her face again. "Do you want a slice?"

"I don't like pumpkin."

He smiled but quickly swallowed it. "But you made it for me?"

"You look like a pumpkin guy."

"I have no idea what that means."

That made two of them.

The truth was the cookbook she'd found in her rental had the recipe and the market had the ingredients. So she made it. She really thought this was more about the gesture than the taste. And since she'd never made a pie—any pie—before, she hoped he didn't base his willingness to forgive on how edible it was.

Time. To. Go. She stood up. "I should get home."

"Dinner."

"Huh?" The keys fell out of her hand. She ducked down and grabbed them. Stood up so fast again that the room spun on her.

"It's the meal most people eat in the evening."

She regained her balance and wrapped her fingers around the keys, refusing to let them go. "No."

His eyebrow lifted. "No, you don't eat it, or no, you don't want to have it with me?"

"I'm not looking for a boyfriend."

He didn't try to hide his smile this time. "Wow."

Okay, that reaction, the aren't-you-impressed-with-yourself tone—all of it was unnecessary. "What?"

"I wasn't offering to be your prom date."

"I . . ." Her mind blanked out. She tried to rewind and replay their conversation. "But you said . . ."

"Dinner." He took a couple steps across the room. Got within about five feet from her, then stopped. "Look, I barely know anyone on the island. You don't get out much. We seem like a good match."

Don't get out much? It was true, but would a bit of tact kill the guy? "Who told you that?"

"The loner thing? Call it an educated guess."

"I do better alone." As soon as the words were out, she realized she'd admitted to the exact thing she had tried to avoid saying.

She shook the keys in her hand. The clanking soothed her but she had no idea why. Probably had something to do with the idea of freedom. She held the keys, and she was closer to the door, which meant she held the advantage.

"I've spent the last two years trying to convince myself I didn't need anyone either, but I was wrong." With each word he grew more serious.

His sister. Her murder. Maddie had read bits and pieces, all filtered through articles designed to gain attention. She knew the ending because the murderer had been caught on Whitaker a few months ago, but that didn't mean she knew anything about Connor. Not really.

She kept repeating that mantra in her head. She might empathize and feel for him, but she wasn't the only one in the room throwing up a defensive wall.

"Okay." That seemed like a neutral response, so she went with that.

"Tomorrow at the Lodge. Six." He finally broke eye contact and walked around the kitchen island until it sat between them again. "You don't have to come. Just know I'll be there and you're welcome to join me."

"Not going to happen." She didn't have dinner. Well, she did, but not with him . . . or dates . . . or whatever he was proposing.

He opened the box and studied the pie. "Is it me or all humans?"

"Yes."

He glanced up at her with a smile that disappeared as quickly as it came. "Then I'll leave you alone."

He moved around the kitchen, grabbing a plate and a fork. Clinking and clunking things together. Then he went back to the butcher block that held the knives and pulled out a small one. He worked with ease, as if the room were a comfortable place for him.

Her comfort zone consisted of a toaster oven.

"Good." He'd stopped paying attention to her but she felt like she should say it.

"Great," he said without looking up.

This is what she wanted—no attachments. Drop and run. Fast and far.

She got the whole way to the front door, keys locked in her hand and her mind ready to move on to the next thing she had to do today, but one question nagged at her. He pricked and poked on the inside of her brain until she looked at him again.

She needed an answer. "Why me?"

He was too busy moving the pie plate around as he shifted the blade, increasing and decreasing the size of his anticipated piece. "Excuse me?"

"You're reasonably good-looking."

He froze before slowly lowering the knife. He didn't lift his head to stare at her until the blade rested against the countertop. "That's so flattering."

"And you seem to make friends fine."

"How would you know that?"

The women. The staring. All that whispering. Come on. He had to know . . . right? "Women lined up to talk with you at the Lodge."

He frowned at her. "Were we at the same Lodge?"

She might call him McHottiePants in her head but some of the things the women in the Lodge said out loud . . . wow. Married. Single. None of that seemed to matter. Connor sat in a room and the gazes zoomed in on him. She noticed. He *had* to notice.

She also wanted an honest answer. "So, of all the choices to run after, why pick me?"

His eyes bulged. "*Run after?*"

"Enough with the self-deprecating crap. Answer the question."

He whistled. "If you insist, the answer is I'm not sure."

She snorted. "Really?"

The question earned her an eye roll. He shot her one, then started talking. "Except that the sadness I see in your eyes looks familiar."

Sadness? Nope. He didn't get to do that. He knew her for five seconds and was drawing conclusions and pitying her. She hated all of that. "Don't analyze me."

"Wouldn't dream of it."

"The answer is still no." She didn't elaborate but she doubted she needed to. The dinner question hovered over them.

He went back to cutting the pie. "Understood."

"You're frustrating."

He lifted a huge wedge of pie—the equivalent of at least three actual servings—and slipped it onto the waiting plate. "Want to go back to talking about my stitches and how I got them?"

Yeah, he was never going to let that unfortunate little incident go.

She opened the door and sent him what she hoped was a look that telegraphed they were even and done. "Goodbye, Connor."

"I'll see you around town, Maddie." He dug into the pie and made a satisfied humming sound as he gave it a try.

The look on his face was kind of cute. All smiling and happy and appreciative.

She refused to be swayed. "You're not getting the last word."

He swallowed the bite. "Yes, I am."

CHAPTER 7

She made a friend.

A random guy who had been on the island for all of ten seconds. A nobody. Nothing interesting about him. Average in every way except that she moved in on him immediately. No games with this one. No pretending. Right to flirting and helping.

Brought him a fucking pie.

Little Miss Needy couldn't control herself. Always investing in the wrong people. Looking in the wrong places for security. Ignoring the warning signs and moving in.

She never learned.

All that careful planning unraveled watching her now. Subtlety had failed. She needed to know this was serious. Deadly, even. Ratchet up the pressure and send a physical reminder of just how shitty her life could be. Make her understand that her behavior, once again, forced them into this position. The way she toyed with men. Her refusal to be honest.

Her life was no longer in her hands. No more games or tricks.

After all that time and the hours of watching her, it was time to move in. No more trouble. No more running. No other men. Ever.

She would pay for this.

CHAPTER 8

"You're standing outside." Sylvia delivered that bit of wisdom as she pushed the hood of her jacket off her head and stepped into the circle of white lighting the entry to the Lodge's double front doors. "And staring into . . ." Sylvia squinted as she looked out over the front lawn, illuminated by strings of dainty lights wrapping around and traveling up the trees lining the driveway. "Nothing. Unless you see something I don't."

Maddie didn't think she'd ever get used to the genuine, homey, too-much-chatter conversation the people on Whitaker liked to engage in. They didn't just say hello. They commented on the weather or what they just ate. Lots of words, all to convey one thought—*hello*—because, for some reason, a plain hello was never enough.

The island thrived on gossip. It fueled every moment and every interaction, even as the people who lived there delighted in reassuring each other that the residents kept to themselves here. Maddie blamed the divorce from reality on the seclusion. Being cloistered together, see-ing only each other for days, weeks, even months at a time, made everyone search out ways to stay alert and keep active.

Unfortunately, her dating life—or the lack of—had moved up on Whitaker's *Most Interesting Topics* list. Lucky her.

"I needed some air." The answer, short and clear, should stop any other—

"The rain just stopped but the temperature dropped below forty and the wind is icy cold," Sylvia said, plowing forward as she shifted to the side, letting the unusual parade of people shuffling in and out of the Lodge pass by her.

"But the air is outside, so here I am." There, that should do it.

Maddie loved Sylvia. Her charm and the way she stepped in to assist, coddle, and apply a bit of pressure when needed, never looking for anything in return. She functioned as the island's welcoming committee, mostly because she ran the one place on Whitaker that any tourist, and they didn't get many, needed to find if they wanted a bed for the night.

She also made the perfect cup of coffee and a banana cream pie that made Maddie's mouth water. She seriously considered going inside just to grab a slice.

"Maddie."

Right. The unwanted conversation. The one that clearly hadn't ended yet. "Hmm?"

"That's not a great explanation."

Yeah, no kidding. "I'm just trying to . . ." What was she trying to do? Part of her hoped a wave of common sense would crash over her and send her running back home. The other part fought the urge to run her fingers through her hair.

She'd worn a dress tonight. Outside. In public. Sure, she'd piled on some leggings and threw on rain boots that screamed sensible, not sexy. But the dress. Black and knee-length and the only one she now owned. The closet in her former life had been filled with skirts and dresses and high heels. Now she lived in jeans and whatever shoes guaranteed she could kick the hardest and run the fastest.

"Maddie, honey." Sylvia snapped her fingers in front of Maddie's face. "I sense it's been a while but there's no reason to be nervous."

She'd lost the thread of the conversation because she thought they'd slipped into a discussion of boots. "What are you talking about?"

"It's only a dinner. Eating with a handsome man doesn't need to produce this much stress." Sylvia ended the comment with a wink.

Well, she could unwink, because no. "I'm not here for Connor."

Sylvia bit her bottom lip in what looked like a failed attempt to hide the smile that overtook her. "Okay."

Maddie blamed Connor for this. Him and his stupid pretty face. His stupid invitation to dinner. His stupid . . . When her mind circled back to his face again, she cut off the thought with a hard blink. "Wait, why do you think I'm here for dinner?"

"I saw Connor sitting alone and asked him to join

me but he said he might have company. And now I see you out here, fidgeting and panicking." Sylvia didn't even try to hide her amusement this time. "I put two and two together."

"It's not a date." Maddie said the line more out of habit than anything. She'd repeated the mantra during the entire walk to the Lodge from her house. That constituted a mile of muttering the same four words to herself.

Yeah, nothing weird about that.

Sylvia looked past her, toward the floor-to-ceiling windows in the dining room. "He hasn't ordered yet."

She would not look. She would not look. "Who?"

Sylvia let out a labored and not-so-quiet sigh. "Your nondate."

"Ah, yes. Him." Mr. McHottiePants. The guy she should have avoided from the beginning. "Any idea when he's leaving Whitaker?"

Sylvia shrugged. "Go inside and ask him yourself."

"That feels like a violation of the Girl Code. You should be helping me."

Sylvia reached around Maddie and opened the Lodge's door. "I am."

CONNOR GAVE HER fifteen extra minutes before he scanned the menu, determined to eat alone and not care. He could take a hint. It's not as if she'd agreed to his proposal . . . or suggestion, or whatever this whole food thing was.

Not interested. Got it.

The whole invitation had been a shitty idea anyway. She'd snuck into his house, hit him, threatened him, and then got grumpy when he expected an apology. Paying for her dinner after that might send a weird message.

Just as he got to the menu's entrée section, he sensed a shift in the room. Looking up, he spied her hovering in the doorway to the dining room. Half in, half out and holding a raincoat that looked only slightly smaller than the oversized one she'd worn yesterday.

He wasn't the only one who noticed her fumbling around but not actually moving. The entire room did a collective stop-and-stare.

Her hair did him in. Pulled back off her face with stray sexy strands curling down next to each cheek turned a rosy pink from the night air. And the boots. Olive and rubber, stopping just below her knees with a dress that hit right above.

The look totally worked for him.

He stared at her until she stared back. For a second their gazes held and she didn't move. A bit of the color left her face before she threw her shoulders back and took on that I'm-going-to-burn-this-place-down bravado she shot at him when they met in Ben's office.

Yeah, good times.

Her eyes narrowed for a second before she plastered a neutral expression on her face and came over to the table. She didn't sit. Nope, not Maddie. She loomed over him, standing at the edge with a death grip on her coat.

There might be some sort of social guidance about how to have dinner with someone who looked like she'd rather be at a funeral, but he didn't know what it was. So he went with the safest option. "Hello?"

She glanced at the folded napkin resting on his unused plate. "You haven't eaten yet."

"No."

"You're still wearing the bandage on your head." She nodded in his general direction.

"I still have the stitches."

"How does it feel?"

Since she was biting on her bottom lip and looking wary about his response, he softened the truth. "Much better."

She hummed before responding. "Interesting."

He had no idea why that would be the case. "I love these little talks we have."

"Right." She spun around and headed back for the doorway.

"Damn it," he mumbled under his breath as he shot to his feet. In a few steps he stood in front of her, blocking her path but giving her plenty of room to maneuver around him and out of the dining room if that's what she wanted to do. "That was a joke."

"I know."

Almost every sentence she uttered confused the hell out of him. For some reason, that intrigued him . . . and convinced him that he was in even greater need of a vacation than he originally thought. "Then why are you leaving?"

She leaned in and lowered her voice. "I don't like the staring."

So she'd noticed. He couldn't deny it, but he hadn't meant to make her twitchy. "The dress and the boots. I liked the combination. Kind of cute and—"

Her eyes narrowed again. "What are you talking about?"

He was starting to wonder. "Your outfit."

She held her jacket away from her body and looked down before glaring at him. "What's wrong with it?"

"Nothing." Not one damn thing.

"I don't understand you."

They finally found something they agreed on. "Yeah, same."

"I meant the room. Everyone in here." She had her back to the room but she wasn't wrong. Most of the eating and talking had stopped when she walked in.

He thought about pointing out how standing in the middle of the room for no apparent reason would only ratchet up the problem but he motioned to his now-empty table instead. "Ignore them."

"That's not so easy."

"They're staring at both of us and you still need to eat. So, dinner?"

She nodded and walked past him. Didn't even stop as she muttered, "This isn't a date."

"Okay."

It took another ten minutes for her to get settled, sip some water, and scan the menu. As far as awkward dates went, he'd had worse. But, as she pointed out numerous times, this wasn't actually a date anyway.

Before he could come up with a half-intelligent sentence to break through the crust of ice growing between them, she looked up. "The lemon chicken, right?"

"Excuse me?"

"The other day." She folded the menu and set it down on her plate. "You said it was good."

"You remembered."

She sighed. "Connor . . ."

"I meant that I didn't think you heard me when I praised it." She had him spinning in circles. The sensation kept him dizzy and off balance, and he didn't hate it. "It's very good."

The waitress broke into the stilted conversation, took their order, and left. Connor almost hated to see her go. With the food-choice part out of the way, that left the slog of conversation until the plates arrived. He'd never felt this on edge with a woman, as if one tiny step would send him sailing into her *off-limits* category.

She leaned back in her chair with her elbows balanced on the armrests. "You're a workaholic."

"Interesting conversation starter." But not wrong. When she didn't say anything else, he decided to go with it. "Who told you that?"

"I read it."

"That's written somewhere?"

"I studied up on you."

He took a drink of water because his brain picked that moment to shut off. He had no idea how to respond without running into trouble and took a few stalling seconds to figure it out. "Because?"

She shrugged. "A smart woman checks on a man before they have dinner."

"Okay . . . yeah, that makes sense." It did. She should investigate him. Ask around. Carry mace. Whatever she needed to do to stay safe. She was fine with him, but she had no way of knowing that and shouldn't take his word for it.

"So?"

He wasn't exactly sure what question he was supposed to be answering. He guessed the work one. "I've spent the last few years building up the family business."

Some of the wariness around her eyes faded. "To keep yourself busy."

He debated going around this subject. If she studied up on him, she knew the horror his family had lived through. Hell, if she'd read a paper or watched one of the two true crime shows that had highlighted his family's pain, she knew. "We all have our coping mechanisms."

She opened her mouth, then closed it again. The stress seemed to leave her shoulders as she leaned forward. "I'm sorry."

"Thanks."

"I can't imag—"

"You can't." The response shot out of him. He winced, but it was too late. While the words floated out there, he exhaled, trying to find the right way to explain, then move them quickly to another topic. Any other topic. "Look, I didn't—"

"No, you're right." She slid her hand onto the table. Her fingers traced over the spoon, then the base of the knife. "It's not my business. Not my life. I couldn't possibly understand. No one else could."

"Basically."

"Sudden, tragic, shocking loss stays with you. The questions. What you could have done. If you'd been faster. If you'd seen the truth earlier. It eats at you."

The churning came back, that anxious dropping feeling that repeated in his stomach. He'd been fighting it for years, pushing it away and burying it under work and concern for his parents. But as she spoke, with each word, tamping it down grew harder.

"Yes." His agreement came out as a strangled whisper. He knew she heard him when she nodded.

"Your salads."

The comment didn't register until the waitress set down the plate of greens in front of him. Like last time, she stayed only long enough to take care of business, refill the water glasses, and go.

"I've debated the right protocol here. Should I pretend I don't know what happened to your sister?" Maddie asked while she moved the croutons around with her fork.

"No." He hated that. He also hated the words of comfort. Really there was no right way or good way to approach him on this subject. The man who killed his sister killed a piece of every family member. Stole their sense of normal, forever tilting it.

"I'm assuming you worked yourself silly to avoid dealing with her death and are now trying to recuperate." She ended the thought by taking a bite of the salad.

"I dealt with her murder," he said, noticing that she swallowed hard enough for him to see her throat move. "What?"

"Really?"

Before he could answer, a visitor popped up next to Connor. The intrusion cut off the uncomfortable topic, and he appreciated that. The older man stood there in a flannel shirt and down vest, both in shades of brown. Connor hadn't met the older man yet and tried to pin down his age. It proved impossible despite the snowy white hair and slight hint of a bend in his shoulders. He could be anywhere from sixty up.

He nodded his chin at Connor. "Are you Hansen's brother?"

"His name is Connor," Maddie said as she lowered her fork to the side of her plate and made the informal introductions. "This is Paul."

"Hi, Paul." Connor assumed the other man would leave after the brisk handshake but that didn't happen.

"My back steps need some work."

Not the usual greeting and not one Connor could maneuver through without some assistance. His gaze traveled from Paul to Maddie and back again. "I'm sorry, what?"

Paul shoved his hands in his vest pockets. "It started as a squeak but now the board gives when I step on it. Could crack at any time."

Connor peeked around the man's slim build to take a quick look at the rest of the dining room. He couldn't be the only one who thought this was odd, but the lack of response from the other diners suggested he might be. "Okay."

"Between the step and loose railing . . ." Paul demonstrated . . . something . . . with his hands before giving up and shrugging. "Well, you get it."

He really didn't. "Do I?"

"Paul, I'm not sure—"

Paul waved off Maddie's comment and kept his gaze locked on Connor. "You're handy like your brother, right?"

He and Hansen ran and were part-owners, along with their parents, of a lucrative design firm back in Washington, D.C. They handled engineering, building design, and construction. Multimillion-dollar contracts. He supervised crews and job sites. Won awards and was responsible for more than a hundred employees. People tended to think of him as a desk guy, the one behind the scenes, making sure every deadline and regulation was met, but yeah. "Related, yes. Handy? Only sort of."

Paul's eyes narrowed as if he didn't like the tone or how long it took Connor to answer. "What does that mean?"

Fair question. "What kind of work are we talking about?"

"Come over tomorrow and take a look. You can work while I make some coffee."

Connor thought he'd be giving more of a diagnosis of what needed to be done than doing it. He didn't have so much as a hammer with him on Whitaker. "I'm not actually a handyman."

Paul made a strangled sound. "What are you?"

"An engineer."

"There you go." Paul snorted. "They build stuff, right?"

"Paul." Maddie's tone sounded like a warning.

Which he ignored. "Bah, he's fine. Young enough and he doesn't have that useless look like some do."

Connor was pretty sure that was a compliment, but who could tell? "Thanks?"

"I'm up by five."

He couldn't possibly mean that . . . "In the morning?"

"There's no need to waste the day." Paul nodded. "I'll give you a break and see you at six."

"Wait . . ." But Connor was talking to air and looking at Maddie's amused expression. "What just happened?"

Maddie reached over to the bread basket and grabbed a roll. "I think you agreed to fix his steps and railing."

"Did I use any of those words?"

A smile lit up her face. "You didn't have to. I think it was assumed before the conversation even started."

He was half tempted to agree to get up at five for this ridiculous back-steps adventure if it meant he got to see that unguarded look of pure joy in her face again. "I'm not going to let him pay me for work I'm not really qualified to do."

"Oh, I doubt he plans to pay you."

Words stuttered to a halt in Connor's brain. It took another few seconds for the cells to fire up again. "Free labor I'm not qualified to perform, and at sunrise. Great."

"Consider it being neighborly."

"This is Hansen's fault."

"I'm afraid so."

A thought hit Connor. "You're a recluse. How do you know everyone?"

"First, stop throwing that word around. I'm careful, not a live-off-the-grid type who shoots people who step on her lawn."

"That's an interesting distinction."

She handed the bread basket to him. "Second, Paul is on the Whitaker Board, which is a sort of demented island council—you don't want to know—and from time to time, I get called in to handle some work for the board, like writing the meeting minutes."

"My brother forgot to fill me in on all of this, including how I'd get roped into free labor for strangers."

Her smile only widened. "While you're at it, I have a kitchen cabinet that needs some work."

"I bet you do." But he couldn't be mad. Helping out was one way to meet people. Helping her guaranteed spending more time with her. "We'll see how dinner goes first."

"You're paying." She toasted him with her water glass.

"Of course I am." When she glanced at him over the rim of her glass, he explained. "I was raised in a family where people dive for the check as soon as it hits the table. I'd say it's cultural, like an Asian thing, but my dad—who is very white—partakes in the tradition."

She slowly lowered the glass. "So, if I tried to pay?"

"Amateur move. They would mow you down to get to the bill first."

"That's endearing."

He found it exhausting. Add in cousins and aunts and uncles and you had forty people body slamming each other for the check. It could get rough. But he was the expert, which meant he planned to pay. "It's a game. And you can't win it."

She made a humming sound. "That sounds like a challenge."

"We can have dinner ten times and I will win every time."

Her eyebrow lifted. "That's a lot of nondates."

Right, because they weren't dating. Neither of them wanted that. "But I don't hear you saying no."

"I don't like to lose."

This he could handle. A healthy rivalry that ended with lemon chicken. "But you will."

"We'll see."

CHAPTER 9

The rain stopped its on and off spurts during the two hours in which they ate and drank coffee. After a bumpy start, the conversation flowed. She avoided talking about his sister and what she suspected was a severe case of unresolved grief on his part, and really avoided any talk about her life. They stuck to Whitaker gossip and landmarks around the island, places he should see and the ones he should avoid.

Connor proved to be charming and kind of adorable whenever she joked about his early morning handyman date with Paul. The whole idea of it made her smile. He could have said no or made a scene with the older man, but he hadn't. He accepted Paul's order to be at his house and took the whole muddled mess in stride.

She found that way more attractive than she wanted to admit.

After they finished eating and walked through the dining room while everyone gawked and more than one pointed, Maddie debated taking advantage of the break in the weather and walking home. The mix of air and quiet sounded good until she remembered the newest threatening note. So when Connor made it clear he'd abandon his car and join her on the walk, she agreed to a ride. Now they walked the last few steps up to her front porch.

The air carried the scent of pine and wet grass. Water splashed as she tapped her boots in the puddles on the rough stone drive leading up to her house. She could walk around them, but why?

"You could have dropped me off," she said without looking at him.

"Just slowed down enough for you to jump out the window?"

She smiled in the darkness, comforted that he couldn't see her do it. "You know what I mean. I'm guessing this is another family tradition. Some form of required chivalry."

"It's about safety." He zipped his jacket up high against his neck. "I don't take risks."

Well, crap. She'd managed not to step on this mine all night and now she tripped headfirst into it. "Right. I didn't mean—"

"Maddie." He stopped at the bottom step up to her porch. Let one foot rest on the edge of the stair above as he faced her. "You don't have to worry that everything I say is about my sister. I'm not weighing your words, waiting for you to mess up."

Tension eased out of her. She hadn't even realized she'd been holding her breath until he talked.

Now that he opened the door on the topic, she tiptoed a bit closer to the emotional wall she sensed he didn't even know he'd built up around himself. "Her death must shape everything."

"But I can't let it *be* everything I remember about her. She was so much more than that."

A sweet yet painful comment. She knew he was right, but she also doubted recovery worked like that or ran according to a plan.

"What was her name?" She knew the answer but wanted to hear him say it.

A faint smile crossed his lips. "Alexis."

"Pretty."

"She was amazing. Fierce and smart. The best of the Rye kids. No question." He pushed up onto the next step then the one after until he stood on her porch.

Whatever signal he meant to send out got jumbled in her head. She couldn't tell if he wanted her to stop or talk more. "Did you think her husband was dangerous before he . . ."

"Killed her?" He exhaled. "No. She'd be alive if I did."

He stood there, waiting as she crossed the remaining distance between them. The light on the porch bathed his face in soft white, while the world around them remained plunged in darkness.

The closeness. The quiet. The threats.

She waited for the panic to come, for the rush of anxiety to overtake her at letting anyone get close. But nothing. Being there with him, alone with her fingers just inches from his, brought a wave of warmth crashing over her. All her training to run and hide, to keep her location and identity secret, melted at her feet. Even out of witness protection she'd been careful not to let her guard down . . . until him.

He shifted his weight and she heard a crunching sound under his foot. Rocks or dried leaves, probably. She didn't know what and didn't care until he bent down. When he stood back up again, he held something.

He lifted his hand toward her. "For you, I guess."

One glance down and reality whooshed back and slammed into her with the force of a careening car. The white rectangle registered in her brain right as she reached out and knocked it from his hand. "Don't touch that."

An envelope. Another one.

She glanced around as she shifted. Her back hit the wall of her house as she strained to listen for any stray noises over her heartbeat thundering in her ears.

"Maddie?" He stood in front of her now with his back to the front yard. His hands held her forearms in a gentle touch. "Hey, look at me. What's going on?"

That familiar trapped sensation overtook her. The energy racing around inside her had her scooting away from him. She fumbled with her keys. The jangling rang out in the silence as she strained to get each lock opened and step inside.

"Wait here," she shouted as she ran into the house without him.

"I don't understand." He followed her to the doorway and stopped, staring at her all wide-eyed and concerned.

He moved fast but she moved faster. Nothing hampered her movements and panic fueled her. She'd left all the lights on, so she could see every inch of open floor from the living area through to her dining room and kitchen.

She tore around the small space, grabbing supplies. "I need to save the evidence for fingerprints, even though there won't be any."

"What are you talking about?"

"Nothing." She brushed by him again, moving outside to pick up the letter by the corner with her now gloved fingers. "It doesn't matter."

He could have pummeled her with questions or taken over. Instead, he watched her, sticking close enough to put his body in front of hers, if needed, but letting her lead. "It clearly does."

Within seconds, she grabbed the envelope before it could blow into the wet grass or tumble into the darkness where she couldn't find it. Her hair fell out of its holder and swooped in front of her face. The sleeve of her oversized jacket slipped down over one shoulder.

She couldn't imagine the sight she presented. A frenzy of action and fear. Even now she could feel her heart thudding as she concentrated on calming her breathing.

The truth hit her with a wallop—he needed to go. She couldn't stand the thought of something happening to him because he'd tied himself to her. She'd started all of this with the idiotic break-in. Without that, they likely wouldn't have met and he'd be chatting with Ben or Sylvia right now, safe somewhere, and not watching a wild woman drip water all over the entryway of her house.

"It's late." A ridiculous excuse to kick him out, but she didn't have the energy to come up with anything else.

"It's not even nine."

"You don't understand." She had to stop pretending the threat was meant to scare her. This, another note so close to the first, felt like an escalation. This was serious, scary stuff and she didn't know where the danger would come from next, or if the words would turn into the promised deadly action.

"If you're hinting for me to leave because you want to be alone or are sick of my company, fine. But we both know this is something else. You're upset. Something is going on. Just tell me." He stared at her with damp hair and skin that had paled a bit since he picked up the envelope.

She had him worried. She could almost see him planning her protection. Him, the guy who lost his sister in the most horrible way.

"I don't want to drag you into this." And she meant that. He'd survived enough.

"What?" His eyes narrowed with confusion as he gestured toward the note in her hand. "And what is that? Help me understand what's going on here."

"A threat."

Every handsome feature pulled taut and the life zapped out of his eyes. "What?"

When he didn't move, she knew she'd lost her opportunity to get him away from this tonight. "You're not going to leave, are you?"

"Not after that comment."

Standing there, out in the open, made him more vulnerable than being inside with her. She tugged on his arm to drag him into the living room. "Come in."

Neither one of them said a word as she locked the locks. Multiple, including the dead bolt and the one that slammed into the floor. With each flick of her wrist and spin of a knob, she felt the heat of his stare. He followed every movement until they stood at her kitchen table with the note lying on a placemat in front of them.

Carefully, she opened one end of the envelope. She knew how to touch it to minimize her exposure to the paper. How to preserve evidence, though there never proved to be any of that left.

No, her stalker or would-be attacker or nightmare from her past—whoever this was—was very careful. She knew the basics of letter forensics thanks to some training, but this person knew how not to make a mistake.

She opened the folded piece of paper. The words sent a new wave of panic flooding through her.

Get rid of him or I will

Connor bent down to get a closer look then stood up straight again. "What the fuck?"

"How did . . . ?" She spun around, half expecting to see someone else standing there, watching them.

"Who would do this?"

Right now the *who* didn't matter to her. Placing him in the line of fire did. "I swear I never meant for you to get involved or be in danger."

She'd pushed her luck with dinner. Hell, she blew it before that. When everything exploded over the summer and the press showed up, she should have run again. Her safe space had caved in around her, and all of her naive thoughts about being able to move on and be normal shriveled. She knew better but she'd stayed, and now Connor might pay a price for that hubris.

"In what? I don't even understand what's happening." His body froze. "Wait. Am I the *him* in the note?"

"You. Maybe Ben. You've both been here. I haven't really seen anyone else. Not a he anyway." But every cell inside of her screamed that it was Connor. She'd implicated him in her messed-up life. "I don't know, but I'm betting it's you."

"Do you know who's writing the notes?"

"No."

"Really?" He lifted his hands slowly, as if giving her a chance to move or bolt. When she didn't, he rested his palms on her forearms and brushed them up and down along her jacket sleeves in a soothing gesture. "We all have a past, Maddie. I swear I'm not judging.

I really want to help here but I can't do that with the limited information I have."

Her insides shook. She could feel her resolve, that thick wall of determination she practiced and shored up around her, crumble. A few more minutes and she'd be on the floor, rocking back and forth while she forced her brain to focus.

Before common sense could blink out, she made herself think. Nonsense chatter filled her brain and she let some of it slide out. "Do you have secrets? From what I can tell you're kind of perfect."

He shook his head. "Not even close."

"Smart. Hot. This super businessman. The stable one in a family that's still reeling from loss." She closed her eyes when she realized she'd said the *hot* part out loud.

"Maddie."

The energy pinging around inside of her wouldn't let her stand still. She broke out of his reassuring hold and paced. "I've worried about something just like this. It's why I don't get involved. I stick to the house. Watch the island for visitors. Weigh every move. I'm careful and always watching. It's the only way to live."

"That doesn't sound like living."

"Surviving, then. Call it whatever you want because it wasn't enough. Not if someone can slip in and leave that, here, on an island where everyone knows everyone and strangers stick out." She stopped and faced him, suddenly convinced she could still save him if this ended now. "You should go. This was a mistake."

"Dinner?"

The note. Those words. How could he not get it?

She pulled and tugged on his arm to get him to move, to run to the safety of his car. Maybe keep going until he got on a ferry headed for Seattle and away from her. "Don't you see? You're a target now."

He outweighed her. All the advantage was on his side. He shifted and took a step or two. Never touched her as she tried to shove him out, but didn't back away either. "This—whatever is happening right now and all the pushing—is because you're worried about my safety?"

Her hands dropped to her sides and she stood there, willing him to possess an ounce of self-preservation. "Of course."

The expression on his face morphed from confusion to more of a frustrated male what-are-you-talking-about look. "I'll be fine."

"You don't know that."

He started to shake his head, then stopped. "You're right. I don't. But I'm not walking away from you because some anonymous asshole tells me to."

Frustration swamped her. It was pretty hard to save a guy who refused to understand he was at risk. But under the grumbling and spiking panic lurked another feeling. A lightness that made her dizzy. Relief. All-consuming, unexpected relief.

All the fight ran out of her. "You don't even like me very much. You know, because of the miscommunication at your cabin."

He snorted. "Is that what we're calling it today?"

She fought the urge to brush his damp hair off his forehead. To cup his cheek and let the warmth of his body seep into hers. "Let me save you from this, Connor."

"Do I look like I need someone to rescue me?"

She dropped her hand. "I've never met a man more in need of a lifeline than you."

His head snapped back as if she'd slapped him. "What are you talking about?"

Yeah, they could dive into that messy conversation another time. Maybe never. She spun around and headed for the kitchen counter and her cell phone.

"I'm calling Ben." She dialed and watched him. "You can—"

"Wait for Ben. I'll do it on the porch, if you want, but I'm not leaving you alone."

"This—us being near each other—could end really badly."

Connor shrugged. "Maybe, but we're in it now."

"What does that mean?"

"The person who sent that note has seen us together. Me going home now doesn't stop that. We're stuck with each other."

She'd almost expected him to say something like that. And he didn't disappoint. "I knew I shouldn't have made you that pie."

CHAPTER 10

Ben rested his palms on Maddie's dining room table and studied the note through the plastic bag. He'd been in the house for ten minutes and hadn't said a word. When he finally looked up, he pinned her with his gaze. "Have you ever received notes this close together in time before?"

"Hold up." Connor cleared his throat. "Did you say *notes*? As in plural?"

Yeah, she'd forgotten to fill him in on that part. Blame the unwanted attraction and blinding panic. The combination took her off her game.

"The number doesn't matter." She turned from Connor back to Ben. "And no."

"How long of a period are we talking about here?" Connor asked.

"The notes started shortly after the excitement and horror of the summer died down and your brother headed back to D.C., so a few months ago. Maybe four."

"How close together, Maddie?" Ben asked.

"They usually come a few weeks apart, then there will sometimes be a break, then a few more, but never on top of each other." Terse and lecturing. They scared her but they were nothing compared to her life before. This felt like a way of letting her know she couldn't hide and would never find peace. A very specific warning not to ever get too comfortable. Last time they skipped the threats and went directly to trying to kill her.

Ben stretched as he stood up, then glanced over at Connor. "This one mentions you."

"No." She refused to concede that part. "Not specifically."

"It's not a big mental leap," Ben said. "We can assume it's about Connor since you two are dating."

Connor winced. "That's not—"

"It was one dinner," she said at the same time.

Ben let out a heavy sigh. "The point is, someone is watching Maddie and knows where she's going and who she's seeing."

"Then it's settled." Connor stared at her, as if daring her to fight with him.

"What is?"

"You're not safe here."

She followed his argument and cut it off before he could elaborate. "I'm not leaving my home."

A screeching sound echoed through the quiet house as Ben pulled out a chair and sat down in it. "That's the wrong answer, Maddie."

Connor gestured in Ben's general direction. "Listen to the man. He's law enforcement. He knows what he's talking about."

These two on the same side would be the death of her. "You don't understand. Either of you."

Connor crossed his arms in front of him. "I get that someone is coming after you. You don't need to tell me why, but you do need to accept Ben's help and then make a decision."

She knew she'd hate his answer but the curiosity ate at her. She'd always been an instant gratification type. When she needed to know, she needed to know *now*. "About what?"

"You stay at the Lodge, you come to my cabin, or I stay here with you." Connor counted out the options on his fingers. "Those are the only choices you get until Ben figures this out."

"When did you become the boss?"

"When some asshole started including me in your threatening notes."

He knew the exact right argument to make. The one that sent a shot of guilt spiraling through her. "Solving this could take forever."

Ben let out a harsh laugh. "Thanks."

"You know what I mean." She looked from Ben to Connor. "These notes . . . they've been happening. I don't see them stopping anytime soon."

Connor's eyes narrowed. "Which is why you need to be careful."

"I am." She'd been over this with Ben, so she waved Connor off. "I watch out for myself and the entire island."

"Maddie."

Ben stood up, drawing her attention. "I thought you two weren't dating. Here's a hint. It kind of sounds like you are."

"You're not helping." She pointed at Ben, then at Connor. "And you're out of line. For the record, I'm not a fan of the guy-knows-all thing you're doing."

"I'll apologize for my behavior once you're safe. Until then, get used to me making some demands because—and I want to be very clear about this—my only goal is to make sure you're here for me to apologize to in the future and not the victim of some deranged psychopath."

"It's just a note." She was trying to placate him and convince herself.

Neither worked.

"The one thing I've learned is that some creep who gets his thrills threatening a woman will eventually try to hurt her, and I plan on standing in the way."

"That's actually my job," Ben said.

She heard Ben mumble about his work but her focus stayed locked on Connor. The concern was sweet, but she wasn't convinced she was the one on his mind right now. "I'm not your sister, Connor."

"No, and your story will have a different, much happier, ending." Connor's voice shook as he spoke. When the last word bounced off the walls, a deathly quiet settled in again.

She could feel his determination. It wound its way inside her and the lure, that temptation to grab on, tugged hard.

A full minute passed before Ben broke the silence. "Maddie, he's not wrong. This guy is escalating."

He was right. They were both right. She hated that. "Why do you assume the notes are from a guy?"

"Do you know who they're from?" Connor asked in a flat voice.

"No." And until she did, she would tolerate the whole hero flex by Connor. She'd protect him right back, without him knowing of course, but the idea of pushing through this with reinforcements kept the panic from settling in. "Your house. One night."

He rolled his eyes. "This isn't a negotiation."

"No, it's not." Somewhere during the discussion she'd moved until she stood just inches away from Connor. Now she stepped back and headed for the bedroom. "I'll pack a bag."

CONNOR PRESSED HIS hand against the bandage on his forehead as he tried to make sense of what had happened since dinner. The night turned from unexpectedly enjoyable to a nightmare. Someone wanted to hurt Maddie. He couldn't fathom that. She could be short and possessed a mile-thick defensive wall, but that struck him as smart. People should be more self-protective.

But the note . . . notes. The idea of her being watched and tracked, potentially hurt, made his stomach roll.

He looked up at the one man who might be able to make the danger go away. "What the hell is going on?"

Ben shook his head. "I don't know."

"Ask her." That sounded like a dead end, so he turned to a more radical idea. "Or, I don't know, can't you force her to tell you?"

"We're talking about Maddie here. How would I do that?"

"I have no idea, Ben. I'm out of my depth." Connor felt useless and that made his temper spike. Sitting there, unable to help . . . he refused to go through that shit again.

It didn't matter that he just arrived on Whitaker or that he barely knew her. This wasn't about timing. It was about making sure he never again played the role of passive bystander when someone was in trouble and afraid to reach out for help. He owed Alexis that. He wouldn't make the mistake a second time with Maddie.

"Her past is locked in a mental vault and she's not sharing." Ben shook his head. "I can't blame her. Not many people on Whitaker open up about their lives before getting here without a lot of prodding, and she is more careful than most."

Connor refused to take that as an answer. "Yet they stared at us all through dinner and feel perfectly comfortable asking me all sorts of personal questions."

"I didn't say they weren't nosy."

Before they got derailed, Connor tried to drag them back onto the main topic. "But you could investigate her past. Call in favors. Right?"

A series of thuds sounded from the bedroom. Maddie's voice followed a second later. "No, don't come running or anything. I'm fine."

Connor shook his head. "Are you?"

A mumbled reply shot right back at him. "I just said so, didn't I?"

Ben stepped in closer to Connor, lowering his voice. "I know you're trying to help, but there are things you don't know about her. Some facts that make all of this more difficult than it would normally be."

More cryptic bullshit. Connor had just about maxed out on that for one day. "Like?"

Ben scoffed. "Things I'm not sharing."

"Someone is leaving her threatening notes. Someone on this island that only has about two hundred residents on it is after her." Connor glanced toward the bedroom before continuing. "That means they're close. She's been lucky they haven't moved in, but they will."

"You want me to do a door-to-door search?"

Connor ignored the sarcasm in Ben's voice. "Kind of."

"Okay, I get it." Ben visibly calmed. The tension ran out of him as he stood there, being far too sensible for the circumstances. "You want her safe. So do I. I'll check with my contacts and call in for some help from Seattle, but we don't have much to go on. I'm willing to give her some time to open up, time we'll—I'll—use to investigate."

"What if she doesn't have time? This person is watching. Could be unraveling." He'd already lived this. One day his sister was fine and talking about going on a hike. The next, she was dead.

"This isn't your fight, Connor. You're here to relax and—"

"I'm not going anywhere." The defiance in his voice shocked even him.

Footsteps caught Connor's attention. Both men turned as Maddie walked out of the bedroom with a computer bag on one shoulder and a gym bag slung over the other.

She kept going until she stood in front of Connor. In a few quick moves she had the bags in her hands and shoved them into his stomach. "Here."

One of the bags felt like she'd packed a piece of furniture in it. He poked at the zipper. "What's in here?"

"Don't push your luck." She broke eye contact with Connor and looked at Ben. "You have one day to solve this."

"That's not possible and you know it. You're going to stay with Connor and at some point you have to tell me something. Give me some direction. If your past is coming back to haunt you, I'll need some details."

"You know there are limits on what I can say."

"What does that mean?" Connor thought his head would explode. They both treated threatening letters as no big deal no matter how much he yelled about it. "Maddie, come on."

"My past might be unrelated."

"Explain," Ben said.

She sighed before answering. "I mean, I don't see how this has anything to do with what happened before."

It was the way she said it that made Connor wary. "Because?"

She stared right at him. "Because the people who tried to kill me last time are already dead."

CHAPTER 11

Once Maddie dropped that verbal bomb, all talk of investigations and her past stopped. No surprise there.

She'd held back, refrained from sharing the final tidbit of truth about her then would-be attackers, but the worried looks on their faces—the absolute determination to protect her no matter what—sent her mind spinning and she caved. She saw weeks of them hunting for answers and walking deeper into danger. If they weren't careful, they would ratchet up an already volatile situation. As of now, the note writer hadn't escalated past tough talk. She hoped to keep it that way.

Connor set her bags at the base of the ladder to the loft. He hadn't said much since she cut him off with the *dead* comment and took her back to his house. She knew he had to be burning to ask questions. She would be in his position. Yet he busied himself with tossing pillows to the floor and removing the cushions on what she now guessed was a sofa bed.

It looked old and lumpy and her insides screamed at the thought of being down here when he was up there, but she wasn't alone tonight. For the first night after so many alone, someone was right there with her. She never expected that kind of togetherness to feel so good.

Anything or anyone could lurk outside. Ben promised to stick nearby. When she tried to question where, to make sure the answer wasn't to spend the night in his car, Connor convinced her to let it go. Ben had a job and he would do it.

Connor had volunteered for his position, but he didn't appear ready to go off duty for the night. That left her in the situation she'd tried so hard to escape two years ago. All the time checking in and having someone watching over her, sometimes close and other times at a distance. The constant surveillance, even if it was for her safety, exhausted her. It confined and suffocated her.

The bounty on her head died when the people who issued it were killed. Days after, she pressed Witness Protection to get out. They wanted to keep her in until they could guarantee her safety, that all threats had been eliminated. She needed her life back. Not her old one, but *a* life.

"You take the bed upstairs." He issued the order without looking up from his work on the sofa.

"I can sleep . . ." His head shot up and his expression suggested she not engage him in another battle tonight. She took the hint because, really, he'd been rock-solid at a time when she needed to fall apart a bit. "Okay. Upstairs it is."

His stark expression finally dropped away. He didn't treat her to a smile, but he no longer seemed to be on the defensive. "Was it so hard to agree with me?"

"You tend to say things like a command. I'm guessing that's because you're used to being the boss."

"Sort of."

"Not here." She wanted to make her position on this matter very clear. "Not with me."

He smiled. "Understood."

She took a minute to study him. Those long legs and broad shoulders. The way his pants balanced on his hips. The way he moved, all confident and in control.

The McHottiePants title fit. When he smiled, she got a little winded. When he frowned at her, she wanted to kiss it away . . . and that was a problem. They weren't dating. She wasn't convinced they even liked each other. But the sparks, the unexpected connection that made her want to cling to him when she hadn't wrapped her life around anyone else's for years, threw her off balance.

When she focused on him again, she realized he'd stopped fidgeting and cleaning up. They stared at each other across the open sofa bed.

Mattress. Sheets. A confined space. Misplaced adrenaline shooting all over the place. This was going to be a long and confusing night.

"I should shower." The sound of her own voice broke the power of the strange pull between them.

He blinked a few times. "What?"

"It's the ritual some folks do before bed." Naked. Okay, yeah, that was also a problem. They'd be in the same small cabin, only a door apart.

She needed the energy arcing between them to stop. He was just a guy and she was a woman with dangerous loads of baggage. This couldn't happen no matter how sexy she found his smile and that ass.

He shook his head as he finally broke eye contact. "Uh, right."

"Are you afraid I'll use all of the hot water?" The joke fell flat but at least the need to sprint across the mattress and crawl all over him had died down. A little.

She needed to get a handle on the adrenaline coursing through her before she did something really stupid. She had been so careful and dateless for so long that temptation rode her hard. The *what-if*s ran through her mind until she struggled to catch her breath.

He exhaled in a way that sounded haggard and a bit out of control. "I didn't really think through the whole living together thing."

She needed to stop his thinking on that topic right now. "We're not."

"Of course not."

Uh-huh. Her voice didn't sound as sure and clear as she needed it to be, so she tried again. "It's one night. Don't make this weird."

He held up both hands as if in mock surrender. "Wouldn't think of it."

"You're kind of . . ." Hot. Perfect. Tempting.

Tall, dark, and smoking.

She could go on for a very long time before she'd reach the not-so-great stuff near the bottom of the list, like his bossiness.

His eyes narrowed. "What?"

She even loved his voice, all deep and serious. Realizing that was enough to snap her control in half. She only knew one way to get it back, and there was a fifty-fifty chance it would backfire. "Okay, this is ridiculous."

"I don't know what you're—"

"Kiss me."

He looked like he'd swallowed his tongue. "Excuse me?"

"You heard me." It was a stupid idea but it was the only one in her head. It had taken over every other thought since they walked in the door and now it pounded inside her. She needed this over, done, and forgotten.

"I can't really hear anything right now."

Okay, that was kind of cute . . . as if she needed to find one more adorable thing about him. "There's some weird charged thing happening between us. Adrenaline. Frustration. Boredom. Whatever you want to call it, we need to burn it off."

He took a step back and rammed his leg into a table. "Shit."

"You okay?"

He waved off the concern. "You think a kiss will do that?"

"That's the only choice we have."

He winced. "Actually."

Was he saying no? That made the need inside her rev up faster. "The only one I'm giving you."

He'd stopped fumbling and running into things and stared at her now. "Okay."

Okay? Not exactly loads of excitement in his tone, but she wasn't about to argue.

"So, do it." She wanted to add *now* but stopped herself. But she was pretty sure she was yelling. That general loudness didn't block out the churning inside her or the ringing in her head, but it would happen. One kiss and all of this would be wiped away.

"Maddie."

She needed this to happen. Now. "Come on."

"I think the charge is gone."

Her mind went blank. All the need rushed right out of her and bubbling frustration settled in its place. "What did you say?"

"Yeah, you killed it off."

Now she could add one very unattractive quality to the list about him. He could be a jerk. Noted.

She grabbed her bag and headed for a door she hoped held the bathroom or this might be the most embarrassing exit of all time. "You had your chance."

HE WAS AN idiot.

She offered and he stumbled around until she started with the shouting. Still, he wanted to kiss her. If his brain hadn't kicked back to life and thoughts about her safety hadn't started running through his head, they might be kissing or on the mattress right now.

And that would have been the wrong move . . . right?

He sat down hard on the end of the sofa mattress. A bar dug into the backs of his legs but he ignored it just like he needed to ignore all the date-like parts of this evening.

Dropping his head into his hands, he tried to focus on protection, not seduction. "This can't happen."

Bare feet appeared between his shoes a few seconds later. She curled her toes under and into the hardwood floor, but not before he got a peek at those bright red toenails. He'd never cared about nail polish before. Now he did.

"Connor?"

Don't look up. Don't look up.

Despite the commonsense advice from his brain, his head shot up at the sound of her voice. "Did you need something?"

She wore pajamas. Navy blue pants with bright pink lip prints all over them and a slim-fitting navy-blue tee that highlighted exactly what she hid under those oversized jackets.

He lost the ability to spell.

"Just this." She dropped to her knees between his open thighs.

Sweet Jesus. "Uh, Maddie?"

He was pretty sure his brain stopped working. Just clicked right off.

"Stop me if you don't want this." She ran her palms up and down his thighs.

Then her mouth closed over his and he didn't care if he ever had a rational thought again. Her mouth, all warm and inviting, traveled over his. Not a quick peck good-night. No, she dove in. Her tongue licked the seam between his lips, pressing them open and deepening her touch.

The kiss raged through him and burned past every defense. He wanted to touch her, taste her, run his hands all over her.

Just as he settled his hands on her waist and toyed with the idea of dragging her down onto the mattress with him, she pulled back. Her mouth hovered over his, teasing. Skimming just close enough for him to smell her.

He tried to draw her closer but she shook her head.

Only inches separated their lips when she smiled at him. She slowly rose to her feet, letting her hands drag along his legs and not breaking contact until the last minute.

"You were right." Her hands dropped to her sides as she stood in front of him. "The charge is gone."

He felt the shot straight to his gut. More than likely, he deserved it.

She headed for the ladder. "Get some sleep. You have an early handyman date tomorrow."

He fell back against the mattress. "Lesson learned."

"Let's hope so," she said in one last parting shot as she climbed the ladder.

CHAPTER 12

Maddie marched into Ben's office the next morning. It's not as if she had a choice. Connor dropped her off early so she could man the answering service, then he headed off to Paul's house. They'd colluded and decided that she needed full-time babysitters. Never mind that she'd been handling the notes and living her life—mostly—without their help and direction for months. The men seemed to believe they were in charge now.

Little did they know it was happening because she was *letting it happen*. Only a fool would turn down protection when danger lurked so close.

Connor had delayed his visit with Paul until after seven. That left plenty of time for awkward shifting around each other in his kitchen. As much as she wanted to pretend the kiss last night meant nothing, that it didn't touch her at all, that wasn't true. Their lips touched and her tongue went numb. Her knees buckled. Her traitorous heart hammered so hard that it blocked every other noise and most of her common sense.

Another few seconds and, head bandage or not, she would have crawled all over him. Not that she ever planned on letting him know that. Sending him the not-impressed vibe was the right answer, no matter how hard it was to hold on to her pretend indifference.

But that was earlier. Right now she had another male problem. This one had a badge and gun.

She stopped in Ben's doorway and slipped off her coat. When he yawned and sipped on coffee, she'd never felt more bonded with anyone in her life.

She dropped into the chair in front of his desk with her tablet on her lap and phone in her hand in case she needed to take a call for anyone. "Any news?"

"We saw each other ten hours ago."

"So, no?"

"I didn't see anyone at Connor's place last night. Repeatedly checked the perimeter. This morning I got in touch with your old friend Evan Williams and sent the new note for testing." Ben took a long drink before talking again. "I also managed to sleep about a half hour, right in this chair because I'm a multitasking genius."

Only one part of all that whining mattered to her. The part that ran headlong into her past. "Go back. Why did you talk with Evan?"

"Really? That's all you got out of that?"

"Humor me."

"I called him because you need round-the-clock protection until we can figure this out."

That sounded far more formal than the babysitting she endured now. And, no. That wasn't happening. She'd lived that life already. Gave up her name and her life. All of her friends and what little family she had. She walked away. Missed her mother's funeral. Maddie was an only child to a single mom, and it had always been the two of them against any threat. But when the end came she couldn't even say goodbye. Every decision made in accordance with the guidelines and rules set by WITSEC, the Federal Witness Protection Program.

The overwhelming majority of the people in the program were criminals. She liked to think her involvement with illegal activity was tenuous, at best. More tangential than actual, but the result was the same. She traded her life for protection, and that's when she met US Marshal Evan Williams, the fortysomething, serious, lethal dude who taught her to shoot and defend herself. She was grateful, but she needed that portion of her life to be over.

"No."

"Maddie, Connor is not a professional and I have one assistant who is off island at the moment and two volunteer assistants with families, so they can't trail you every minute of every day."

Guilt. Ben had to be exhausted from wielding that weapon. It worked on her every time, but that wasn't the point. "I gave up the life."

"The safe one?"

He had to know how the program worked. If he didn't, he should be able to guess. "The one where I was hunted and on the run."

"Those notes you keep getting say differently."

"In WITSEC a handler tells you what you can and can't do. Where there were rules and practice drills." She fought back the memories of those days, crawling in the mud and visiting shooting ranges. "Where every move was checked and double-checked, even as they assured me that I could leave at any time . . . and be killed."

Ben set his coffee mug on his desk blotter calendar. "I could argue you should still be in."

"But that's the point. I'm out because the danger is supposed to be over."

Ben exhaled. "This is the part where I ask you why you were in. Why did you need WITSEC protection?"

She was tempted to sigh right back at him, but she got it. Her failure to provide more information made it hard for him to do his job. "And this is the part where I remind you there are limits on what I can say."

She'd learned not to share. Secrecy was so ingrained that she didn't know how to turn the warning switch off in her head. She also wasn't convinced she should break the rules and drag anyone else into the danger she'd wallowed in for years. The notes proved it still lurked out there, and that held her back from opening up.

"Say something, Maddie."

Her throat tightened but she kept going. "The people who wanted me dead are no longer around to pay for someone to do the job."

"They have friends and family."

"That's not . . ." She hated the way Ben looked at her, as if he were analyzing her moves and dissecting each one to figure out her past. The flash of doubt almost stopped her, but she needed him to understand why she held back. "You know Maddie Rhine isn't my name, right?"

"Yes."

Her throat continued to close but she forced the words out. "It's the persona WITSEC set up. On purpose, I didn't go back to who I was before. So divulging all the information, spilling out every detail, is a waste of time. All it does is mentally put me back there."

"Hey, I get it." He stood up and moved around the desk to stand in front of her. "But you need to point me in the right direction."

His hands found her shoulders and squeezed. The comforting gesture came and went. That's who Ben was. Dependable and nonthreatening.

He also had a job to do and as much as she wanted to ignore that part, she couldn't. "Nothing is different from when I received the first note."

"Your point being?"

"Someone wants to scare me." She folded her arms across her stomach. "Believe me, it's working."

"Good."

Of course he would say that because it fit his needs. "But no one has approached me."

"Yet."

She let her arms fall to her sides again. The energy bouncing around inside her didn't let her stand still. She needed to move, to burn off some of the anxiety pumping through her veins. "Aren't you the optimist?"

"It's no longer just about you, though that would be enough for me to call in reinforcements. Connor could be in danger, too." Ben exhaled as if he sensed an argument on the horizon. "My thought for your protection was, better the guy you know, one who understands your history, than a security guard without any background. That person is Evan."

"Okay, but one question." She waited for him to nod before starting again. "At any time during all this thinking did you wonder if you should ask what I wanted?"

"It's a fair question."

He capitulated so quickly that it put her on edge. She kept pushing her point, just in case. "I have a job and I've had to ask my back-up person to step in and take over the answering service for me the last few days, and I sense she'll need to do it in the future because everything is so unsettled."

"Until we know who is sending those notes it's not exactly safe out there. You need to be careful, and if that means taking a few days off, is that really a big deal?"

She liked to have money, so yeah. "I feel like I've spent most of my life being careful."

A small smile came and went before his expression switched to unreadable again. "You won't even tell me what we're dealing with, Maddie. I can't protect you without facts. Evan has those facts."

She hated that he used common sense against her. It was tough to battle that. "I just want to forget."

"I understand."

Not possible. "Do you? I'm not trying to be a jerk. I'm just saying you weren't there."

"I know about crime and bad choices, about wishing you could go back."

She waited for the phones to ring, for any interruption. None came. So early in the day on an island without much crime, the office might remain quiet for hours. She took the opportunity to broach a difficult subject.

She reached out because touching him, being his friend, seemed right. With her fingers covering his, she waded into what could be a messy situation. "You never talk about your time in the military."

"Army. Military police."

She squeezed his warm fingers. "That must have been tough."

"I've seen some shit."

The door opened behind her, knocking into her and pushing her into Ben. She grabbed on to his shoulders to keep from falling on her face.

Connor's gaze flicked from her arms to Ben's face. "Sorry."

Ben steadied her before returning to his chair on the safe side of the desk. "Connor, come in."

With the sharing mood broken, she gave up trying to understand Ben and what made him tick. It wasn't exactly fair anyway since she did whatever she had to do not to give him the chance to work that mental move on her. "You missed the you-need-to-be-careful speech."

Connor stood there, not moving. "Interesting that he had to deliver it again."

She ignored that because he looked pretty adorable with his hair hanging over his forehead, hiding most of the damage. The bandage was gone today. She could only see the faint bottom edge of the injury through strands of straight black hair.

"This is new," Ben said.

Her gaze followed Ben's to the floor. To the Jack Russell terrier with the brown face and white body sitting half on Connor's sneaker. She'd recognize that plaid bow-tie-shaped collar anywhere. "Why are you walking Mr. Higginbotham?"

Connor held the leash. "So, everyone on Whitaker knows this dog?"

"He's Winnie's dog." She looked at Ben. "Though, come to think of it, I have no idea what Winnie's last name is."

Ben shrugged. "Probably not relevant to the story."

"She came over to visit Paul while I was fixing his step, which was perfectly fine, I would add. It barely squeaked." Connor rolled his eyes as he described his morning. "While I was putting the tools away, she said she needed to talk to Paul and asked me to walk Mr. . . ."

Maddie couldn't help but smile at the picture they made. Connor, tall and looming, watching over the spoiled fourteen-pound dog belonging to a person he didn't even know. "Higginbotham. A perfectly respectable name, by the way."

"Of course it is." He sounded defensive on the dog's behalf. "I put him in the car and brought him here to check on you first."

She laughed. There was just no way to hold it in. When she glanced at Ben, she saw he was right on the edge of losing it as well. "She got him."

Ben nodded. "She did."

"Excuse me?" When Mr. Higginbotham started sniffing Connor's sneaker, Connor picked him up and put him on the chair next to him. Right across from Ben.

"Winnie and Paul are . . ." It was an open secret but Maddie realized that, being new, Connor hadn't heard it yet. "Let's use the word *dating*."

Connor made a strangled noise. "I'm still confused."

Yeah, she was going to have to spell it out for him. "They like to meet for sex but, apparently, Mr. Higginbotham barks if they're too loud, so Winnie tries to convince other people to take him on a long walk while she and Paul do the deed."

Ben kept nodding. "I think they know we all know, but they act like they don't."

Connor's mouth dropped open. It took him a few seconds before he said anything. "Let me understand this. I was scammed by a seventysomething woman who wanted to have a noisy booty call."

Finally. "Yes."

"That sums it up nicely," Ben said.

She waited for Connor to get ticked off but he smiled.

"Good for her." His smile grew wider. "For Paul, too. Although I'm now thinking the handyman job was a ruse for the real job, dog walking."

An odd sensation flooded her. One she hadn't felt in so long that she barely recognized it. Happiness. He got scammed by some well-meaning older people who wanted some time alone and he was fine with that. He didn't yell or cause a scene. He hadn't when he found out she hit him either. That's who Connor was. He stayed calm and handled things. It's likely what made him such a good businessman.

"She'll be happy to know you like walking Mr. Higginbotham," she added, unable to stop herself.

His smile faded. "This is a one-time thing."

"You poor, naive darling. Sure it is."

Ben shook his head. "Sucker."

"That, too." She took pity on Connor and reached for the leash. "Here, let me take him."

"Where?"

"See the circling thing he's doing on the cushion?"

Mr. Higginbotham walked around, sniffed the fake leather, then circled again. She took that as a sign to get moving. "I think he has to go to the bathroom and Ben will get testy if it happens on his office chair."

Ben snorted. "Yes, he will."

AFTER MADDIE HANDED Ben her tablet, she grabbed the dog and headed for the door. Connor just stood there. He could see her through the open door to the inner office and the one to the outside. She stuck to the area right out front, in the patch of grass before the parking lot.

He was about to go with her when Ben spoke up. "You doing okay?"

Connor spared Ben a quick glance. "I don't like getting up this early during what's supposed to be my vacation."

"That's not what I meant."

"I know."

The desk chair creaked as Ben stood up. His footsteps thudded on the concrete floor as he walked around the desk and leaned in the doorway, joining Connor in watching over Maddie from a distance.

Ben lowered his voice to a whisper as he continued. "If the thought is to bolt, you should do it now. Don't get any more entangled with her. Your brother waited too long and now he's engaged, though I think we both agree that's a good thing."

A great thing, but Connor didn't really focus on that part of the comment. "I'm not looking for a wife, but thanks."

"If you say so."

The uneasiness Connor tried to block kept kicking to the surface. The hold or hug or whatever it was looked innocent enough when he walked in, but it wouldn't be the first time he'd read a relationship wrong. He glanced at Ben. "Unless you need me to leave the island."

Ben continued to lounge against the doorjamb. "I'm not sure what you're suggesting."

"Come on."

"Ah, that." Ben let out a long, exaggerated breath as he finally gave Connor eye contact. "There's nothing between us. I asked Maddie out to eat once and she did everything to avoid letting it happen. Even pretended she didn't understand the question. I got the hint. I'm firmly in the friend category, and that's the right answer. There's no us, Connor."

So, he'd tried. At one point, Ben showed an interest and made a move. Connor wasn't sure what to do with that information, so he tucked it away to analyze later. "She hit me with a stick and I keep coming back."

Ben laughed. "Maybe you should ask yourself why."

Footsteps dragged Connor's attention back to the office reception area, saving him from having to reply to *that*.

She walked up to Connor and handed over the leash. "He did his business. You're welcome."

Right. The dog and Winnie. He was supposed to be running an errand.

He rubbed the area around his stitches. "I guess I should take him back."

Ben winced. "Uh . . ."

Maddie's expression didn't look any more positive about his suggestion. "Let's treat him to a long recreational walk first."

"Why?"

She shot him a why-aren't-you-getting-this frown. "Do you want to walk in on Paul and Winnie before they're done?"

Sweet hell. "Some exercise sounds good."

"Now you get it." She winked at him. "Smart man."

CHAPTER 13

They avoided any discussion of the kiss or the spark between them, or anything of substance for two full days. Connor walked a fine line between longing and wanting to run like hell before he got in too deep.

The days played out in a standard pattern. They got up and she went to work but instead of answering calls from the comfort of her house, she did it from a small desk in Ben's office. To avoid hearing her complain, Connor stayed away, doing odd jobs for people he barely knew who assumed he was handy. And tried in vain to relax. Sleep and rest didn't come easy when he spent most of the night dreaming of the woman one short ladder away.

Not that the days passed easier. Maddie grew restless. She insisted that his cabin was a safe enough place for her work. This morning she snapped because he said he didn't like crunchy peanut butter. She took the offhand comment as a personal affront. Acted like he'd kicked a puppy.

Yeah, they needed some space . . . or a long talk about the kiss and the possibility for a repeat, maybe with some touching thrown in. The tension strangled both of them.

He contemplated the options while he sat in his car in the Whitaker library parking lot. He'd dropped Maddie off at Ben's office next door for the new workday, listening to her grumble as she got out of the car. He'd only driven a few feet away before pulling into an empty space. That's all he could manage while memories of her cute pajamas floated through his mind.

He let his head fall back against the seat. His eyes closed, but only for a second before they shot open again. Coffee. He needed more coffee. Maybe a pep talk from Sylvia.

He straightened up, ready to turn the car back on and really drive away this time, when he saw her. She'd been inside all of two minutes and now she walked out the front door and snuck around the side away from him. Didn't look up. Didn't wait for Ben to follow.

What the hell?

He slipped out of the car and jogged to the edge of the building. Toyed with the idea of grabbing Ben, but Maddie moved at a clip. He couldn't afford to waste time and lose her.

After a few feet, she scooted off any recognizable path. She wound her way through the trees. She stopped only once and that was to tie her shoe. One quick glance around and she was off again. Sure that she was messing with him, he waited behind the tree for a few extra seconds. When he peeked around it again, it took him almost a minute to find her. Her jacket hood flapped, but the olive coat otherwise blended in with the bushes and grass.

Now he didn't care if he got caught or not. The important thing was to keep up with her. Not let her stretch out ahead and run smack into danger.

The tall trees blocked out most of the sun, leaving the area underneath shaded and the sounds inside muffled. He slid on the slick forest floor of moss and dead leaves. But he could see a break in the branches ahead and a pool of light. Picking up speed, he slipped through the opening.

It took him a few seconds to get his bearings but then his sense of direction kicked in. From this position, he hid in the trees off to one side of Holloway Harbor. He could see the marina attached to the Yacht Club in the distance and the dock for the ferry in front of him.

Workers bustled on the pier. He knew from experience the ferry from Seattle would pull in there today on one of its two weekly runs. The loading and unloading lasted less than a half hour. Then the ferry took off again, hitting two other islands before setting back for the city.

The ride to Whitaker had been frigid but scenic. Water lapped against the sides of the boat and the view from the open deck gave way to a vast sea of blue with tiny dots of land that grew bigger the closer you got. Most people sat inside, gathered around the small snack bar. Despite the wind and pelting of water droplets, he viewed being trapped in there when he could be out here, around all of this, a waste of a ride.

"What are you doing?" Her voice rang out from behind him.

He almost jumped out of his skin. "Jesus, woman."

She stepped in front of him with a scowl that suggested he tell the truth. "Why are you following me?"

No, he refused to play this game. He wasn't the one who should be answering for their behavior today. "Why did *you* pretend to go to work, then sneak out?"

"I do not sneak."

He refused to dignify that. "Who's answering your calls?"

She stared at him for a few seconds, not saying a word. "The woman who covers for me and handles Mondays so I can have a day disconnected from the table and phone."

"Did you tell her in advance that you needed the morning off to run around the island but then forget to tell me?"

"I don't like being tracked."

As far as dodges went, she'd done better, but he let it slide . . . for the moment. "I don't like being lied to."

"You have an answer for everything, don't you?"

"No, because I have no idea what you're doing."

She sighed at him.

He sighed right back.

"Fine." She threw up her hands. "Checking."

She stopped after that, as if the cryptic remark explained everything. She was determined to make sure he never wanted to take a vacation again. "On what?"

"Who comes on and off that ferry."

He followed her gaze to the empty pier but it didn't help. The visual, the words, none of it made sense to him. "You're going to make me ask."

"I need to know who is on the island."

Some of the tension ran out of him. Each muscle relaxed as he realized this was part of some ritual for her. Not completely relaxed because the idea that she thought she needed to keep that kind of watch on people made him ache for her. Only fear could push a person to those extremes.

"All two hundred nineteen people," he said, keeping his voice neutral so that he didn't upset her more than he already had.

"That's a specific number."

"It's on the brochure in Ben's office."

"Speaking of Ben . . . Before the two of you insisted that I needed a babysitter, this is how I protected myself."

He wanted to touch her, make it better somehow. He ignored the instinct and let her say what she needed to say with minimal interference from him. "And then you go to their cabins and hit them with sticks."

"That only happened once." She brushed the sole of her boot along the small stones lining the division between the grassy area and the start of the parking lot for the ferry. "You were quicker than I expected."

The pieces still didn't make sense but the picture cleared a bit. "You thought I came to Whitaker to hurt you and you wanted to, what, check out the cabin and maybe attack me before I could attack you?"

She shrugged. "I didn't know who you were, and your visit was unexpected."

"This is no way to live, Maddie."

"It's the way I've survived." Her eyes widened. "So?"

That ended the conversation he thought they were having. "What are you asking?"

"Are you coming with me to get the ferry manifest or not?"

"No one has ever asked me that before, so yes. I'm intrigued." And he guessed it took a lot for her to suggest he tag along. He vowed not to take that trust for granted.

"Try not to be too"—she looked him up and down—"you."

She sure knew how to kill a mood. "I'm ignoring that snide comment."

"People on Whitaker don't trust strangers."

"You've all made that clear."

"I'm serious."

"Trust me, Maddie. I am taking you very seriously."

CHAPTER 14

Maddie got the information she needed about the ferry, but it hadn't been easy with Connor standing there. As promised, he didn't talk much but that made it worse. The North kid, her contact in the ferry office, barely twenty and the paranoid type, kept glancing at Connor while they talked. She finally gave up and said he was her bodyguard, which was only a little lie. She feared Connor would take that role seriously and she'd never have a minute of peace on Whitaker again.

Now they were inside, where it was warm. Late breakfast patrons sat in tables around the Lodge's dining room. It looked like a lot of people got a late start today, but Maddie knew better. She didn't venture out often, or hadn't until recently, but every time she did this happened.

This was the eavesdropping crowd. They lingered and pretended to eat, all while watching every move Connor made. An unsettling amount of staring.

Sylvia stood on the other side of the bar at one end of the dining room. Her gaze traveled from Connor to Maddie, who both sat on stools, not saying a word.

"You two are glaring at each other." Sylvia put two cups of coffee on the bar, one in front of each of them. "Keep that up and people will think you ran off and got married."

Maddie ignored the comment as she reached for the sugar packets and decided she needed two to get through this morning. The paper ripped and she searched for a spoon, which ended when Connor held one in front of her face. He even managed to make that seem snotty.

"I'm trying to think of a nice way of telling Connor to back off." She stirred, then clanged the spoon against the side of her mug for emphasis.

Connor didn't seem upset by her words. He stayed slouched over his mug with his elbows resting on the edge of the bar. "She means—"

"The notes. I get it. Those would make anyone twitchy." Sylvia sighed as she poured herself a cup of coffee to match theirs. "My guess is you're suffocating her with much-needed, but likely a bit stifling, protection duty."

"Wait." Maddie lost hold of the spoon and it thudded against the counter. "How do you know about the notes?"

"Oh, that." Sylvia drew out the answer by taking a sip first. "Ben."

For a guy everyone trusted, he sure did like to chat about secrets. Good to know. "Did he put it in the paper?"

Sylvia moved around behind the counter, and when she turned around to face them again, she held a tray of breakfast pastries. "I'm the head of the Whitaker Board. We meet once a week and he fills me in about what's happening and cases I need to be aware of, which usually consists of people who refuse to pick up their dog poop and unexplained garden trampling. That one was last week, by the way. Louise Stone wants to know who messed with her carrots."

Connor nodded, looking all serious as if this were a weighty discussion. "Probably the same dog that did the poop-and-run."

"But still. Isn't there a confidentiality thing here?" Well, there was no reason to miss out on a doughnut, so Maddie took the one covered in chocolate.

"Ben also knows he can count on me to keep quiet and to be on the lookout for new faces around Whitaker."

Connor turned down the offer for food. "Maddie has that under control."

Maddie stopped right before taking a bite. "It wasn't a big deal."

She almost toppled off the barstool when Paul stepped between her and Connor and sort of pushed her to the side. "Uh, hello?"

But Paul's focus centered on the pastries. It took him what felt like forever to pick out the bear claw before turning to Connor. "Thanks for the help the other day. Maybe you can come around next week. I think another porch step is on the fritz."

Connor shook his head. "I don't—"

"Wednesday, but don't sleep the whole day away this time. Be there before seven." Paul snatched the napkin sticking out from under Connor's arm. And then he was off.

Connor didn't try to stop him. He just watched the older man go. "He certainly moves fast after he issues an order."

"Did they trick you into walking Winnie's dog?" Sylvia asked.

Connor lifted his coffee mug. "I don't want to talk about it."

"Okay. What were we saying before Connor remembered his role in helping a lovely older couple have loud sex?" Sylvia asked.

Between the look on his face and Sylvia's obvious amusement, Maddie lost it. She laughed. Just when she got it under control, she burst out a second time. "That will never not be funny."

"Anyway." Connor sounded the exact opposite of amused as he gave his explanation to Sylvia. "Our dear Maddie was supposed to be with Ben this morning and lied to him about running late. Blamed me."

"Wait." Maddie's amusement dried up. "Lied? That's a strong word."

"What you did is the definition of lying," Connor pointed out before turning back to Sylvia. "I didn't know about the lie, so when I dropped her off at Ben's, she snuck out and went to the ferry."

Sylvia nodded. "Right. Her regular check on the ferry passengers."

The Whitaker gossip chain was working at full speed and Maddie didn't like it. "Did Ben tell you about that, too?"

"Some of the ferry workers did." Sylvia looked at one of the tickets a waitress handed her and loaded a Danish on a small plate to be delivered to one of the tables. "You're not exactly subtle."

Maddie closed her eyes and wished for this day to end. "Great."

"If it helps, on Whitaker that behavior isn't considered weird." Sylvia made another run for the coffeepot and refilled Connor's mug.

Connor signaled for her to stop when it was half full. "Thanks, but that can't be true."

Maddie didn't appreciate the shot of sarcasm or the eye roll he sent her way. "You're the one who caused a scene at the ferry."

He scoffed. "How is any of this my fault?"

Sylvia held up a hand as if trying to referee the ridiculous argument. "Not to worry you, but my guess is she also goes to Stark's Marina to check on the water taxis."

He glared at Maddie. "What water taxis?"

Sylvia waved to a few newcomers who walked into the dining room, but never missed a beat in the conversation. "The ferry only comes twice a week but there is a taxi service that brings people back and forth—for a steep price—from some of the smaller islands nearby."

There were only a few ways on and off Whitaker,

and all except for private plane required water. No bridges or tunnels, only boats. That made her job of watching over how people got on the island and how long they stayed much easier. "Dom tells me who is coming and going."

Sylvia frowned. "I doubt that. Talk about lying."

"What does that mean?" Connor asked.

"He thinks it's his job to prevent Whitaker from being overrun by tourists, so he tells tales. He tries to throw people off the truth." Sylvia lowered her voice as a group of customers walked by . . . very slowly. "He once told me the taxi sank. I found out later that he lied because he thought too many people arrived on the ferry that week and the lie was his form of crowd control."

Connor shook his head and his expression said he wanted to comment on the oddities of Whitaker residents. "What would make him act like that?"

"Rumor is he used to work for NASA. So, I guess the answer is he's an actual rocket scientist. Maybe they're cranky by nature." Sylvia shrugged. "Don't know."

Maddie had been listening and stammering and trying to think of a good way to respond to this new information. She gave up and went with the one response that summed up her thinking. "That's ridiculous."

"Sounds consistent with the rest of Whitaker," Connor said as he took another sip of coffee.

Sylvia smiled. "Right?"

They didn't get it. Maybe no one could. To understand, you had to live the life she led, and lose everything. Because this was not funny. "I depend on Dom's intel."

For the first time since they sat down, Connor smiled. "Intel?"

"Most of it is probably accurate, but not all," Sylvia said. "While he's watching over the island, he's making sure he's the only one with the correct information."

"All this time . . ." Maddie didn't even know what to say. She thought she had all of the information she needed, that she was being careful. "I've been so sure the person writing the notes lived off island."

"Because?" Connor asked.

"There really isn't a reason for someone living here to hate me. Until recently, I've mostly just been a voice on an answering machine. People didn't know or see me."

"Before you, she kept to herself and never walked into the Lodge and sat down for dinner," Sylvia said to Connor.

"Anyway." Maddie heard the edge to her voice and fought to even out her tone. "I assumed the person came in on the water taxi or ferry, but anything is possible, and it's all scary."

Sylvia nodded. "Now you're worried the person might already be on Whitaker."

"Any chance the threats and not knowing where they're coming from or who is on the island means you'll be more careful?"

She seriously considered ignoring Connor's question. She would have if she had any control over her thoughts right now, but she didn't. New worries pummeled her. All these doubts she kept at bay flooded her.

"I'm watched by you and Ben every single minute of the day." By the time she got to the end of the sentence she was yelling and everyone in the room stared at her. No one pretended not to notice her now.

Sylvia's eyes widened. "Oh."

"Wow," Connor said at the same time.

Maddie swallowed a few times, struggling to get her firing emotions under control. "I appreciate the concern."

"Sure sounds like it."

Great, his dripping sarcasm had returned. Lucky her. "You have to be sick of me by now."

"I'm getting there, mostly thanks to this conversation."

Maddie slid off the barstool. It was time to go. She preferred the idea of sitting in Ben's windowless, suffocating office to this.

Sylvia reached across the bar and touched Maddie's arm. "You can set up here."

Connor slammed his mug down on the bar hard enough for it to make a rattling sound. "She's sleeping at my place."

That seemed to get everyone's attention. They stopped staring at her and looked at him. More than a few of the older ladies smiled.

Maddie wanted to crawl back into bed . . . Of course, she wasn't even sleeping in her own bed right now.

"I meant the answering service. During the day." Sylvia cleared away the mug and dish in front of Maddie. "Instead of being in Ben's small office, right on top of the investigation into who is leaving the notes, she can be here."

"Is that safe?" Connor sounded skeptical. He opened his mouth as if he was going to speak for her and turn down the offer.

Sylvia stopped him cold. "Do you think I'm going to let anything happen to her on my property?"

Connor whistled. "No, ma'am."

"Good answer. Then it's settled." Sylvia's don't-mess-with-me expression morphed into a smile as she looked at Maddie again. "At night you're all Connor's."

She winked at them and headed for a table by the window before they could respond. She had a pad out and was taking the orders of the couple who ran the Yacht Club.

Maddie liked Sylvia's style. She also knew more about what happened on Whitaker than most people, which made her a valuable ally and credible source of ongoing information. "She said it that way on purpose."

"Of course."

He didn't get it. She spelled it out for him. "She thinks we're dating."

"We kind of are . . ." He tried to take another sip of coffee but his mug was empty. "Without the good parts."

That fast, her focus shifted. She switched from worrying and wanting to smack Dom for lying to her to . . . something else. A warm sensation. A hit of interest she'd repressed for a very long time. "Meaning?"

"The kiss."

"Ah, finally." It took the man more than two days to circle around to this topic. "I thought you'd tiptoe around it or ignore it forever."

He traced his finger around the rim of the empty mug. "You made it clear it wasn't that great."

Men. "You can't be that clueless."

She thought about the kiss all the time. When she watched him get onto that lumpy sofa bed. When he scowled at her. When she brushed her teeth. It was a nonstop total annoyance, but she couldn't fight it. Not when they slept twenty feet and one ladder apart.

He shifted on his stool to face her. "Really? You want to do it again?"

"And other stuff." Before she got the words out, he knocked his mug over. "You okay?"

He cleared his throat. "I'm listening."

Yeah, she could see that. The spark of light in his dark eyes. The way he leaned forward, inching closer to her, and his voice dipped lower than usual.

She had his full attention now.

She ran a finger over the back of his hand where it lay on the bar. "But first . . ."

"Yeah?"

She lifted her fingers, ending the light touch. "We visit Dom and make him tell me the truth, then I believe you have an appointment with Doc Lela about removing those stitches."

Connor continued to lean toward her. "That's the least sexy thing I've ever heard."

She was going to kiss the crap out of him later. Forget being careful and smart. She tried to push him away and protect him, but he didn't want to be left alone. Now he wouldn't be.

"You want some sexy times?" She dropped her voice to a soft whisper. "You've got to earn them."

Their bodies stayed locked in that position. Just inches apart.

His gaze traveled over her face like a caress. "That's a valid point."

"I'm a smart woman."

He held up a finger between them. "You get one conversation with this guy."

Honestly, she would agree to anything he said right now. "Yep."

"No other stops or detours."

He smelled good. She couldn't name the scent but it was a fresh, clean smell. A scent of soap that seemed to be magnified by his general hotness. "Right."

"There are no hidden pieces here, right? Like, he lives four islands away and it will take two days to get there."

Why was he still talking? "The errand will take no more than an hour."

"Then?"

She liked that he wanted to be sure on consent. She was more than willing to give it after two days of pretending not to notice each other. "I'm all yours. And so that we're clear? It's been a long time, so I am ready."

He jumped off the barstool and held out a hand to her. "Let's go."

DOM CLEMONS SHOVED the dirty rag he'd been using to clean a wrench into the back pocket of his too-baggy jeans. He glanced up as Connor walked Maddie down the pier to him.

"You're back," Dom said, not sounding particularly excited by the idea.

Maddie walked a bit faster and ended up standing slightly in front of Connor. "We need to come to an understanding."

Dom pointed over her shoulder. "Who's this?"

For a second, Connor thought about not answering. Maddie ran this show. Having Dom ignore her to talk to him was pretty annoying. Connor couldn't imagine how much that sort of thing ticked Maddie off. "Connor Rye."

"You related to the other Rye guy who was here over the summer?"

Looked like they were back to that question. It had been a few days since he had to field it. "Yes."

Dom shook his head. "Not good."

Sibling protectiveness surged through Connor. He could think Hansen was a pain in the ass sometimes. That didn't mean he liked anyone else thinking it. "Any specific reason you say that?"

"He showed up on Whitaker and people died."

Yeah, that. Connor couldn't really argue with that point. Well, not much. "He didn't actually kill them. He helped solve the case."

"Irrelevant."

Connor was not a big Dom fan so far. "Is it?"

With a big sigh, Maddie stepped on Connor's sneaker and shifted even more in front of him. "You've been hiding information from me."

Dom shrugged. "Of course."

Connor hadn't expected that response. From Maddie's stuttering, he didn't think she did either.

"You're not denying it?" she asked, sounding stunned by the idea.

"I thought you knew."

"Why would I . . ." As soon as her voice grew louder, it cut off. After a few noticeable breaths, she started again. "Dom, I need to know who comes on and off the island."

"So you've said."

Since her plan about reasoning with the man wasn't working, Connor took a shot. "She's in danger."

Maddie stepped down harder on his foot. "Don't tell him that."

But it was too late. Dom had his arms crossed in front of him and his full attention on Maddie now. "From what?"

"It doesn't matter."

"Someone's threatening her. She needs the intel so that she's prepared." Connor swore under his breath. "Now I'm using that stupid word."

Intel? Her flair for the dramatic was rubbing off on him. If he didn't have the promise of more kissing and the potential for some serious touching ahead of him, he'd be tempted to demand answers and generally take over. But he knew she would hate that, understandably, so he refrained. But it took a lot of effort to do it.

Dom nodded his chin in her general direction. "Who'd you piss off?"

"I'm not sure."

Dom made a humming sound, as if he were mentally debating his options. "You don't think the person lives on Whitaker? Makes sense they would. You're on everyone's calls, up in their business. Some people don't like that."

"I run the island's answering service."

Dom snorted. "Why are you telling me things I know?"

And they had circled back to Dom being short and annoying, so Connor stepped in again. "In the last few months has anyone come onto the island without Maddie knowing?"

"How do I know what she knows?"

This guy . . . "Did you tell her about all of the people who came here?"

Dom touched the brim of his hat, lowering it despite the lack of sun. "About some."

"I told you I needed to know about everyone, whether they stayed or left the same day." The words rushed out of Maddie now, raw and uncontrolled.

"I figured you were nosy. Don't like nosy people."

Her glare matched the lack of patience in her voice. "This is unbelievable."

"Only one guy came onto Whitaker and didn't leave again. Actually, he came here three times. He only left again twice, so I'm thinking he's still here unless he left on a private boat."

"Who is it?" Connor asked.

Dom shook his head. "I don't know his name."

This time Connor believed him. Whatever game he was playing before, he seemed to get that Maddie needed the information. This wasn't about being nosy. "Do you know where he is?"

"No."

"What island did he come from?" Maddie asked, sounding a bit calmer now.

"Arnold. Didn't get the impression he lived there because he needed directions both times I dropped him back off on Arnold."

Every time he ended an answer, Maddie fired a new question at him. She didn't back away from Dom's gruff voice or the body language that flashed a *keep out* sign. "What does he look like?"

Dom looked Connor up and down. "Kind of like him."

For the first time since he got to Whitaker, Connor didn't mind having his ethnicity pointed out. "He's Korean? Biracial? How exactly does he look like me?"

"None of those. I guess he's nothing like you."

Maddie let out a rough growl and turned away to walk back up the pier. "This isn't helping. Let's go."

"Five-ten. Brown hair."

Connor and Maddie both stopped moving and looked at Dom.

"Was smart enough to wear clothes that made him blend in. Informal. There wasn't anything memorable about him."

Now, that information helped. It at least set some parameters. Connor hoped Ben could work with those. "Did he say why he came to Whitaker?"

"He said he had a job to do."

"Yeah, threaten me." Maddie's voice had flattened.

The lack of emotion in her voice tugged at Connor. "You don't know that."

"Are you willing to bet I'm wrong?"

Dom's arms dropped to his sides and some of the gruffness left his voice as he talked. "Check the open house rentals. A man smart enough to hide and cover his comings and goings won't go to Berman's Lodge for a room. He'll be keeping quiet. Probably paid in cash for an out-of-the-way place. Isn't going out to dinner, so he'd be buying groceries."

For a guy who didn't talk much he suddenly had a lot to say. Connor guessed it had something to do with the lost and broken expression on Maddie's face. He had to believe Dom wasn't immune.

"How many houses on Whitaker fit that description?" Maddie asked.

After a few seconds of quiet, Dom handed out his final bit of information. "That's your problem, not mine."

CHAPTER 15

She finally knew she wasn't alone, that all of her tricks and games and lying to her neighbors to figure out who visited Whitaker and who stayed had failed. She ran right up against her failure. Had it rubbed in her face.

She wasn't so fucking smart now.

So much for instincts. It took her long enough to gather the information she needed. All those days being led around by the new guy and the useless pretend cop. She hung on to them, flirted with them. Got deeper into trouble and refused to take any responsibility for her actions.

She would learn.

CHAPTER 16

The day went on for what felt like a week. By the time Maddie dragged her butt back to Connor's cabin, she wanted to throw off her coat and not think about ferry schedules or people or anything. Except him.

During the last two days she'd thought about him all the time, whether she was stuck in an office away from him or right beside him. His scent. The way the wind blew his straight hair around. The line that appeared between his eyebrows when he got lost in thought.

The unexpected daydreaming started as a minute here or there. Her mind would wander to him or some stray comment he made. Then those minutes grew closer together. The time got longer. Her thoughts veered in a different direction, one that involved being naked.

She'd had chances for easy, hot sex during the last few years of solitude. The kind that wiped out her worries for a few hours but didn't mean much. It had never really been her thing but it was her only real option when her life imploded. Still, her needs always battled with her fear and being careful won out every single time.

With Connor, all the reasons not to take the next step slipped away. The only valid excuse to maintain separate beds centered on his safety and her worry that she was dragging him to a place he didn't deserve. Into danger he shouldn't have to handle. But the excitement in his voice when she made the offer earlier, the way his whole body snapped alert and those beautiful dark eyes stared right into her, said he knew and didn't care. He understood the risks, maybe not *the* risk, but he'd made some sort of mental calculation and decided she was worth it. She didn't get it but she didn't have the strength or the will to keep him at a distance either.

She heard him clear his throat from across the room. For the first time she realized she stood there, holding her coat, just inches inside the front door.

"One question."

She tensed, waiting for him to say something that would steer them off course and back into danger talk. "Go ahead."

"Why are your jackets so big?"

Not expecting that. "What?"

"I'm not a fashion expert but it's like you're wearing the wrong size."

"I am. They came with the house." As far as explanations went it wasn't the most rational, but it was the truth.

He smiled. "Excuse me?"

"They were in the closet. Well, in a box in the closet."

He continued to stare at her, wide-eyed and waiting.

"The jacket I brought with me when I moved here wasn't warm enough." She hung the one she was holding on the hook by the door and stepped down into the living area. "At first, I thought there was something wrong with me because I was freezing all the time, even in summer. Then I realized the chill here is different. It whips off the water and blows through you. Never experienced that before."

"Two years in and you haven't acclimated?"

Then it dawned on her. She'd been staring into space and the mundane conversation eased her back. He was giving her time and space because that's who he was.

She'd picked the right man to attack that first night.

"Maybe I've been waiting for the right person to come along and warm me up."

He visibly swallowed. "I want to be clear."

"I'm listening . . . watching. Ready." She walked toward the ladder. Rested her hand on it as she kicked off her boots.

"I'm not holding you to anything you said today. Things happened and . . . you know, emotions."

He was extra cute right now. All windblown with rosy cheeks. The sweater he wore hugged his chest and highlighted his trim waist. She'd seen him in a T-shirt and sweatpants. That's as close to undressed as he got when she was still downstairs each night. He didn't strike her as shy. His clothing choices were likely out of deference to her.

Now she wanted to know what he hid under there. "Such as?"

"The flirting, some dirty talk. I'm all for it. But that doesn't mean we have to—"

"Stop talking and come with me." She turned and started up the ladder. That put him below her.

Let him look.

She took her time getting up the rungs. Shook her hips a bit and heard him suck in air. The energy pinging around inside of her threatened to knock her off those rungs. Then his hand skimmed along the small of her back, waking up every nerve and every cell. His fingers caressed her spine.

She had no idea how she made it up to the loft without falling. She spied the unmade bed, then turned in time to see him slip up behind her. His footsteps echoed on the hardwood as he moved to stand in front of her.

The urge to touch him overwhelmed her. She gave in, smoothing her palms over his chest while fighting the need to pull that sweater off him. "I'm here with you because I want to be here with you. Got it?"

"If that changes, you tell me?"

Consent had never been sexier. "You're irresistible."

His hand closed over hers in a gentle touch. "I'm serious."

"So am I, and yes. I want you. With me, over me, in me." She met his gaze without blinking. "Clear enough?"

His breathing ticked up. His chest rose and fell, faster and more labored now. "Very."

She brushed her fingertips gently over the edge of his new scar. "The stitches are gone."

"Doc thought about keeping them in a few more days but my manly whining stopped her."

The way he said it and the thread of amusement in his voice made her smile. "I bet."

She slipped her hands down that long torso to the bottom edge of his sweater and tugged it over his head. The move pulled on the white tee he wore underneath, dragging it up and treating her to a healthy glimpse of his flat stomach and the dark sprinkling of hair there.

Her fingers moved without any message from her brain. Teasing along his bare skin. Sliding down to rest on the button of his jeans.

One second she stood there and the next, the room whipped around her. She dropped onto the mattress in a sprawl. The comforter bunched beneath her but all she cared about was the six feet of hotness on top of her.

His skin warmed under her hands as she yanked his T-shirt up and over his head. The sight in front of her had her brain clicking off. Shoulders that blocked the light on the ceiling. Skin that looked touched by the sun.

The way his hair fell over his forehead and those intelligent eyes. She lifted up to kiss him, and when their mouths met she wondered why she spent days delaying their second time. Heat bubbled up inside of her and she wrapped her arms around his neck. She couldn't get close enough, or touch him enough to satisfy her.

Their hands wandered as the kiss raged on, burning through her and sending her mind spinning. She pressed in closer, put every part of her into showing him how much she wanted this.

They broke apart to the sound of heavy breathing. He rested his forehead against hers. "Has it really been a long time for you?"

Not now. Those words shouted in her head and she almost said them out loud. "This isn't the time to hunt for personal intel."

The tip of his tongue traced her bottom lip. "There's that word again. It makes me feel like I'm in a television show."

The sensation of his tongue grazing over her skin had her shaking from the inside out. She slipped her leg around his, bringing their bodies together everywhere she could.

"Why are you still talking?" She whispered the question against his lips.

"I have no fucking idea."

He rolled them until she sprawled over him. The position let him sweep off her sweater until she straddled him, wearing nothing more than her bra and a pair of faded jeans.

"I'm a big fan of this position." His fingers slipped through her hair and brought her mouth down to his again.

The second before their lips met, he looked at her, not bothering to hide the heat welling inside of him. She saw it in his eyes and the curve of his mouth. It radiated off him. Then she dropped her head and slipped into a blinding kiss. Let it pulse through her.

Those knowing hands slid over her, learning every curve. Fingers touched and caressed. Skimmed over her and landed on her jeans. She expected him to unbutton them but he didn't. His hand traveled lower, against the seam. She felt the touch through the fabric to her underwear.

That finger moved. Back and forth over her. The layers of clothing didn't matter. She felt him, every pressure and every push.

Her head dropped forward and her hair brushed against his chest. "Connor."

"Close your eyes and feel."

She rested her forehead against his cheek and gave in to the rhythm. Shifted her hips back and forth. The touch was both too much and too little. The friction of the material over her softness had her insides clenching.

On instinct she tried to open her legs even further, give him room. And when the pressure rubbed the cotton against her already sensitive skin, she let out a gasp.

She turned her head until her mouth rested against his chin. The scruff teased her lips. "Please touch me."

"I am."

Her breath hiccupped in her throat. She had to drag in air before she could cough out a word. "Inside."

"Show me." He pressed his mouth just under her ear. Against that soft patch of skin and all those nerve endings that jumped at the contact.

Energy pounded her. She shifted with her hands moving and mind turning to mush. The slide of the zipper ripped through the room. Then she had her jeans open. Her breath rushed through her. The pumping need had her scrambling for his hands and those knowing fingers.

She plunged his palm into the open space between her zipper and her underwear. "Please."

That's all it took. His finger slid under the elastic band of her tiny bikini bottoms. Slid over her, then into her. She tried to gulp in air at the contact but her body refused to obey.

She crushed her body against his, plunging his finger deeper. When that didn't give her what she needed, she lifted up and pushed down hard again. A second finger joined the first. While she wiggled and shifted on top of him, searching for the perfect amount of pressure, he pushed his fingers in and out.

She heard a humming sound and realized it came from her. That her body craved this from him.

Need spiraled inside of her and every muscle tightened in anticipation. She squeezed against his fingers and pressed her thighs into his sides. Nothing relieved the pressure. It built and heated until she threw her head back and pushed down hard against him.

"Maddie."

The rough sound of her name on his lips nearly sent her flying over the edge. She opened her eyes, forcing them to focus. A sprinkle of sweat covered his forehead and that sexy crease where his throat met his collarbone.

When he lifted his other hand, she thought he might pull her down for a kiss. When he slipped it into the tight space at the opening of her jeans and rubbed in circles right over that sensitive spot that sent her reeling, she lost it.

The orgasm slammed through her. Her body bucked and her thighs pressed even harder against him. The shaking and pulsing wouldn't stop. She bit back a scream and kept the chanting of his name in her head.

By the time the waves of pleasure died down, she no longer had any strength. Her muscles gave out and she collapsed on top of him. A heap of hair and heavy breathing.

The soothing caress of his fingers tracing circles on her back made her eyes drift shut. All thoughts of getting up or rolling off him or saying something that made sense left her mind. He'd wrung every ounce of energy out of her.

After a few minutes of silence a few things hit her. A slight chill in the room. The bulge pressing against her stomach.

Yeah, she really wanted to do something about that but she needed a second.

She lifted away from the hand that still rested against her and slid off him. A few kicks and her jeans hit the floor. One roll and she was on her back, staring at the ceiling and listening to their labored breathing die down.

"You are so good at that." She meant it. He seemed to excel at everything and this proved to be no different.

"Maybe I am a handyman."

She laughed as she rolled to her side and snuggled against him. "That was a terrible joke."

"I bet Paul would have liked it."

They both laughed that time. She had no idea where she found the energy to make the noise. "Give me a second."

He looked at her. "For?"

He was either the least selfish person on earth or he thought she was the greediest one.

She lifted up with her head resting in her palm and looked at him. His body stretched out on the bed. Those long legs were still packed into those jeans but the rest of him, every impressive inch, was open to her view. "Do you think we're done?" she asked.

"I'm following your lead."

"So sexy."

She lay there for a few more minutes, stunned at the comfortable silence. Brushing her fingers over his bare chest. Trying to ignore how right this felt.

Her hand dipped lower, down the front of his pants. Skimmed over his length and watched as his eyes eased shut. He was hard and ready but still he waited.

Every article she read about him raved about his business sense and his work ethic. They described him as tough and energized and ready to walk out on any deal if he didn't get what he wanted. She didn't know how that lined up with the man beside her now, but this was who he had been with her since they met. A little bossy and a bit grumbly, but charming and decent. The kind of man who would walk a dog so a couple could have a booty call.

She smiled at the memory.

Finding a reserve of energy, she climbed back on top of him, careful to cradle his hard length between her thighs. His eyes popped open and he watched her. That gaze took in everything from the way she unhooked her bra to the way she slid it off and dropped it on the floor.

"Your turn."

WHEN SHE CLIMBED on top of him the second time, his mind went blank. All he saw was her, and that body and that beautiful face. Miles of bare skin.

The memory of touching her still played in his mind. So wet and ready. The way she trembled and leaned into him. Her hips shifting in time to his hand. She didn't hold back or play games. She wanted to be touched and begged for it, and he couldn't remember ever seeing anything as sexy as her open mouth and pink tongue as she came.

He rubbed his hands up and down her soft thighs. "This is a hell of a view."

She covered his hands with hers. Trailed them along her lean muscles to the insides of her thighs. She still wore those sexy blue bikini bottoms. They didn't block his gaze. He could smell her excitement.

She guided his hands higher, up her stomach to cup her breasts. Her body intrigued him. So firm yet so soft.

He held her, brushing his thumbs over her tight nipples. "Beautiful."

He caressed her until a tiny growl escaped her throat. He was already rock hard, and the sound pushed him right to the edge. The way she shifted on top of him, purposely rubbing against him, tested his control. It faded with every passing second.

Without warning, she leaned down and brushed her lips over his. Deepened the touch, treating him to a scorching kiss that sent his temperature spiking.

"Ride me." His plea came out as a rough whisper.

"Condom?"

He swore his heart stopped. He dropped his head back into the pillow. "Oh, shit."

"Amateur." She winked. "The drawer."

"What?"

She nodded in the direction of the nightstand. "I bought them yesterday."

No wonder everyone stared at them at the Lodge. The whole town likely knew about her recent purchases. But he liked her style. "Nice job."

"Get one."

Just as he reached over, he felt her move. She shifted and slid, traveled down his body and went to work on his jeans. Shimmied them down his legs.

His breath caught in his throat as he watched her fingers trail over him. Saw her hair cascade against his thighs. The sight held him there. Speechless. And when she slid her mouth over him, took him deep inside after licking along his length, he had to fight not to lose it.

"Maddie." His fingers slid through her silky hair. He guided his length in and out of her mouth, slowly torturing himself.

When she lifted her head, wetness glistened on her lips. "Now, Connor."

The sexy growl to her voice got him moving. He threw out an arm and tugged on the drawer knob. The contents thudded as he jerked it closer to him. He sighed with relief when his fingertips touched the condom.

He had it out and the wrapper open in record time. Before he could roll it on, she took over. Slipped it over him as he twitched and bit back a moan.

He wasn't sure when she stripped off her underwear, but she traveled back up his body naked and determined. His hands settled on her hips and he guided her down. She slipped over him and sank down with her inner muscles grabbing him and pulling him in deeper.

Praise gravity or her expertise, but the plunging inside her wiped out the last of the hold on his control. His hips lifted off the bed as he moved in and out. Her fingernails dug into his chest and her knees pressed against his sides. Heat swirled around them and his breathing hitched.

He barely felt or heard any of it. His body took over, a sensation so primal and raw that it ripped through him. His hips shifted and her body wrapped around his. By the time he let go and let the orgasm overcome him, he no longer saw anything but her body covering his. That face so close to his as he threaded his fingers through hers.

It took more than a few minutes for his brain to blink on again. When he finally opened his eyes he looked up at the off-white ceiling and tried to regain his breathing.

Her hair rested against his cheek and her head fit into the space under his chin. She had pulled up the comforter, somehow wrestled it out from under their bodies, and it now covered their legs.

"Okay," she said into the quiet darkness.

That was a pretty big understatement as far as he was concerned. "Okay?"

"Not a reflection of anything other than the fact it's the only word I could form right then." Her voice sounded breathy and uneven.

"That's less insulting than saying *okay*. Sounds better."

The sex knocked the life out of both of them. All that heat and friction. He was happy Paul didn't expect him tomorrow because there was no way in hell he was getting up early.

She lifted her leg higher against his until every part of her touched a part of him. "You know, there's a secondary benefit to us having sex."

"I'm pretty happy about the main benefit," he said.

"You don't have to sleep on the sofa bed."

That sounded promising. A little like progress, actually.

He lifted his head and stared down at her. "Are you inviting me into your . . . well, technically my . . . bed from now on?"

The second he said the words he wondered if he'd gone too far. Presumed too much.

She kept her eyes closed and her hand over his heart. "You've been very good."

A part of him loved her chattiness after sex. Another part of him wanted a nap. "Then my plan worked."

"This was all about getting a better mattress for you, wasn't it?"

She rarely showed this side of her—playful and uninhibited—and he was a fan. "Of course."

"You evil genius."

"Give me fifteen minutes and I'll prove what a genius I am." When she groaned, he figured that was one step too far. "Too much?"

"I'm willing to ignore the cheesiness."

"No one has ever accused me of that before." He tried to imagine what the people he did business deals with would think of that.

"You didn't know me before."

"I'm much luckier now." The words slipped out but he meant them.

She smiled with her eyes closed. "Yeah, you are."

CHAPTER 17

Connor didn't get up the next morning until after nine. He hadn't slept that late in years but Maddie had worn him out. Two more rounds, including one this morning, and he needed more than coffee to get him moving. The eggs helped. So did the fresh air.

He stood about twenty feet from the front of his cabin, in a small clearing near a clump of trees. He'd retrieved some of the dry wood from the shed at the back of the property and started cutting. It had been years since he'd wielded an ax. When he was growing up, his parents had a small place on a lake in Maryland. His father's workaholic tendencies had relaxed there. He sat outside and tutored his kids on the fine art of fishing and firewood collection.

The years passed and the memory faded. Now it made Connor smile.

"How long are you staying? On Whitaker, I mean."

At the sound of Maddie's still sleepy voice, he looked up. She sat on the bottom step leading up to the porch. She'd thrown on his sweatshirt, which looked like a tent on her. Her tablet rested on her lap, meaning a call could interrupt them any minute.

She looked relaxed while she sipped her coffee, but that was a loaded question. Connor treaded carefully. "That's out of the blue."

"Is it?" She tapped her sneakered feet against the step and cradled her mug. "You're supposed to be here on vacation, which usually would mean relaxing. I haven't seen you sit still since you got here."

Her gaze wandered over him. He felt every move and every frown. Looking down, he didn't see anything odd. He wore jeans and a T-shirt. Too light for the weather, but he'd been chopping wood for a half hour. Not exactly the desk work he was used to.

"A lot has happened." That struck him as the truth. He'd been here about a week and it felt more like months.

"Including the part where you got roped into helping me."

He leaned the ax against a stump and walked over to her. The conversation walloped him. He hadn't seen it coming and struggled to answer. "Let's be clear about one thing. If I didn't want to be with you, I would leave."

She looked down into her mug. "Right. Okay."

"You don't believe me." What the hell was that about? They'd been all over each other the night before. There wasn't an inch of her that he hadn't touched and kissed. Seemed to him the time for an interrogation was *before* they climbed into bed.

"You're a rescuer. I landed on your doorstep and . . ."

"What?" Every word she uttered ticked him off. The reaction was overblown and irrational but his temper ran away and he had trouble dragging it back under control.

"Sometimes you look at me like a bird with a broken wing."

"That's not true." He didn't see her like that at all. Mysterious and sometimes careless. Not as worried about her safety as she should be, but a survivor. The person who would rush into danger to keep anyone else from getting hurt. Not a bystander. Definitely not broken.

Her eyes narrowed as her head tipped slightly to one side. "Be honest. Is there a part of you that looks at me and sees your sister?"

Sweet hell. "You're asking that after last night?"

"Don't be weird. Not the sex. I mean . . ." She stared into the trees as if she were searching for the right words. "Is this really about a driving need to make sure I survive when she didn't?"

The words sliced through him. "Wow."

"Are you stalling while you think of an answer?"

"No." He was trying to figure out what kind of asshole she thought he was. Pathetic, stumbling around. Not knowing what he really wanted.

What the fuck?

The more frustrated he became, the calmer she looked. She set her mug and tablet on the step beside her and folded her arms on her knees. "Have you let yourself grieve at all?"

He shook his head. The conversation had taken off on this gallop. He didn't understand where they took a wrong turn or what changed since breakfast. She went to get dressed and he came outside and—*bam!*—she now thought of him as some sort of . . . he didn't even know what.

"What's happening right now? How did we go from showering together to this?" He really didn't get it.

"We can't avoid the topic forever."

"But when did I become the topic?"

She lowered each leg until her feet rested on the grass below. "Because it's more comfortable when all the focus is on me and protecting me and watching over me, right?"

"I feel like we're fighting and I'm not sure why."

She stood up and walked over to him. Stopped a few feet away. Close enough to touch but they didn't. "I don't want you to look at me like someone you need to fix."

"Sweet hell, Maddie. I look at you and my breath stops. I want to drag you home and strip you naked, and none of that has to do with rescuing you."

Some of the tension left her face. "What is it about?"

She looked as confused as he felt. Nothing about last night prepared him for this topic. They kept flipping around and now they'd landed on something that sounded like *what are your intentions?* and he couldn't get his bearings. "I don't know. I don't really get why you have me spinning in circles when no woman in a year even piqued my interest enough to ask her out for coffee."

"Spinning?"

"Confused. Off balance." Did she really not know the definition? "I haven't focused on anything but work and my family for almost two years. Then you come along and . . ." He didn't know how to describe these feelings for her because he didn't understand them. They hit him out of nowhere and kept knocking him down. "You're in my head all the time. From the moment we met in Ben's office."

She blinked at him a few times. "No one has ever said that to me before."

No, he didn't want the soft eyes and lighter tone. She had him revved up and ticked off and maybe he needed to stay that way for a while. "Yeah, well, I didn't expect it. I sure as hell didn't plan on you."

"But then I lured you into my mess."

Enough about that first meeting. He'd let that go a long time ago. "With or without what happened that first night in the cabin, I would have found you on Whitaker. This—us—was inevitable."

She frowned at him. "How do you figure that? I'm a recluse, remember?"

She just kept picking a fight. She would wind up and unload, then calm down. The emotional roller coaster confused him. "You've been all over town with me. That's not what a recluse does."

"Or, maybe, I haven't had a choice because of the babysitting."

No way was he letting her tag him as the bad guy in this scenario. "Ever think that you're sticking to my side because you want to be there?"

She snorted. "Of course."

Somewhere between the yelling and the answer she lost him. "Wait . . ."

"If I didn't want to be with you, kiss you, get to know you, I would have run and hid the second after we met." She reached up and pushed the hair out of his eyes.

He waited for her to circle back to angry again but it didn't happen. "What are you saying?"

"I'm surprised you feel the same way."

The last of the anger and tension ran out of him. "It's a weird thing to have in common."

"There's something about you."

He should let it go and not ask. But he wasn't that guy. He sought out answers. "Is that a good thing?"

"The hotness. The charm."

Those sounded good. "Nice."

"The pain."

He groaned. "You ruined it."

"You don't even see it, do you?"

The conversation was over. He was not tiptoeing back into that mess of a topic. If she wanted to psycho-analyze someone, she could pick Ben.

He turned around and picked up the ax. "I need to finish this."

"It's possible we're attracted to each other and pulled together by this weird unseen force because we're not so different. We're both in a type of mourning we still haven't fully processed."

He didn't have any destination in mind but he started walking. Headed for the thick patch of trees. "Uh-huh."

"We're both trying to survive the aftermath."

That's it. He turned around to face her. "What are you surviving exactly? You know about my sister. I'm clueless about your past."

"I got sucked into a crime and witnessed a murder. I want to say wrong place, wrong time, but I was where I was supposed to be. Missed the clues and then . . . there was so much blood."

She said it right out, without prompting. The words sat there. He didn't know what to say next. "Jesus."

"Yeah, exactly."

"I'll listen if you want to tell me more." Whatever she said, he would handle it. She didn't need him judging or rushing in with a thousand questions. She could take her time, but he wasn't going anywhere.

"Not now." She chewed on her bottom lip for a second. "But I will. Just give me a little more time."

"Done." His mind spun with possibilities. He tried to mentally put together the few facts he knew, but he couldn't get a picture. All he knew was that the danger was real and sounded deadly. "But is the murder, what you saw, tied to the notes you're getting now?"

"Must be since I don't have any other big secrets in my past, even though I still don't get how. All of that should be over."

She seemed determined to tell him the part about the secrets. It's the exact reason he didn't buy it. That and the tone. Her voice dipped as if she was trying to convince both of them. "Really?"

"Which part?"

"I think you know." When she continued to stare at him, he filled in the blank. "The secrets, Maddie. Do you really only have one?"

All of the emotion left her face. "Don't analyze me."

Apparently only she could play that game, or so she thought. But she was wrong. "You just said I was stuck in my grief."

"You haven't truly mourned your sister. That's obvious."

He blocked the words. Didn't let them in his head. "Yet you're fine."

"I never said that."

He had enough. He turned back around and continued walking.

She called after him. "Where are you going?"

"Not far."

"It feels like you're running away."

"No, just going deeper into . . ." He saw the flash of red a few feet away and thought it was a shirt or a piece of trash. A few more steps told him he was dead wrong. "Oh, shit."

"What?"

He heard the crunch of her sneakers against the dead leaves and warned her off. He needed her away from this. Far away. "Are you carrying your cell?"

"Of course, why?"

She stood right behind him. He turned to tell her to go back to the cabin. "Maddie."

It was too late. Her eyes focused on the spot over his shoulder and her mouth dropped open. "Oh, my God."

Connor followed her gaze to the man lying face-down on the ground. Blood pooled around him. Connor tried to look anywhere but there. One glance and his stomach heaved. Seeing blood did that to him.

"Who is that?" Her voice vibrated with shock.

He understood exactly how she felt. "Call Ben."

CHAPTER 18

Most people went their entire lives without seeing a dead body. This was Maddie's second experience. She didn't handle it this time any better than the first.

She sat in the conference room off of Ben's office. She'd called her fill-in and asked her to take care of the answering service for a few days. There were only so many responsibilities she could handle at one time.

The dead body changed everything.

Sylvia had arrived and stuck a coffee in her hand then disappeared again. The caffeine helped. So did sitting across from Connor. He grounded her. They'd been in the middle of a difficult discussion. She'd kept pushing, couldn't stop herself. The questions rolled out of her. She wanted to know about him, to make him see that the sister he loved was never really far from his thoughts, despite his insistence he was fine. Then they found the body and nothing else mattered.

He reached his hand across the table and covered hers. "You okay?"

"No." She knew he wasn't any better. He'd gagged more than once waiting for Ben to arrive at the cabin. "Are you?"

"Seeing blood makes me queasy."

She understood. It's why she looked away. The idea that the poor man lay out there all alone while his life ran out of him doubled her over. "I guess you didn't play sports growing up then."

"I played soccer from the time I was little through college. Had my share of injuries. Once saw Hansen snap a bone to the point where it poked through his skin." He stared at a spot on the table. Kept all his attention focused there. "Ever since we lost Alexis, I can't see blood without thinking of her."

Her heart flipped over. The pain stayed there, right at the surface. Spurred him on. Changed him.

She squeezed his hand. "I'm sorry."

"Me, too." He sat back in his chair. The move had his palm sliding against the table, away from her, until he put it on his lap. "So what happens now? I don't fully get how this island works. Do the police fly in or what?"

She wasn't in the mood to give a history lesson but the nonsense topic might keep both of their minds off of what they'd seen. "Ben is in charge but with something like this, at least last time, state investigators arrived. For a few days, they swarmed and asked questions and spent a lot of time with Ben."

Connor tried to imagine how much the residents must hate the intrusion. "Damn."

"I'm not sure exactly what the chain of command is, but Ben basically *is* Whitaker's law enforcement. After last summer, he hired a full-time assistant, but he's in training off Whitaker right now. So he's no help."

"Convenient." When she stared at him, Connor realized he sounded a bit off. "I wasn't saying it was a conspiracy. Just throwing out a word."

"Maybe some of Whitaker's paranoia rubbed off on you."

"Let's hope not." *No, really.* He hoped not.

"Anyway." She cleared her throat as if she were about to launch into a long speech. "Ben also has a few voluntary assistants and Doc Lela handles the forensics."

"It's a bit of a patchwork of people, isn't it? You'd think Ben would have more permanent help."

She shrugged. "Never needed it until recently."

"You mean, until the Rye brothers arrived."

"We're all thinking it, but thank you for saying it." She winked at him. "Whitaker is just odd, in general. It's a privately owned island. A rich benefactor— mysterious and unseen—owns it and runs it through a corporation. All of the property is leased and the Board, of which Sylvia is now the president thanks to a financial scandal with the last one who is off island for some *me time*, makes most of the rules."

"Very dramatic."

"Right?"

"Does anyone know who the owner is?"

"If they do, they aren't talking." But, man. She really wanted to know. More than once her curiosity got ahold of her and she asked around. No one had any answers and Sylvia just smiled instead of responding. It had been an exercise in frustration.

"That's consistent with my experience so far." He shook his head. "There are some odd folks here."

"Despite the weird circumstances and tales about in-fighting by some of the original families that moved in, Whitaker is pitched as a bucolic, quiet island where people can go to start over. Reclusive and cut off with very few activities to attract tourists, so visitors beware."

"Is all that on a brochure somewhere?"

"It's what sold me." WITSEC placed her in Portland. She loved the buzz but needed more quiet. She thought living on Whitaker would be temporary but when the months stretched into years, she realized she liked the quiet. "The Board oversees Ben. Ben reports to someone in Seattle."

"And the whole system works unless and until someone turns up dead."

"That seems to be true." She thought back before the summer. "Literally nothing happened here until last summer. I know because I answer most of Ben's work calls. A kid causing trouble now and then. Someone trampling on someone else's garden. Not death."

"Death is everywhere."

"I wish you were wrong."

"Hey." Ben walked into the room and closed the door behind him. He held a file and the deep lines around his mouth spoke to the pressure he was under. Again.

Connor's eyebrow lifted. "Well?"

"Doc Lela is doing an autopsy. Her initial assessment is that our victim was stabbed to death."

"There was so much blood." Maddie regretted the comment when she saw Connor flinch.

Ben stared at Connor. "You don't know him?"

"Never seen him before."

"Me either." And she would know because she made it her business to know these things. "When did this happen?"

Ben took a quick look in his file before closing it again. "With the rain and cold temperatures, she couldn't give a definite answer yet, but she's thinking twenty-four to thirty hours ago."

That meant someone killed the man while they were living together in Connor's cabin. "And he's just been out there, in the woods. All alone."

"Damn." Connor shoved his chair away from the table and took a long breath.

"You okay?" Ben asked.

"I'm not great with blood."

Ben frowned at him. "It's been hours."

"Yeah, well, I'm not great with dead bodies either, I guess."

Maddie knew Connor's reaction was about more than the man in the woods. This reached back into his memories and his frustrations. Not that he would fully admit it, but after knowing him only a short time she could see it. She wondered how his family missed the distress he was in.

She tried to change the subject. "Does this mean we're about to see more police on Whitaker?"

Ben nodded. "I have to make some calls, but I suspect I'll have some patrol and investigative help by tomorrow."

"Who's the guy?" Connor asked.

Ben didn't check the file for that answer. "Owen Pritchard."

Nothing about that sounded familiar to her. "Never heard of him."

"Sylvia says he's not registered at the Lodge. She's never seen him either."

Connor tapped his fingers against the table. "Dom."

Whatever Ben had been about to say cut off and he focused on Connor. "Excuse me?"

"Maddie and I talked with him." Connor glanced at her before continuing. "He talked about bringing someone over from Arnold Island a few times and that he thought the guy was still here. Probably in a rental."

And now dead. That reality started churning deep inside Maddie. A fear everything would start spinning. Tilt until she'd be unable to straighten it again.

Ben nodded. "I'll check with him and about the rental properties. Thanks."

She tried to hold her questions in so she could analyze and prepare, but they came spilling out. "What was he doing out there? Other than the cabin, there's trees but he was off the hiking trail and not really dressed for that anyway."

"Well, that's the interesting part," Ben said.

Connor groaned. "I'm almost afraid of what you'll say next."

"One thing first." Ben held up a hand as if to calm her racing thoughts. "Keep in mind that he could be a tourist. This could be innocent."

"Well . . ." Connor drew out the word for a few extra seconds. "He was stabbed to death."

Her mind had already jumped ahead. She could feel that Ben was about to drop some huge information bomb on them. "But?"

Ben stopped looking around the room and following the conversation and stared at her. "Owen Pritchard was a private investigator."

And there it was. The expected fall. "What?"

"His driver's license is from North Carolina. I did a quick check into his background and he's from—"

"Wait." The trembling started in her hands but it would soon overtake all of her. All those memories would crash in and haunt every hour. She'd lose the ability to keep it together.

Connor stared at her. "What is it?"

"He's from Winston-Salem or somewhere close." She could hear the faraway sound in her voice but not the fear. Somehow, she disguised that. Probably from years of practice and pretending to be someone else. Someone with a boring life and no drama.

Ben confirmed her worst fears with a nod. "That's right."

The chair squeaked as Connor shifted position. He leaned forward, balancing his elbows on the edge of the table. "I'm thinking that wasn't just a really good guess."

"You said you didn't know him," Ben said.

Their voices echoed around her. She tried to concentrate, to stay in the here and now. "I don't, but this is about me. This guy being here, possibly his murder—all me."

Ben's eyes narrowed. "We don't know that."

"There's no pretending. It's too much of a coincidence." This wasn't about this one guy. This was bigger. So much bigger.

"What are you saying?" Ben asked.

She lifted her head and stared at two of the only people she trusted right now. "That past I'm running from? It's in Winston-Salem."

CHAPTER 19

Ben called Sylvia in from the hall. Connor heard him say her name and the door opened, but all of his focus stayed on Maddie. The color had left her face. She sat there, pale, looking small and vulnerable. Not anything like the woman who stormed around the island asking about outsiders and talking about hiding places. This was the Maddie who had all those locks on her door. The terrified one.

"What's going on?" Sylvia glanced around the table, and when her gaze landed on Maddie, her mouth flattened into a thin line. "Are you okay?"

"Fine." Maddie's hand shook as she reached for her coffee mug.

Connor wanted to take her home. Not to the cabin because the police tape and gawkers made that impossible. Maybe to hers or the Lodge. He looked at Ben. "Do we need to be here?"

"Yes." Ben only spared Connor a quick look before turning to Sylvia. "I need a list of open properties on the island and a second list of short-term rentals. The rent likely would have been paid in cash."

"You have that as board president?" Connor asked because he still didn't understand the way Whitaker ran or how all of these pieces fit together.

"Yes." Sylvia nodded. "This is about the man you found?"

"Dom suggested someone came onto the island and didn't leave. Someone he didn't know." Maddie visibly exhaled a shuddering breath as soon as she finished the sentence. "That person could be our victim."

"Okay." Sylvia said the word, but she didn't move.

"We have some questions we need to get through."

The comment was as close to a dismissal as Connor had heard from Ben. He opened his file and took out a pen. He didn't clear the room but his body language said *get out.*

Connor understood Ben had a job to do, but not like this. Not now. Maddie had made it clear she was ready to talk but she looked too shaky to get much of value out. "Can this wait?"

"No, Connor." Ben stopped writing on his notepad and looked up. "I've waited long enough to hear this. You and Sylvia can step into the hall."

"It's okay." Maddie rested her hand against the table with a soft thud. "They can stay."

"Maddie." Ben's tone held a warning.

She didn't look impressed. "Let's not pretend we can keep this a secret. If Owen Pritchard is connected to my past, everyone will know soon enough. People here have a skill for ferreting out information, even though they all claim not to be nosy."

"I don't understand," Sylvia said as she sat down next to Connor.

"Maddie believes the victim is tied to her past." Ben looked around the table and stopped at Maddie. "And I'm trying to figure out how."

"But now?" Connor asked.

Ben nodded. "Right now. And to be clear, everyone gets interviewed separately about their whereabouts when this death occurred. This is about background." Ben waited for everyone to acknowledge his statement before he nodded at Maddie. "Go ahead."

She traced her finger over some invisible pattern only she could see on the table. Watching her sit there, struggling to find the words, made Connor ache for her. She'd gone from being painfully private to having her life laid bare. Maybe not all of Whitaker would know, but he knew from experience that talking about events like this took a toll.

Everything would change now. She might sneak back to her reclusive ways. He just hoped she didn't walk away from him.

MADDIE LOCKED THE information away long ago. Kept it pent up in that tiny part at the back of her mind. The dark space of things she wanted to forget. Cracking the vault open now took all of her strength, but it gave her something to focus on. If she could just repeat the words, describe the details as if they happened in a movie or to someone else, she could survive this.

There were things Ben needed to know. Details she should have given him when she handed him the note. She'd opened the mental door to let him peek in but still kept him out. He hadn't pushed because he was Ben, and because he likely thought he could either find what he needed or get it from Evan . . . or wait her out for a week or so. Either way, not talking might have led to this PI's death and she couldn't find a way to process that.

"Maddie, do you need a few minutes?" Sylvia asked.

No, because time wouldn't make this easier to say. "Up until three years ago, I worked for the Edgmont Company in Winston-Salem. Commercial real estate development. Big projects, like shopping malls and university buildings." She glanced at Connor. "It was one of those family businesses. Very insular. Handed down from their father to the two sons—Grant and Ned. I worked for Grant."

Ben made notes but Connor just watched her. She looked for judgment but didn't see any. Then again, he didn't know what was coming. Or what pieces she'd held back.

"I started as an assistant and worked my way up really quickly during the five years I was there. Grant talked about me being like family. He and his wife—" She choked over the word and had to swallow a few times to start again. "Allison. That was his wife."

Connor frowned. "Was?"

Maddie didn't respond. Sticking to the timeline was the best way through, so she kept talking. Letting the rambling in her head flood out of her. "The company did well under their father but business exploded with Grant and Ned's leadership. They kept the management team small. Made everyone feel special."

"Including you," Ben said.

Especially her. "They gave me more responsibility. Promoted me. I started doing some financial work for them. I didn't have a background, but I took some classes on my own. It was all so new, and I had no idea if I would like accounting or be any good at it, so I didn't tell them. It was a thing I did for me, but the more I learned, the more concerned I became about the company's accounts." She shook her head, lost in the memory of that moment when she put it all together. "Maybe I always knew because the accounts never added up right. There was money for jobs that didn't exist. All this paperwork that didn't match up with what I knew was really happening in terms of actual projects."

"Were they laundering money?" Connor asked.

Of course he knew where to focus. He'd know what to ask because he dealt with large contracts all the time. "They got into the business of bribery, dealing information on their competitors and former friends. On politicians. They collected intel and used it. Money flowed, so much more than from the real work that they switched their focus to the dirty money."

"Wait a minute. This sounds familiar." Connor squinted as if he were pulling the pieces of the story out of his memory. "The wife and husband . . ."

"Died. Killed each other. Were killed." None of the words fit. "The initial thought was Allison found out about an alleged affair and confronted Grant at the office. He killed her, then himself."

"Was any of that true?" Sylvia asked.

"No." Maddie inhaled, waiting for the moment where talking about this would become a relief. But it never happened. "Thinking we were like family, or at least friends, I had talked with Allison about my suspicions. Showed her the tracing I'd done, walked her through the accounts and showed her the evidence that the money didn't match with the work orders, all thinking she'd work with Grant to get the truth out. She said we'd go to the police or the FBI together. And that night . . ." She swallowed hard. "Well, there was an affair, but it was between Ned and Allison and she warned him about my worries."

Ben groaned. "Shit."

"Before I left the office that night, Ned tried to kill me. The whole thing ended with Allison and Grant dead and the police called."

"Ned killed them?" Ben asked.

She couldn't really answer, so she nodded.

"How did you survive?"

"In the middle of the chaos, I hit the alarm for security." She swallowed over the lump in her throat. "They got there, but not in time for the others."

Connor continued to stare at her. The look morphed from concerned to assessing. Just as she feared. He would see her differently now. They all would.

"What happened next?" he asked.

Time blurred in her head. "Ned blamed me. He made up the affair story. I was arrested."

"What?" Sylvia sounded appalled on her behalf.

"Technically, I did help move the money around. The accounts didn't match up and I ignored the signs until I couldn't anymore." If she could go back and replay all those moves, call the police in sooner, Allison and Grant might be alive. That awful bit of timing changed everything and she'd never figured out a way to live with that.

"But someone followed your tracing, agreed with you, and you became the star witness," Connor said, filling in the pieces for her.

Sylvia hummed. "Good guess."

"It's not a guess. I remember the story now. A city politician is in jail. Others were implicated. A lot of powerful people started scrambling and pointing fingers." Connor let out a long exhale. "And Ned died in prison while waiting for trial."

"Not before he paid for someone to kill me so I couldn't testify about what happened in the office that night."

Ben put his pen down. "And that explains your time in WITSEC."

"He hired a guy he knew who had worked on his car. Some people say the guy wanted more money and turned on Ned when he wouldn't agree. Others say the guy was decent and only agreed so that he could go to the police and turn Ned in. The *why* didn't matter to me. I was just grateful he talked." The one piece of luck she was ever thankful for. "But Ned was desperate and a lying narcissist, and everyone believed he would try again."

"But when he died in prison, the threat against you, conceivably, ended."

Maddie understood Connor's careful wording. The notes suggested someone out there still viewed her as a threat.

"Being in WITSEC is voluntary." And suffocating. It filled her with fear and paranoia and she couldn't live that way one more day. So when she got the out, she took it. "I left over the objections of Evan, the marshal assigned to my case."

"Are you still in legal trouble?" Ben asked.

"No. When I answered the questions, that helped put the politician and another businessman in prison. Unlike Ned, they took a plea and my charges went away."

Connor's mouth dropped open. "Why in the world do you think it's safe for you to go around without protection?"

"Most trial witnesses don't get WITSEC protection. It was the breadth of the case that opened that option. Like you said, a lot of powerful people paid a price."

"And some of them have the money to hire people to kill you." Sylvia shook her head. "It's called revenge."

"They want revenge on the old me, Ellen Samuels, not Maddie Rhine. Ellen is gone." That was the price she paid for not calling out the problems she saw sooner.

"You can't believe that." The edge to Connor's tone mirrored the disbelief on his face. "Someone is sending you threatening notes and a PI was here looking for you or following you."

She couldn't do this.

"Okay, enough." She stood up so quickly that she knocked her chair over. It crashed against the hard floor. "I just laid it all out there. You all wanted to know, and now you do."

The look of concern on Sylvia's face spoke for the room. "Maddie . . ."

"I'm done with show-and-tell."

Maddie stormed out of the room. The words spewing out of her were unfair and she knew it. But the fire in her head and the mash of memories running through her mind—the ones she tried so hard to pack and put away—knocked her off balance. Her fingers tingled and her heart raced.

She made it the whole way to the outside of the building before she doubled over. Balancing her butt against the wall, she braced her hands on her knees. Took deep, cleansing breaths. Forced her mind to think of good memories, but hunting those down zapped her strength.

She slid down the stucco wall until her ass hit the wet grass. Last night's rain soaked through her jeans on contact, but she had bigger problems. Tipping her head back, she let the cold breeze blow over her. Above her all she saw was a solid gray sky. No rain but something was coming. She felt it to her bones.

A door banged shut in the distance. She could hear a dog barking and assumed someone walked by and got a front row seat to her messy reaction. She closed her eyes, not wanting to know who or how many people stood around or waited in their cars to see what she would do next.

This was what mental exhaustion looked like. All that running and energy spent convincing herself she was fine when she felt anything but. The anxiety built and grew and just walloped her.

"You forgot your jacket."

She opened her eyes and saw Connor standing over her. He held out her raincoat but his expression was unreadable. She looked for anger or disgust but got an emotional void. It was as if he felt nothing and that realization punched into her, stealing the last of her will.

She took the coat. "I'm fine."

"Yeah, you look fine." He glanced at the wet ground, then sat down beside her.

"You're going to have wet underwear."

He shrugged. "Won't be the first time."

"That sounds like a story." She turned to look at him and half hoped he'd tell it.

He sat in a sprawl with his long legs bent at the knee and his feet flat against the ground. His arms hung between his legs and a slight smile crossed his lips.

"He's a hotel guy now, but when I was growing up, my dad had a thing for camping."

"What about your mom?"

The smile grew. "She did not. She was always pro-hotel. But he would get us out there, to this cabin in the woods that he loved, and we'd go boating and swimming."

The longer he talked, the more the tension eased from her body. "In your underwear?"

"Hansen thought it was funny to try to throw Alexis in the lake. When he couldn't find her, he'd come after me. Lots of sibling wrestling happened on that dock in Maryland."

"You're close to your family."

"My parents are good people. Not perfect, but clear." He glanced at her then. "Do you know what I mean by that?"

She realized she'd snuggled up next to him but didn't care. Didn't try to move away. "Like, honest?"

"Sort of. It's like I know who they are because they've always been true, even when they messed up. Hansen lost it when Alexis died. His temper raged and he couldn't work. The most natural thing was for Dad and me to step up and to get Hansen out of there so he could find peace. We didn't debate it. We filled the void."

They were good people. She knew that from what she knew about Hansen, from the articles she read, and from being with Connor nearly nonstop since he arrived on Whitaker.

He closed his eyes for a second before opening them again. "Years before we lost Alexis, my dad had a drinking problem, so none of us drink. My mom had a cancer scare when I was in college, so we all vowed to shave our heads, even Alexis. Never had to, but that's how it worked. We were a team, still are, but we're down a player."

"Losing Alexis must have been devastating."

"My mom changed. Retreated emotionally. She describes losing a child as this sucking pain that never goes away. She is pretty stoic and not outwardly emotional, but it's as if a part of her heart was ripped out and she never refilled the hole. Never wanted to. She talks about not being able to breathe some days."

Maddie leaned her head against his shoulder. "I can't imagine."

"You've known loss."

She thought about the secrets she'd just shared. "My mom died while I was in witness protection. Ovarian cancer."

He pulled back a few inches and looked down at her. "Were you able to see her?"

She choked back the unexpected rush of tears. "Too dangerous. But it had always been us. My parents divorced when I was young and my father immediately moved on to a new family."

"What the fuck kind of father is that?"

Of course that would be appalling to him. He only knew family acceptance. She'd learned long ago that the concept of unconditional love had its limits. "Some guys leave."

"Some guys suck."

She wanted to reach out and take his hand. Forget that they were right there, in the middle of town, sitting on wet grass in the freezing cold, and her with a jacket on her lap but not on. Let them watch and wonder. "Does it matter?"

He looked confused. "What?"

"My past. The money. Being involved in that mess."

"It wasn't your mess, Maddie." He sucked in his breath. "Should I still call you Maddie?"

"I'm Maddie now . . ." There were so many *but*s that went after that. She wasn't sure where to start. "You're honest and decent and . . . I get it if what I told you is too much."

"Would it surprise you that many of the people I deal with in my job every day think I'm a ruthless dick?"

"I can imagine you being successful, but that description doesn't really fit you."

"Don't let vacation Connor fool you. I fight pretty hard for what I want."

It was the way he said it. His voice dipped deep and heat flashed in his eyes.

The last of her panic subsided. "What do you want?"

"You. From the first day I talked to you."

She smiled because he made the distinction between meeting her and talking to her. That was her fault but the guilt over the hitting had also eased. That's what Connor did. He made things better.

"My underwear is wet." She had to fight off a laugh as she said the words.

"We should do something about that." He jumped to his feet and held a hand down to help her up.

That lightness she sought, the sensation that was supposed to hit when a person told the truth they'd been hiding, still eluded her. But the burden wasn't as heavy now.

"You're smiling." He helped her into her raincoat. "It's good to see."

He put it there. She knew it and she sensed a part of him knew it. "I'm tired of running."

"We'll move into your place." He reached for her arm. "And we'll—"

"Touch her and you die."

She heard the voice and looked up. That's when she saw the gun pointed at Connor's head.

CHAPTER 20

Connor froze. The pressure of the barrel against his skull held him in place. He thought about all those boxing sessions and ways he could trip up the man next to him, but every option led to a bullet to the brain.

The other option was to call out for Ben. Yell, then take Maddie to the ground, hoping Ben would get out there in time to stop whatever came next, but that put Maddie in danger.

Both choices sucked.

He tried to send Maddie the silent message to duck and run, but she wasn't looking at him. Her focus centered on the man over his shoulder and there wasn't an ounce of fear in her frown.

"Evan?" She sounded as confused as she looked.

"Police." Ben shifted into view from around the side of the building. He had his gun and walked alone, careful and determined, while Sylvia pushed bystanders back into the parking lot and out of the way. "Put the weapon down."

Tension still snapped through Connor. Too many people hovered and all of them had guns. That was too many guns for his comfort.

"It's okay. Let's stay calm." Evan's voice remained even and placating. There was a rhythm to his words that was almost hypnotizing.

"You heard me." Ben kept his gun raised with his aim clear. Nothing in his demeanor suggested he was ready to back down.

"How did you even know we were out here?" Evan kept the conversation light despite the tensions slamming against them. "Impressive."

"Four people came into my office to report you the second you got close to Maddie and Connor." Ben's voice didn't waver. "Now, put the gun down."

Color flooded into Maddie's cheeks. She looked at the men around her, the weapons, and held up her hands. "This is the marshal. Evan Williams."

Ben hadn't moved. "Lower the weapon, Evan. Now."

Evan hesitated another few seconds before dropping his arm. Relief flooded through Connor a second later. Every instinct in him screamed to punch this guy but he pushed it down. He still was the only one other than Maddie without a weapon.

"He was bothering Maddie and I stepped in." Evan slipped his weapon into the holster he wore at his side.

She shook her head. "He really wasn't."

"It's good to see you." Evan stepped forward and hugged Maddie.

She stilled and he clapped her shoulder a bit harder than normal. The touching struck Connor as one of the more awkward welcomes he'd ever seen. He guessed that made sense since Maddie and Evan had a relationship based on danger and safety. Add to that her reluctance to have protection and it was not exactly a recipe for a close friendship.

"I'm Ben Clifford and that needs to be the last time you draw your weapon on this island." Ben's shoulders relaxed as he shifted out of battle stance but his voice stayed firm.

Evan shook his head. "I can't promise that."

"Do it anyway."

For a second Evan just stood there in his dark pants and slim black down jacket. Then he nodded. "Happy you called and filled me in about what's been happening. Looks like it was just in time."

Connor's dislike of the other man was immediate and unrelenting. He tried to nail down what bugged him. The guy thought a lot of himself, which wasn't a surprise. That tended to come with the carry-a-gun-so-I'm-in-charge vibe. He walked into danger without hesitating. That level of self-assurance sometimes bled over into asshole.

He was fit and tall, probably in his late forties, and wore an expression that suggested he viewed himself as Maddie's savior. No wonder she wanted out of the program as soon as possible.

"This is Connor Rye." Maddie moved to stand next to him and touched his arm. "He's a . . . friend."

She had to be kidding. "Are you serious right now?"

Evan looked from Maddie to Connor. "What am I missing here?"

"Everyone." Sylvia joined them, lowering her voice after her initial greeting. "We have an audience. I think we should head over to the Lodge. I can get Mr. . . ." She looked at the marshal.

He shot her a wide smile. "Williams, but call me Evan."

Yeah, Connor didn't like the guy at all.

Sylvia gestured for Evan to come with her. "We'll get you settled in. I'm thinking we can all use some pie or liquor. Maybe liquor and pie."

Sylvia had guided Evan toward the parked cars and the small crowd that had gathered there, eavesdropping with abandon. Not even pretending to hide they were listening in. Even Paul stood there with Mr. Higginbotham.

Evan and Sylvia only got a few steps before Evan turned around. "I get that we have a crowd issue but I need to talk with Maddie. Just a few minutes alone. We can get a lot of this straightened out and let the people on the island get back to their lives."

Connor had to give the guy credit for knowing his target. He knew where to aim. He had to know she felt guilty about upsetting people on Whitaker and he drove right there. The asshole.

But if Maddie felt obliged to go with him, she didn't show it. She waved off the concern. "We can do that at the Lodge. Get checked in and then we'll run through what's happened and some new information that might have come up while you were on your way here."

Evan's eyes narrowed. "Interesting."

Connor enjoyed seeing her deny Evan's order and ignore the emotional blackmail more than he wanted to admit. "Isn't it?"

"Then we're all agreed." Sylvia had her hand under Evan's elbow and got him moving back toward the parking lot again. "Let me show you the way."

A wave of exhaustion hit Connor, but he welcomed the release of tension. Maddie's outpouring about her past. Her breakdown right there in the grass. All that sharing took a toll. He'd spent two years blocking every emotion and keeping as far out of people's private lives as possible. He'd been on Whitaker little more than a week and he'd been roped into investigations and protective details . . . and being with her.

"*Isn't it?*" Maddie said, mimicking his tone. "Really?"

If she wanted to do this, they would do it. "*Friend?*"

She shook her head as she walked past him, following in Sylvia's footsteps. "Behave yourself. He's here to help."

He thought about pointing out how she didn't want the marshal here but he let the subject drop. No use getting into a battle he couldn't win because she'd keep changing the rules anyway. "Yes, ma'am."

He tried to remember where he'd put his keys. Before he could take a step, Ben shifted in front of him.

"Careful." Ben made a show of glancing in Evan's direction and Maddie's retreating back before looking at Connor again. "I'm serious. This is good advice, so take it."

He sure looked serious. Stress showed in every line on his face. Adrenaline likely still thrummed through him following that standoff with the marshal.

But that didn't mean Connor understood the message Ben was trying to send. "Meaning?"

"The man carries a gun."

"Yeah, I know. He aimed it at my head when he threatened me."

Ben finally seemed to relax a bit. "You do have that effect on people."

"Now that we know about Maddie's past and what happened, is he really needed?" Connor knew the answer—no. The guy should leave, go back to his desk. Go help the other people he was supposed to watch over. The ones actually in the program.

Ben smiled. "You're pretty transparent."

"How?"

"You're jealous of the marshal."

No way was Connor engaging on that topic. His feelings for Maddie were on constant fire. His brain misfired and fogged around him. She generally had him running in circles. Something he never did. He stayed focused, so focused that he'd nearly worked himself to death over the last two years. This constant blur of mental confusion . . . he blamed her.

But none of that was the point. This was about some jackass bursting into her life and trying to take it over. That way of existing was behind her and she was clear that's where she wanted it to stay. "She doesn't want to be in the program anymore."

"He thinks she should be. I know that because we've talked several times. He's convinced someone from her past, from that case, wants revenge." Ben sounded like he agreed.

Connor got it. All of the responsibility for Whitaker landed on Ben's shoulders. Having Maddie gone meant less danger. But there was another answer. The one where they found out who was messing with her and stopped it. "Did he tell you who might want this revenge? Because it sounds like most of the key players in what happened to her are now dead."

"He didn't give me any details but I got the impression he's been watching over her from afar out of concern."

Of course he was. He acted like he owned her, or at least got to decide how she reacted to the situation in front of her. So, it wasn't a surprise. "Creepy."

Ben let out a long sigh. "It's probably a habit."

Made sense but Connor wasn't in the mood to be practical or fair. "Well, he can go back to watching her from a distance."

Ben whistled. "He's right about one thing."

"What?"

"This is going to get interesting."

THEY ALL JAMMED into Sylvia's office twenty minutes later. Evan sat in her leather desk chair, because of course he did.

The reasons for Connor to dislike the guy kept piling up.

Sylvia and Maddie took the other chairs and Ben and Connor stood by the door. Connor thought it might be good to be this close to the exit. He didn't see a reason to be trapped in here any longer than necessary.

"We have notes without fingerprints." Ben took over the conversation after the initial passing out of water and coffee. Liquor and pie would need to wait. "Threats that might link back to the dead PI, but why would he leave them for Maddie? What does a PI gain from that sort of behavior?"

"He could be working for someone else," Evan said. "Completely unrelated. It's possible we're jumping to conclusions."

Ben shrugged. "Possible but not likely."

Maddie had turned her chair around so she could face everyone in the room. Up until that point she'd been busy staring into her coffee cup, but at Ben's comment she perked up. "There is no way the PI on an assignment thousands of miles away from home—a home where I once lived—just happens to pick this island where I'm hiding out. That coincidence is too much to believe."

"Agreed. That's why I've made a request for a review of his client files and computer." Ben talked in clipped sentences, fully back in command and clearly not ceding the floor to Evan. "Tomorrow I'll start a search of the island to figure out where he was staying before he was killed and see if we can find anything to direct us there."

"I can do that," Evan said, as if anyone asked him to step up.

Connor shook his head. "You're out of your jurisdiction."

"Maddie is my responsibility," Evan shot back.

"Okay, let's stop this." Maddie raised her hand. "And, Evan? Not anymore."

Evan ignored her comment and kept his attention on Connor. He sat back in the big chair. Lounged there, looking like he was running a meeting. "Are we in the middle of a turf war?"

Because that's probably how the guy saw this, as some sort of battle. "My only goal is to keep her safe."

He was trying to prove another point. He wasn't even sure what it was but he hated the idea of letting Evan win at anything.

Evan folded his hands over his stomach. "And your qualifications to guard her are what?"

"That's enough. Evan does have the expertise. No one is debating that." Ben made the point, then winced as if to apologize after the fact.

Maddie sighed at him. "You're not helping."

"I want you safe." Evan delivered the comment as if it was news. "I'm not going to dick around, feeding your boyfriend's ego at your expense."

Fuck this guy. "You being the only competent male on the planet."

Maddie looked at Sylvia. "Do you notice how none of them bother to ask me what I want?"

Sylvia nodded. "Typical."

Okay, yeah. She made her point. Both women did. Evan might have him revved up and pissed off but the person he was trouncing on was Maddie. "Message received."

"Between the notes and the dead body, your choices just got limited to one. You need to be back in the program." When Maddie started to respond, Evan talked over her. "We'll relocate you, set you up with a new name and—"

Sylvia looked confused. "Wait."

Maddie didn't. "No way."

The marshal looked ready to blow. "We should talk about this alone."

"She gets a choice." Jesus, this guy and his attitude made Connor want to hit something.

He wasn't the violent type, but the way Evan mowed over Maddie and her feelings pissed Connor off. Danger or not, there were better ways to handle this. Hell, he'd issued some orders of his own when it came to her safety and gave her little choice, but he didn't do it this way . . . damn, he hoped he hadn't because this was bullshit.

Evan turned on him. "Did you read the fucking notes?"

"I'm referenced in one, dumbass."

Evan didn't say anything for a few seconds. He stared at Connor as if assessing how much of a rival he might be. "And just who are you in all of this? I mean, I've done a background check and got the basics."

"Evan." Maddie's stern voice sounded like a warning.

"You don't exactly have a great track record for keeping women safe, now, do you?"

The shot landed but Connor refused to flinch. He kept his expression neutral. He would not let all this ranting get to him. Not from this guy.

Maddie stood up. "Evan!"

Even Ben, who had been silent and watching, straightened away from the door. "That's out of line."

Connor appreciated the show of solidarity. He hadn't expected it and wasn't sure he'd earned it, but he vowed not to take it for granted. "Do you think you can intimidate me, Marshal?"

"You're a businessman on a mandatory vacation." Evan smiled as if he'd scored some sort of victory. "Right?"

Ben started moving. "We should take a break."

The only acknowledgment from Evan was that he sat forward in the chair. But his glare never left Connor. "Your family sent you here. Didn't give you a choice because they thought it was here or a hospital."

He had the information mixed up and turned around, but Connor guessed that was the point. Evan wanted everyone in the room to know that his family had conducted an intervention. He might not know that much, but he knew too much.

Connor acted like he didn't care. "You done?"

"Am I wrong?"

"No, you've proven you're an asshole."

Maddie stepped around the outstretched legs and all the bodies in the way in the twelve-by-twelve space and headed for the door. "You really have, Evan."

Connor almost smiled. Evan had overplayed his hand. He launched an attack, not realizing that it would drive Maddie further away from him.

Evan's jaw clenched. It looked like he wanted to go on, to blow, but he reined his temper in. He lowered his voice and brought back that singsongy calming tone. "Maddie, you know I can't tiptoe around the danger. My language is harsh because what can happen to you is harsh."

"She fired you already." Connor had been holding that one but he enjoyed dropping it now.

She nodded. "Yes, I did. Sort of."

Before Evan could fire back, Ben took over by talking directly to Evan. "By tomorrow other police officers will arrive. You can take a look around the island with them. I'll start the house search and we'll meet up after that."

Evan swore under his breath. "None of that deals with Maddie's safety."

If the argument upset Ben, he never let it show. "I will have someone watching her. Me, one of my people, or one of the police officers who are on the way."

She appreciated all of the help but wanted to make one thing clear. "I'm staying with Connor."

She shifted until she stood beside him. Their arms touched but she didn't make a move to show any more affection in front of Evan.

"Your boyfriend?"

Connor waited to see how she'd react to the word.

"He is."

All of the amusement ran out of Evan. He didn't look quite as self-satisfied now. "We talked about distractions and the risk they pose."

Maddie shook her head. "It's my life, my choice."

"You could do better."

For the first time since they met, Connor agreed with Evan.

CHAPTER 21

The day dragged on forever. Between the talking and Evan and moving her stuff back to her house, Maddie had reached her limit. So when Connor offered to cook dinner, she jumped on it.

She loved the idea of watching him cook. She also looked forward to seeing him busy in the kitchen and maybe a bit distracted. Him off guard meant she could ask some of those questions she'd been holding inside.

As sucky as the day had been for her, it was equally sucky for him. Evan had acted like a jackass. More than once she saw Connor visibly restrain his anger to keep from going off. She appreciated the effort and guessed that was for her benefit. Maybe he sensed she could only take so much more without having a few hours to refuel. Because that was true. She'd run out of the energy needed to keep fighting this fight. All those years of running, all the lying, raced up behind her and knocked her flat.

Now she needed quiet. A few hours of relaxation. It might be temporary, it might not even be real, but she borrowed the time. She no longer knew what counted as normal but she could try to find a version of it. With him. Tonight.

The plan started with comfortable clothes, some food, and bed. Tonight it would be her own sheets, but he would be with her.

She'd changed into lounge pants and an old university T-shirt from a school she didn't actually attend. Sitting on one of the two stools at her kitchen island, she had an open view of all the cooking.

Everything about this cottage appealed to her, from the weathered white walls inside and out, to the riot of purple flowers in her front yard in the spring, to this kitchen. The one-bedroom house measured less than seven hundred square feet, but the kitchen had been upgraded well past the value of the rest of the house.

The area spanned most of the open floor plan she could see when she walked in the door. Marble counters. Every appliance and every type of pot and pan. Rumor was the person who lived there before her refurbished the kitchen, then spent a year working on recipes for a catering business. She now worked at a wedding venue in Northern California and Maddie benefitted from both her determination and her passion for food.

"What are we having?" The ingredients fascinated her. A package of noodles, various vegetables, and strips of beef. Bottles and spices sat off to one side.

Mushrooms soaked in a bowl of water. She wasn't sure what was going on there, but she also wasn't much of a cook. She was more of an expert eater.

"*Japchae*."

The word sounded like *chopped chey*, but she had no idea what it meant. "My food choices have been limited on Whitaker, so fill me in on what this is."

"Basically, noodles and vegetables." He held up the package. "Glass noodles. They're made from sweet potato."

Sounded good so far. "You got those on Whitaker? I couldn't find garlic at the store a few weeks ago."

"Brought them from home."

She basically brought underwear and she was staying forever. "You're a serious cook."

"Not really." The water boiled and he dropped the noodles in. "I can make the basics. That was a rule in our house growing up. Mom taught everyone. No one got a pass."

"I like her already."

"She refused to let me be a useless husband one day. At least, that's what she repeatedly said." He heated a pan and added some oil. "I think she was afraid I'd get married, wouldn't know how to cook, and the whole mess would reflect poorly on her. Either that or she worried I would never move out, and that was not okay with my Korean mother. My job was to work and not just sit around."

The story made Maddie smile, in part because it made Connor smile. "Sounds like you shouldn't cross her."

"Ever."

"But that doesn't explain why you travel with food."

"Mom shoved the package in my hand when I stopped by before heading for the airport to come here." He acted out the scene and mimicked her voice. *"Here, take these."*

"She was afraid you'd starve."

"Probably more afraid I'd eat fast food. She is not an eat-out type of person." He cleaned off the knife and put it back in the butcher block.

Everything looked set. A bowl of sauce he'd made there. Those vegetables, lined up and cut into even slices with precision. Much more of this and she would never let him leave again. And that was tempting even without the food.

She waited for him to start cooking—cutting the now cooked noodles and starting the stir fry of vegetables and sauce—before broaching the unspoken subject between them. The kitchen filled with intoxicating smells. The meat and the soy sauce. The sesame oil and the onions. It came together under his hands and all she wanted to do was pounce on the pan.

"So, about Evan."

Connor looked up but kept stirring. "He's a dick."

"Very true." When he transferred the cooked mushrooms and beef to a bowl she reached over and snuck a few pieces. Then some more.

"Not sure how you tolerated working with him."

"Well, he kept me alive, so there's that."

"That's his only redeeming quality as far as I can tell." Connor put stir-fried vegetables in a bowl. Next went the sauce and some spinach.

The kitchen smelled like heaven and it took all of her restraint not to dive headfirst into the food. "You know he's supposed to be a bit of a jerk, right?"

"Is that a job requirement?"

"More like a type of guy. Not the type you'd want to date or even have dinner with—"

"Agreed."

"He's an expert. He thinks a lot of his abilities because he has helped so many people stay alive, which is no small thing. But the only-I-can-do-this attitude is exhausting." It had worn her down after a few months. The blowhard narcissist breed was her least favorite breed of guy.

"I'm not disagreeing."

After cooking everything separately, he now put it all in the pan. The noodles went in last and he mixed all the parts together. Her mouth actually watered. And she would get to the food, but first she had to get this piece out. "The stuff he said—"

Connor rested his hands on either side of the serving bowl on the counter and looked at her. "My family did think I was on the verge of work burnout."

Not a surprise. From everything she'd read about him and that award he'd won, it sounded as if he worked all the time and only caught a few hours of sleep at his desk each night. But she didn't get the impression he believed he'd gone too far. That's what scared her. "You didn't?"

"I knew from my doctor the bigger issue was my heart."

She dropped the noodle she'd stolen for a taste test. "What?"

"Apparently when you plunge your brain into nonstop stress, work twenty hours a day, don't sleep, lock yourself away, and rarely venture out in the sunlight, you get high blood pressure and your body starts to break down." He grabbed two bowls from the cabinet. "Who knew?"

"Everyone?"

The joking tone didn't fool her. He'd pushed his body right to the edge. She'd bet the doctor gave him an ultimatum. She also doubted that Connor realized that work frenzy kept him from mourning.

"You're not wrong . . . sort of. What you said before. I did cope with Alexis's death by overdoing. Being the best son. Best businessman. Being at work all the time."

She feared the self-destructive behavior went deeper than that. A sort of post-traumatic reaction he still hadn't dealt with . . . not really. "I'd argue with the word *cope* because I don't think you have, but talking about this is progress." When he shot her an are-you-done frown, she tried to clean up what she said so he would keep talking. "Sorry. Go on."

"I saw the worry on my parents' faces. Got yelled at for weeks straight by Hansen when he came back and realized I'd taken on a workload that was usually handled by a group of three—"

"Connor."

He held up a hand as if he understood her concern and got it. "I gave in to their request that I take time off—extended time—because I didn't want them to worry."

So Evan's comment about a forced sabbatical of sorts wasn't wrong. His ability to track down information, things he should not know, made her twitchy.

"But they don't know you screwed up your body. Right?" She wanted to call Hansen, make him fly here, then shake him a bit for letting his brother go through this.

"My body is on the mend."

"It's fantastic, but that's not my point." She retrieved the dropped noodle from the counter and popped it in her mouth. "Good grief, that's good. A little sweet mixed in with the soy."

She stopped talking long enough to take another noodle and a piece of the beef. She might never eat fast food again.

"It's easy to make. Takes fresh ingredients and some cutting, but not much else." He served a portion into each of their bowls.

"Says the man who had an expert in Korean cooking train him on how to make it."

"Good point." He smiled as he set a bowl in front of her, then finally stopped moving around. "Want to go back to the part where you talk about my body being fantastic?"

She could talk on that subject all day.

"It's ridiculous. And what you can do with that tongue? It's sinful." She reached for a fork because she didn't have chopsticks. She thought about just sticking her face in the bowl, because who needed utensils of any sort? Then the silence hit her. She glanced up to find him staring at her. "What?"

"I forgot to tell you one big benefit of this dish."

"What?" If he said it tasted even better naked he would make her day.

That sexy smile of his grew impossibly wide. "It reheats really well in the microwave."

Even better.

A HALF HOUR and no eating later, Maddie grabbed the underside of the headboard. The force of her grip made her palms ache. Her fingers clenched and unclenched around the wood while Connor's tongue swept over her. Back and forth. His fingers and those licks.

She looked down the length of her naked body and saw him lying between her knees. His dark hair contrasted with the sensitive skin of her inner thighs. That scruff around his chin scratched against her. Every touch, every brush, made her muscles tighten and her body heat. Warmth and need mixed and pulsed through her.

She shifted until one leg draped over his shoulder. Still he didn't stop. His fingers plunged in and out of her. His tongue flicked over her. The combination had her hips lifting off the mattress in an effort to get even closer to his hot mouth.

Lost in need, she dropped a hand and wove her fingers through his soft hair. Let the strands fall over her hand as she pushed him in closer. Her eyes drifted shut as she gave in to the sensations shaking through her.

She was so close. Pleasure swamped her and her muscles tightened, screaming for relief. His name danced on her lips and the satisfaction she chased so hard hovered just out of her grasp.

"Connor, please."

He slid his fingers out of her and blew a cool breath over her already sensitive skin. She gasped at the contact as her shoulders lifted off the bed. Her eyes popped open and her plea for him to keep going died on her lips.

On his knees now, he pushed her thighs open even wider to fit his body between them. She fought to calm her breathing but he stole it again when he pressed against her opening. She didn't know when he'd grabbed the condom, but he wore one as he slipped inside her now. Slow, inch by inch.

Her tiny internal muscles pulsed around him. The fullness, the heat. She felt him everywhere and wanted more.

She held on to his forearms as he moved back and forth inside her. His speed increased and her body tightened. She felt raw, exposed, and uninhibited. The need to scream his name surprised her, and she started to when the orgasm overtook her. Her fingers tightened on his arm and her nails dug into his skin. Control exploded and all she could do was savor the sensation as he sank into her.

Her hips shook as the last of the pleasure moved through her. No longer able to hold back, she ran her palms over him, slipped a hand down to the small of his back, and urged him deeper inside her. Her skin, so sensitive from his touch and kisses, had her mouth dropping open.

A groan rumbled from deep inside his chest. A sexy sound that made her want to watch him. His shoulders stiffened and his hands tightened on the backs of her thighs. The pleasure hit him and shook through his whole body. When he finally collapsed on top of her, she wrapped her legs and arms around him and held on.

Minutes passed, maybe more. Without moving, she closed her eyes and let the heat from his body seep into hers. His body grew heavy and her stomach rumbled.

That last issue needed to be addressed. She couldn't ignore that sound for very long. After that workout, she needed food. "Connor."

"Yeah?" He mumbled the question into her hair.

The hot puffs of air against her skin tempted her to put food off for just a little longer. "I am so hungry."

He laughed as he lifted off her and rolled to the side. "Lucky for you there's food just a few steps away."

"Good. I need my strength."

He flipped over to his back and lay there in a sexy sprawl with his eyes closed. "I'm hoping that means we're doing this again tonight. Maybe a few times."

She sat up and rested a hand on his very impressive chest. "Definitely, but I meant for tomorrow."

He opened one eye and looked up at her. "What happens tomorrow?"

She traced a circle on his bare, damp skin, prolonging the inevitable. "I tell Evan to go home."

Both of Connor's eyes opened now. "I really want to celebrate that idea, but you weren't wrong earlier. He is the expert. Asshole or not, he knows what he's doing."

Wow. That probably took a lot for him to admit. She could almost hear him grit his teeth in resignation.

"He can be less of a jerk while doing it." Maddie didn't actually have any proof of that. Evan had always been heavy-handed. But she could hope.

Connor must have sensed her doubts because he smiled. "Is he actually capable of that?"

"He will listen or he's gone." And she meant that. Whatever it took, danger or no, it was time for her life to move forward.

CHAPTER 22

Maddie met Evan for coffee the next morning. She'd rather be home with Connor, relaxing in bed and eating leftover noodles, but she didn't have that choice. She had no interest in refereeing a battle between Evan and Connor, so the male posturing nonsense needed to stop. The biggest perpetrator was in front of her.

They sat away from the window because that's what Evan always did. He found a corner and faced out to the room with his back protected by a wall. She doubted he realized he did it. The move probably was a habit by now but it was one of those things she could count on. For instance, the fact that half the room stared at them but pretended not to. They likely thought she was cheating on Connor with a man they didn't know . . . as if that would ever happen.

She ignored the interested looks and the older ladies who ran the yarn shop. They sat at the table two down and literally leaned in.

Let them listen.

Her focus stayed on the man in front of her to whom she owed so much but still couldn't stand most days. "We need to come to an understanding."

Evan leaned back in his chair and let out a long this-is-boring breath. "I agree, but the terms are clear."

Not to her. Not to Connor or Ben or anyone who knew about her past. "I'm no longer in the program."

"That's your choice and a bad one."

The same refrain. He jumped over her feelings and the limits of his job, which brought the question that had been pricking the back of her mind right to the front. "Once I'm out, I'm out. That's how the program works."

"Not necessarily."

"Is it standard procedure for you to leave the office and try to convince someone to get back in?"

"My boss gave me a few days to come here and talk some sense into you." He took a sip of coffee. "Since I have other work and other people under my protection who aren't running from my help, I'm hoping I won't need the full five days I was given to get you back in the program."

He always did that. Zoomed in on her weakness—other people. Fed her guilt and used it against her.

Not this time.

"Ned, Grant, and Allison—everyone involved in the incident in the past—are dead." She stumbled over the word. She knew she always would. "The people in prison who were messed up with Ned and Grant and their bribery schemes are in prison because of evidence the FBI uncovered, not because of me. None of them should be looking to me for revenge."

"Yet you're being threatened." He leaned forward, balancing his elbows on the table and closing the distance between them as he kept his voice low, just above a whisper. "You left that part out."

"Someone found me and is trying to scare me. Someone wants to make sure I never forget what happened, as if I could."

"I missed the note that explained all that. Do you have it?" His voice dripped with sarcasm.

"I can't do this anymore. I don't want to live in the shadows and peek out now and then. Panic about everything and everyone." She'd said the same words in different ways so many times. Thought them. Wrote them. Signed paperwork forfeiting WITSEC protection. Still, no one listened. Certainly not Evan.

He didn't know what it was like. None of them did. Safety stayed foremost in her mind. She lived and breathed it. Panic and danger followed her, suffocated her. All those years of pretending to be this new person, being cut off from everything she'd ever known and the people she loved—her mother, friends—took a toll. She morphed from human to shell, never getting close to anyone. Never trusting a person or a thing she heard.

They told her she would adjust. She'd make new friends and create a new life. Maybe that worked for other people, but not her. She entered the program alone and she knew if she didn't get out, she would die alone. That simple fact combined with Ned's death in prison made her leave.

"Please tell me this is not because you found a boyfriend. Like, he wants you to go to business dinners and join the country club or some dumb shit, so you have to take the risk for him."

It struck her that Evan didn't think very much of her. He saw her as weak and easy to lead around. That she could ignore. Targeting Connor she wouldn't. "Don't take shots at him."

"I've read his file. He can handle it. Or he could until recently." Evan shook his head. "The family is very worried about him."

He'd tried that tactic before and it hadn't worked. She didn't know why he thought it would now. "Connor has nothing to do with this."

"He makes you reckless."

She tightened her grip on her coffee mug. "He makes me strong."

"You're a survivor without him."

But he didn't believe that. Connor was the one who did. "That's exactly what he says about me."

Evan made a low harsh sound before sitting back in his chair again. "This is ridiculous. If you weren't so busy thinking about getting under him, you'd be more concerned with your own safety."

Anger spiked inside of her. It hit her with a shot of heat and spiraled through every vein. "Watch it, Evan. That tough talk might work with other people you handle. Not me."

Their voices must have risen because a few diners sitting close by didn't pretend to be busy with their breakfasts. They actually stared openly now. One of the older yarn store ladies frowned at Evan. Looked like she might smack him with a spoon.

The mood in the dining room shifted. Curious whispers took on a more pointed feel. Evan lowered his voice again. "Look, you're right. I've overstepped, maybe gone off when I should have stayed silent, but all of this is because I'm concerned."

Those few words were as close as she would ever get to an apology. "I get that, but Connor is off-limits."

"He's got a pristine reputation. If he knew what you did—"

"He does."

That seemed to stop Evan for a second. He sat there, scowling but not talking. "Okay, but do you really know him?"

He pummeled her with every argument. Hit her from every angle. None of it would work.

"I will. But from him, not you." Because that was the point of being whole again. She got to live her life, and that included making mistakes and going into free fall over a guy she barely knew.

"What if we confirm the PI was here for you? And we both know we will." All of the anger had left his voice. He sounded reasonable and concerned now. Genuine in his need to get through to her. "Chances are he's working for someone from your past. Someone who wanted to track you down and kill you."

"Why would that be the case?"

"Does that matter?" He pushed his coffee mug out of the way and leaned in closer, dropping his voice so low that she had to strain to hear him. "The bottom line is you're in trouble and because he's sleeping with you, Connor is a target, too. Can his family really survive losing another child in a violent and unexpected way?"

This time the guilt slammed into her. Evan finally drilled down and hit on the one thing guaranteed to make her rethink everything.

"You made your point." She closed her eyes for a second before facing him again.

"Answer my question."

She thought about Alexis and Connor's parents. About how Hansen had fallen into an angry spiral after losing his sister. So much pain and none of it their fault. She would not be the reason they experienced more. "If all of what you think is true and Owen Pritchard was hunting me down so that someone else can literally stalk me . . ." She swallowed hard and said the one thought she couldn't kick out of her head. "I'll reassess my decision on the program."

Evan nodded. "Then you should start packing."

CONNOR TAGGED ALONG with Ben to Stark's Marina. He didn't really give Ben a choice about taking him since the idea of sitting in on Maddie and Evan's conversation was out of the question. Maddie never would have agreed.

The plan was to be there if Dom needed a reminder of their previous conversation about the man and the water taxi. Ben seemed to think Dom might suffer from convenient amnesia in an attempt to avoid questioning. No doubt that Ben's job really sucked.

They got out of the car and didn't say much. Sipped on the coffees in their hands and listened to the thud of their footsteps as they walked to the pier.

A few cars lined the parking lot and boats bobbed in the water. The clanking of metal and splashing water sounded all around them. It was almost as strong as the stark smell of water and fish. The fishery business was alive and well here. Connor could see the last of the boats taking off, heading to more open water.

Ben broke the silence. "You okay?"

"Ever notice you spend a lot of time worrying about me?" That fact worked on Connor's nerves. He hated being the one people worried about. He'd never lived his life that way. He stepped in, he handled whatever needed to be handled, but for the last few months, and for almost every minute since he stepped on Whitaker, people had been looking out for him. Never mind that he could take care of himself.

Ben laughed. "You are a full-time job."

"I'm the easy Rye brother."

"So you keep saying."

Connor stopped and wasn't surprised when Ben did, too. One thing Connor wanted to be clear about before much more time passed. "That Evan guy . . ."

"I'm not a fan either, but don't miss the main point."

"Which is?"

Ben walked over to the trash can and threw his empty cup away. Drew out his answer by waving to a family walking their dog and to a group of men who looked like they were playing cards on crates stacked on the pier.

He finally turned his attention to Connor. "Evan is a pain in the ass but his only job is to keep her safe."

Dom appeared out of nowhere and walked right between them, breaking their conversation. "Ben." He nodded, then looked at Connor. "And you. You're back."

As charming and welcoming as the last time. Connor lived all of his life in and around cities. People walked past each other, not seeing anything. Here everyone had something to say all the time, relevant or not. "We had such a nice talk when we tried before."

Dom snorted. "If you say so."

"I need to ask a few questions," Ben said.

"Uh-huh." Dom used his chin to gesture toward Connor. "Why is he here?"

Before he could answer, Ben did it for him. "Woman trouble."

"Ah, I get it." Dom whistled as a look of sympathy briefly crossed his face. "They worm their way in and mess things up."

Ben joined in the commiserating. "Amen to that."

"Go ahead. Be quick with your questions. I've got business."

"The man you told Maddie about, the one you brought to the island and think is still here. Is this him?" Ben showed Dom a photo.

Connor didn't look because of the blood and death thing. He'd seen enough of that person on his property.

Dom shoved the photo away. "That guy's dead."

"That's the problem, yes."

Dom looked at Connor. "He's the one you found?"

The Whitaker gossip seemed to be moving at its usual high-speed pace. "Yes."

Dom sighed before plucking the photo out of Ben's fingers and studying it. "Shit, yeah. That's him."

"You're sure?" Ben tucked the photo back in his shirt pocket. He didn't wear a uniform. Only the badge on his jacket indicated who and what he was on Whitaker.

"I said I was."

Ben didn't get sidetracked by Dom's gruff response. He pushed on, doing his job. "Do you have any records about his trips? Credit card receipts. A log. Anything?"

"He paid cash." Dom shot Connor a frown that said *this is your fault*. "I checked after you came snooping around."

"Did he give you a name?" Ben asked.

"Why would I need a name with a cash transaction?"

Connor lost his patience. He had no idea how Ben held on to his. "Are you trying to make this discussion difficult?"

Dom let out a long sigh. "There's not much to tell. This guy and the woman came on the island and didn't leave."

What the hell? "Woman?"

The question didn't stop Dom. He kept telling his story as if he hadn't added a new piece of information. "I don't know anything about them or where they've been or who stabbed him, but maybe Connor here isn't the only one having woman trouble."

"What woman?" Ben asked.

"The one with him."

Connor started to think the good people of Whitaker got together and planned how to be obtuse. They were very skilled at it. "You didn't tell us about a woman when we talked to you before."

"You didn't specifically ask about her."

He sounded so rational that Connor wasn't sure what to say in response. Conversations were an endless game here. He blamed the isolation and boredom because just when he thought he knew the answer, the objective changed and he had to switch strategy. "You've got to be kidding."

Ben's usual neutral expression slipped. "Dom, what the hell?"

"I didn't know this guy." Dom threw his arm out in Connor's general direction. "Hell, I barely know Maddie."

That wasn't right. Connor remembered Maddie talking about visiting Dom. "She comes here all the time and asks you questions."

"She bugs me, but we never talk for more than ten minutes. Even then, she's focused on one topic only." Dom made a grumbling noise. "Why should

I go talking about people's private stuff with her or with you?"

Connor gave up trying to explain. "So you lied to us."

"No," Dom said. "I was careful about what I shared. That's what smart people do."

Connor took a step in Dom's direction. He had no idea what he was going to do, but Ben's arm held him back.

"What did she look like?" Ben asked.

"A woman." When they both stared at him, Dom continued. "Look, I don't have a memory for details unless it's stuff I care about. I didn't care about this couple or people in general."

Connor refused to let that be the end of the conversation. "Try."

"She was younger than him. More attractive than him. All I remember is thinking they didn't match as a couple."

"I'm going to need you to come in and give a better description."

"That's a waste of time."

"That's what you get for lying to Connor and Maddie." Ben started to walk away. "I need you in by the end of the day."

"This is why I don't get involved."

Ben ignored the comment and so did Connor. He'd had enough of Dom and the quirky Whitaker types for the day.

He waited until they neared the parking lot and moved out of earshot. Where Dom's grumbling wasn't quite so close or so loud. "Now what?"

"I check the open properties, looking for a woman."

That didn't sound like a real plan to Connor. More like a hope. "But what woman? How does she fit in?"

Ben shook his head. "I have no damn idea."

CHAPTER 23

It was early afternoon before Maddie saw Connor again. They'd met back at home with a kiss but nothing else. Once she heard the story about the woman, and Dom keeping secrets for stupid reasons, she couldn't think of anything else. But she had a plan.

Now to convince Connor to help her.

She waited until he walked into her kitchen and got a glass out of the cabinet. He poured a glass of water while she watched. When he offered her one, she declined. She couldn't afford to get sidetracked right now.

"It will be faster if we help him." As she talked, he eyed her over the rim of his glass but didn't say anything. She took that as a sign to keep pitching. "We can search some of the places this woman might hide."

He drained the glass before setting it on the kitchen island. "And by accident we could walk right up to a woman who wants to hurt you and hand you over. Make it very easy for her."

An excellent point. One she decided to ignore. "Or she could be injured or not involved in this. There are hundreds of possibilities." Okay, more like two, but this wasn't about numbers. "This is really about ruling her out."

"Your argument isn't convincing at all."

The blank look on his face told her that, but she kept trying. "Humor me."

He didn't say anything for a few seconds. He seemed to be engaging in some sort of mental debate about what to say next, but then he leaned back against the sink with his palms resting on the counter on either side of his hips. "You think you know where she is?"

"Yes." Because when it came to hiding on Whitaker, she was the expert.

"Ben is out there with his volunteer crew. Evan— the supposedly most competent person on Whitaker, just ask him—is checking on places with two officers that landed on Whitaker this morning." His eyebrow lifted. "Do you see where I'm going with this? In case you don't, tell them and let them handle this."

"The one person on this island who runs drills where she practices hiding and who hid out when the killings started over the summer is me."

His mouth flattened into a straight line. "Jesus, Maddie."

"It's trained behavior. A reflex." And weird. She could admit that, but not now. She needed him to listen and agree. "That's not important."

"It is to me. I hate that this has been your life."

She needed his thoughts moving in a different direction, so she worked to get him there. "Your last two years haven't been any better."

"It's not a competition."

"Just trust me." She sighed at him to let him know she was serious and had no intention of letting this go. With or without his help. "We search two places. That's it."

He hesitated but then held up two fingers. "Two houses only."

"That's not quite what I said."

His arm dropped to his side again. "Maddie."

She rushed to explain before he launched into a lecture sure to tick her off. "One is an abandoned prison."

"Hell, no." He stilled. "Wait, there's a prison here?"

"The remains of one." Kids drank there on weekends. A few people hiked around it. She was one of the few, and she thought only, who ventured over to the rocky side, past the gate. The part with all the warnings and signs that Ben and his assistant patrolled sometimes. The part with the hidden door that she knew how to open. "That was once the purpose of the island. But the good news is, the other hiding spot is a house."

"Fine, we'll do that one."

She had a feeling it would be harder to sell him on the prison. "Agreed."

"Why do I think I didn't really win that round?"

That sexy smile of his got her every time. "Of course you did."

HE'D BEEN PLAYED, but he knew that when he agreed to come to this house. Maddie kept secrets and handed out bits of information at a time. Connor went along because he wanted to see where this ended. He just hadn't expected it to lead to a big house on the edge of the island. Finding it made him realize how little he'd explored Whitaker since he got there.

He could see the long drive and the two-story stone house at the end of it. The compound—and that's what it looked like—sat behind a wall and a gate. Trees lined the front yard. And the landscaping said some-one lived here.

"You forgot to mention the fence." Kind of a big detail in his view.

She stood at the security box next to the gate where a car would normally enter. "It's not electric."

"Is that the test for disclosure?"

She glanced at him but kept fumbling with the lock on the box. "This house belongs to the person who owns the island. It was the first one built here."

"It doesn't look abandoned."

She shrugged as she opened the metal box at the bottom of the panel, exposing wires and circuitry. "Gardeners come. Cleaning people come. Everyone else stays away."

"Is it haunted?"

She froze before turning around to face him. "I can't tell if you're kidding."

He guessed that would get her attention and wasn't wrong. "It's a valid question. As valid as this being the hiding place for a woman who only has been on Whitaker a few times. How would she even find this place?"

"No one touches the property because, of course, that's not how people on this island act."

"Of course. Them being so rational and neighborly and all."

"And there's a general fear that if you tick the owner off you'll lose the lease on your house. No house, then you have to leave."

The way ownership and housing worked on Whitaker didn't make a lot of sense to him. The only thing he knew for sure was that one person owned all of this and everyone else lived here at his or her pleasure. Which made him wonder why they were running the risk of ticking off that person.

"That's all very mysterious and weird. Totally fits with the rest of Whitaker." He glanced up at the towering trees before looking at her again. "But seeing this place does make me wish we tried the prison first."

Her eyes lit with excitement. "It's amazing. The cells and the ruins."

"We need to talk about your definition of *amazing*." He heard a click and one of the gates opened. "Wait. We're breaking in?"

"Did you think it would be unlocked?"

"Not sure what I thought."

"We're not knocking." She pushed open the gate and started down the rocky path.

He followed because there was no way he'd miss this. The property also fascinated him. He could hear a stream and see the expansive water view behind the series of buildings—the house, the garage, and one he thought might be a gardener's shed.

He caught up with her in a few steps. "You do realize we are, right now, increasing the crime rate on Whitaker."

"How do you figure?"

"Do you think this is legal?"

"It's a technicality."

The L-shaped house had a small garden out front. In the right season, flowers likely bloomed. Now a piece of furniture sat there with a cover over it.

His gaze switched to the house. The dark red trim contrasted with the gray stone. A breezeway lined with doors seemed to separate one wing of the house from another. He couldn't get a sense of the size, but this place loomed over the smaller cottages and cabins dotting the island.

"Nothing." Maddie wiped her palms on her jeans after touching every inch around the front door and overturning the flower pots on the small porch that surrounded the oversized door.

"You thought the person would leave a key?"

"It was worth a try."

He wasn't sure he agreed. "We have two choices."

"I pick the one that guarantees we get inside."

She exhausted him in and out of bed. "You don't know what the choices are yet."

"Fine." She crossed her arms over her chest, bunching her oversized jacket underneath. "Go ahead."

He'd been on enough job sites and checked out enough abandoned and on-sale buildings to know how to get inside. Trespassing bothered him but so did the idea of her sneaking back here once he fell asleep and throwing a pot through one of these expensive windows. And they were. For a place where no one lived or visited, it was pristine. High-end and stunning, with an open view on all sides. The engineer side of him appreciated all of it.

Between the fence and the intimidating gate, the house was protected. Add in the historically low crime on the island—until recently, at least—that protection should have been enough without a deadbolt. He slipped his wallet out of his back pocket for this next part.

He looked for signs of cameras or other surveillance and didn't see any. Like most people on Whitaker, it looked like the owner took safety a bit for granted.

"What are you . . ." She leaned over his shoulder and watched. "Interesting."

He slid the credit card into the gap between the door frame and the edge of the door, right by the lock. A few bends this way and that and the card slipped under the latch. He turned the knob and opened the door. "There you go."

"Did they teach you that in business school?"

"You develop skills when you have siblings." He and Hansen used to practice to see who could do it faster.

"Fascinating."

They stepped into the two-story entry. The entire inside opened up and he could see straight through to the stone fireplace at the far end of the living area, to the water that was visible through the floor-to-ceiling windows on either side.

A curving staircase off to his left traveled to the second story. To his right was the kitchen, complete with every high-end appliance and an indoor pizza oven. The person who didn't live here liked nice things.

But that was the problem. It didn't take any snooping around to see the plastic bags on the oversized woodblock island or the travel bag resting on the floor by the sectional sofa.

Damn if Maddie wasn't right. A person hid here . . . which meant they could still be there.

She smiled at him. "See?"

He didn't share her amusement or satisfaction. "We should call Ben."

"We're already here." Her smile dimmed.

"And so is someone else. Do you know what the word *reckless* means?"

"I do." Then they heard footsteps.

He glanced up in time to see a woman descending the stairs. Walking slow . . . carrying a gun. She looked to be in her early thirties. Dressed in dark pants, a sweater, and rain boots. Nothing fancy, but there was nothing panicked or disheveled about her to suggest she was on the run.

He circled back to Dom's words. He'd said something about the woman with Owen being younger and prettier, like maybe they didn't match as a couple. This woman seemed to fit that description.

Owen had been about fifty. Every photo showed dark circles under his eyes and a strain around his mouth. Fit but not muscular. Tall but not too tall or too short. Utterly unremarkable.

She had a round face and big brown eyes. Very pretty except for the weaponry.

He said the first thing that came into his head. "You don't make a sound, do you?"

"What are you doing here?" She got to the bottom step and stopped. That put about ten feet between them.

"Welcoming you to the island," Maddie said.

The woman didn't blink. "Try again."

"I'm—"

"Maddie Rhine," the woman said, filling in the very scary blank before Maddie could.

Maddie's eyes widened. "Uh . . ."

"That's upsetting," Connor said, but the word didn't come close to what he felt right then.

The woman looked at him. Let her gaze bounce up and down, as if assessing whether he would be stupid enough to dive for the weapon. "And you're Connor Rye."

Yeah, just as scary when she did it to him. "Want to tell us how you know who we are?"

"No."

"Why are you here?" Maddie asked.

"Also not your business."

"Call Ben," Connor said to Maddie without taking his eyes off that gun.

The woman smiled. "Yes, call Ben."

Maddie made a strange sound. "You know Ben?"

"You can tell him about your trespassing."

"He knows we're here."

"I doubt that, Maddie." The woman used the tip of the gun to point toward the front door. "Call him and wait outside. This time on the other side of the locked door."

BEN GOT TO the house ten minutes after the call. Maddie wasn't sure where he had been or how fast he drove, but he had to break records. She appreciated the urgency. She hadn't stopped shaking since that woman appeared on the stairs.

Now she was inside and they were outside and that didn't work for Maddie at all. Not that they had a choice. In a verbal battle the person holding the gun tended to win. She'd stepped outside at the other woman's command out of fear Connor might try to be a hero. She couldn't let that happen.

All three of them stood on the front porch. Ben leaned on the buzzer for a second time after trying the knob again. He looked in the windows on either side of the door. "I don't see anyone in there."

"Break the door down." That sounded like a reasonable response to Maddie, or Connor could mess with the lock again. She didn't care which option so long as the woman didn't sneak off before they could ask her questions.

Ben stepped away from the windows. "This isn't a television show."

"She knew our names," Connor said in a firm voice. "That's—"

"Suspicious." Connor nodded. "Yeah, exactly."

Ben looked at the door, then down the lane to the gate. "I need you two to go."

That was not happening. She didn't come this far to turn back without talking to this woman. "Where is she?"

"I might have an answer if you hadn't played amateur detectives and scared her away."

"That woman didn't scare easily."

Ben frowned at Connor. "Do you see her now?"

Her patience expired. "This isn't a joke, Ben."

"No, it's not." Ben's voice stayed even. "Sit this one out. That's an order for both of you."

Maddie usually appreciated Ben's calm but right now it annoyed her. She needed him running and shooting . . . or whatever had to be done to end this. "She might get off Whitaker and we won't—"

The front door opened and the woman stepped out. "I'm not going anywhere."

Ben reached for his weapon but she no longer held one. She'd put on a jacket and held a set of keys.

"And you are?" Ben asked.

She took her time locking the house behind her before facing them again. "The person who owns this island."

CHAPTER 24

Connor wasn't sure how they made it back to the Lodge but the woman—and she still didn't divulge her name despite repeated requests from Ben—insisted they talk there.

They sat in a small private dining room off the entry that Connor hadn't even known existed until that moment. Since the tables weren't set and no one came in and out, he guessed no one used it. But he and Maddie sat at a round table meant for a much larger party, with the woman on the other side. Ben being Ben, he manned the door.

Sylvia came flying around the corner and into the room. "What was so urgent that . . . Jenna?"

"You two know each other?" Ben asked as he straightened up and closed the door behind Sylvia, trapping them all inside.

"For a long time. She's the . . ." Sylvia's voice trailed off and she didn't look inclined to finish the sentence.

Connor was tired of all the secrecy on Whitaker. The weirdness was cute at first. Now it made him want to yell. "Owner of Whitaker. Yeah, she told us that part before she suggested we all head to the Lodge to talk this out."

Sylvia looked around the table. "Talk what out?"

"Wait a second." Maddie held up a hand as she watched Sylvia take the seat next to this Jenna person and cross her legs as if they were all having a calm conversation. "You knew who the owner of Whitaker was and never said?"

Ben made a noise that sounded like a groan. "Good question."

If Sylvia noticed the iciness in Maddie's voice or the question in Ben's, she hid it well. "Those aren't my answers to give."

"No, they're mine." The woman none of them except Sylvia knew finally piped up. "It's part of the deal. We talk about island business. Sylvia votes my proxy on the Board. I get to keep my privacy."

That sounded like a convoluted mess to Connor. "Does that make sense to you?"

"I have my reasons, which aren't your business." The woman shrugged. "But the one thing people on this island appreciate is privacy about their pasts."

"Including you?" Maddie asked.

"Including me." The woman didn't flinch from Maddie's barking tone. "So, why did you break into my house?"

Sylvia's leg fell and her boot thudded against the floor. "You did what?"

"We didn't mean to . . . I mean, there are dangerous things happening on the island and we didn't know
if anyone was in the house or in trouble. Or maybe
someone was using it as a place to stay while they ran
around the island." Maddie had lost the ability to do
anything but babble.

"The door was locked." Jenna looked at Sylvia. "So
was the outside gate."

"We can deal with the details later." Ben pulled out
the chair next to Jenna and faced her. "Right now I'm
confused about why you're here."

"I live here."

He shook his head. "You actually don't. Since you're
technically my boss and it hasn't been quiet around
here, I think we would have met."

She smiled at him. "That's kind of the point. Over
the last six months there have been more murders on
Whitaker than during its entire history." She ended the
comment by glancing at Connor.

Connor's defenses rose. "Why are you looking at me?"

"The last name of Rye seems to be connected to all
of them."

Maddie scoffed. "That's not fair."

"What exactly are you saying?" Connor asked. Because if he was going to be accused of something, he
wanted to know what.

"I came because I was concerned that Whitaker
isn't the sleepy comfortable island it once was." Jenna
pointed at Connor and Maddie. "And I was welcomed

by you two standing in my entry which did not ease my concerns."

Ben didn't look any more impressed than Jenna did as she shot Maddie a you've-been-warned look. "That's why you should stay out of the investigation business."

She shook her head. "I was checking in. Nothing more."

"Your job is safe. I'm not questioning your methods, even though I could since you technically do work for me," Jenna said.

Ben frowned. "I didn't realize my job was in jeopardy."

"What do we know about the man who was murdered?"

Before Ben could answer Jenna, Maddie cleared her throat. "Shouldn't we . . . I don't know, check to see if you are who you say you are?"

Sylvia's eyes widened. "Maddie."

"I'm sorry to sound paranoid but my trust isn't running high right now."

"Understandable." Jenna nodded. "Mine either. I'm a victim of trespassing."

"Funny." Connor had to give the woman credit. She didn't shake easily. She had people coming at her from all sides and she stayed calm. He doubted she was the mystery woman and nothing about her suggested she was hiding at the house . . . her house.

Sylvia swore under her breath. "She is Jenna Hughland. She owns the company that owns this island." She looked around the table. "If you don't trust her, trust me. She is who she says she is. I've known her for years."

Jenna smiled at Ben. "Now it's your turn to share."

He hesitated as if a mental battle were warring in his head. Saying no to his boss would not be a wise career move. Connor could appreciate the position. If he had any information he would have offered it to take the pressure off. As it was, tension clogged the room, making it hard to do anything other than be on the defensive.

After a few seconds of silence, Ben started talking. "Owen Pritchard was working for a woman named Daria Jones."

"Is that her real name?" Connor asked because no one around here seemed to be who or what they said they were.

Maddie was the one who answered. "Yes."

All attention turned to her. Connor could see the answer written in the wariness on her face but he asked anyway. "You know her?"

"She was Ned's fiancée."

Ben looked at Jenna. "I'll fill you in on the details later."

She waved him off. "Sylvia already has."

Of course she had. More secrets. Connor almost suffocated from them. "What was the part about privacy?"

Maddie leaned closer to Ben, reaching her hand out to touch his arm. "Are you sure it's her?"

"Definitely. There's a file in Owen's office. There are checks, and phone records show constant contact over the last four months."

Connor waited for relief to flood him but it didn't happen. Knowing who she was only answered one of the many questions floating out there. Still, he saw the strain on Maddie's face and rushed to put a good spin on the new information. "That sounds like confirmation. And she would have a motive."

"No. That's where you're wrong." Maddie leaned back in her chair and rested a hand on Connor's knee. "She was a victim in all of this. Ned cheated on her. She lost her job and her reputation was a mess because everyone thought she was involved."

He winced, hating to add to her distress but not really having a choice. "Maybe she was?"

"She supported me. She vouched for me."

"Okay, but she hired Pritchard specifically to find you. He's been tracking you for months and only got a break after all the press this summer," Ben said.

"Someone saw me."

Some of Sylvia's earlier anger vanished. Her voice softened as she talked. "We had a lot of press and photos. People were digging up residents' pasts. It turned into a circus."

"But there's a bigger clue." Ben moved his chair closer to Maddie. "Pritchard had a copy of one of the notes in his file."

Her expression went blank. "What notes?"

Connor could almost see her brain trying to process the information. She had to know what Ben referenced but reality refused to settle in and she squeezed his leg even harder.

"*The* notes. To you," Ben said in a reassuring voice. "Evan is trying to verify if the one in the file is one of those he's seen before."

Any note sounded relevant to Connor. "Does that matter?"

Ben kept his gaze on her. "It could, but now we know who we're looking for."

Maddie shook her head. "Why doesn't that make me feel any better?"

The answer came to Connor and he said it before he could weigh whether he should. "Because we still don't know who killed Pritchard and why."

AN HOUR LATER, Maddie sat on the edge of her couch. She'd taken her coat off and kicked off her shoes. She thought about unlocking her safe and grabbing her gun. Stashing it nearby. But she didn't have the energy.

A mix of panic and confusion zipped through her. The memories of Daria in tears as she found out the truth about Ned three years ago. How she pleaded Maddie's case to the prosecutor. The night they sat and drank wine, exchanging stories and trying to make sense of the way their lives had imploded because of the men that ran through them.

She heard a clanking sound and looked up to see Connor washing their dishes from this morning. He didn't push or pepper her with questions. He had two speeds and neither amounted to coasting. He kept busy, kept moving. He didn't even know it was a form of running. But she did because she was an expert on running.

She twisted her hands together on her lap, massaging her palm with the thumb of her other hand. "Maybe I should leave with Evan."

A mug crashed into the sink as he turned around. "What are you talking about?"

The answer was obvious. "My past is responsible for one man's death here on Whitaker."

"You didn't do anything to the PI."

"Connor, come on." She appreciated his attempt to keep things normal but they'd passed that line long ago. "I've been in denial, insisting the danger was over and I could live like everyone else. Worry about electric bills and argue with the news."

He dried his hands on a towel, then threw it on the kitchen island. "Some woman is searching for you. That's all we know."

Her head grew too heavy. She dropped it in her hands and stared at the Wedgwood-blue carpet under her feet. Stared at the swirling pattern and couldn't look away. "I can't be responsible for any more deaths."

The seat cushion dipped as he sat down. "Whose death are you responsible for? You didn't announce who you were and challenge people to find you."

The swirls blurred the longer she stared. "You know what I mean."

"Do I?"

She lifted her head and looked at him. "The note references you. Maybe not specifically, but we know it's you. You're the one I'm sleeping with. You're the only person I've let get close to me on Whitaker, and look what happened."

"I'm fine and have no complaints. The time with you . . . it's been good." He brushed the back of his hand against the side of her leg. The gentle touch soothed. Didn't demand anything.

"It's great for us but not for Owen Pritchard." She thought about the man she didn't know and the end he suffered because of her. "Now there are people who know who I am and what I look like. I no longer blend in. People who come in contact with me might be in danger. Nothing about this is clear or easy."

Connor reached over and took her hand. Slid his fingers through hers. "We're talking about one woman on a small island of roughly two hundred people. She'll be noticed."

Reality punched into her. Days had passed, more than a week since Connor came to the island. The ferry had come and gone. Dom continued to do his job. "I haven't been checking for people coming on and off the island."

"Hey, listen to me." He covered their joined hands with his other one. "Ben is in charge. Evan, as much as I dislike him, is an expert. The owner of the island is here, and she's pissed. This is not your job, Maddie."

She rested her head on his shoulder. "I'm exhausted."

"Then rest." He whispered the words against her hair, then kissed her there.

"It's not exactly safe to close my eyes." But she did. There with him. Let her muscles relax and her body sink into him.

After a few minutes of quiet, she felt him move and lifted her head. His hand slipped out of hers.

He leaned back against the stack of pillows and opened his arms to her. "Come here."

The invitation sounded so good. Picking him over analyzing her options could be another form of running, but being with him, blocking out the past, was all that calmed her lately.

"You are so comfortable." She lay down against him, flat on his chest with her head tucked under his chin. With her arms wrapped around his waist, she inhaled, letting the tension drift away and her mind go blank.

Falling into him was so easy. So natural.

"And by comfortable you mean sexy." His fingers slid through her hair before massaging the back of her neck.

"That's undeniable."

"Close your eyes."

"I'm never going to sleep again." But they were already closed and her breathing evened out.

He kissed the top of her head. "You will."

The heat from his body lulled her. His heartbeat thumped under her ear, so reassuring and affirming. She brushed her palm over his chest, back and forth. Pure intimacy but not the sexual kind.

She let her body melt against his. "You're very good at cuddling."

He laughed and the sound rumbled under her cheek. "That kind of talk will ruin my negotiating position back home."

The longer they sat there, wrapped up in each other, the more the peace settled in. The connection, with him like this, made every worry and fear slip away.

"I hate to think of you leaving here." She hadn't meant to say the words right then but she did *mean* them. She wanted him here.

He didn't react. His hand kept smoothing over her hair. "And I hate when you talk about disappearing forever."

"I told Evan I would consider getting back into the program." After years of keeping things to herself, she wanted to share that. Not hide anything from him.

"Don't be a martyr." He kissed her head again. "Go back because you're scared for yourself and need to do it for you. No other reason."

"I have to think of other people."

"For once, think about what you need."

The words sank in and she opened her eyes. She needed to hear every single one. They grounded her, made her regret she ever gave Evan hope that she would do anything but stay and fight. "It's a balance."

"And you'll figure it out, but not tonight."

"*We'll* figure it out." She felt him smile against her hair in response.

"Yes, we."

CHAPTER 25

All **the** pieces fell into place. She'd thought she was safe but now she knew the truth. She'd gotten cocky and now her past found her.

No more secrets. She couldn't lie her way out of this. She had to face up to her mistakes and her failures. Make an admission because it was time.

At least she finally looked scared. No more false bravado. About time.

She'd lost her edge, which was good. Less lethal, less careful might finally put an end to this.

The threats. The visits. The murder. She could no longer run or avoid. She needed to understand that her future skated on a very fine line. No more living as if the horrors of her past hadn't happened.

It was time for her to deal with the consequences of her bad choices.

CHAPTER 26

Something jolted Connor out of a deep sleep. He glanced at the clock on the bedside table. It felt like he'd been out for hours. A little after five in the morning. Nowhere near time to get up. The sun wouldn't be up for at least another two hours.

The dark sky and dark room blended. He could make out the shadow of her open closet across the room and the small flower-print chair in the corner.

He inhaled, dragging the scent of her shampoo into his senses. He lay behind her with an arm draped over her and his hand on her stomach. They relaxed on the couch for a few hours, not saying anything. Just breathing and sleeping. He let the silence wrap around her and calm her jumping thoughts.

The talk about her leaving and changing identities again had ripped through him. The response he wanted to say—*fuck no*—died on his lips. He tried to sound neutral and not let her see how much the idea of not seeing her again bothered him. Hell, the slicing sensation that tore into him at the thought surprised him.

They were seeing each other. It was new and shouldn't mean that much yet, but it did. He hated the idea of losing her before he could really know her. He hated that loss of independence even more for her.

Wanting out didn't mean getting out and she'd driven that realization home tonight.

Long after they showered and she drifted off to sleep, he stared at the ceiling of the quiet room. Thinking and trying not to think at the same time.

Life was easier when he kept his head down and sat at a desk almost all day. He hadn't planned on her or how she would flip his life inside out. The few weeks of vacation he promised to take vanished and she became his focal point. How to help her. How to protect her. How to make her happy . . . how to stay with her.

He listened to her soft breathing and relaxed again. Another round of tension would guarantee a night without sleep and he needed a few hours. His focus had to be on getting through the next few days. Watching over her and working with her as Daria and Evan and whoever else from her past washed up on shore.

Minutes ticked by and he forced his eyes to close. He inhaled, trying to clear his mind. The locks on the door helped. So did Ben's promise he'd patrol the area all night. Stay on call.

That sucked for Ben but it was the job and he'd do it. That provided Connor with some sense of security.

With one last kiss on her bare shoulder, he drifted. Sleep came in and out. He'd finally started to fall under when he heard the clicking. A scraping sound. The same one he realized woke him earlier.

His eyes opened again. He concentrated on figuring out where the noise came from but he couldn't track it. He lifted up on his elbow and strained to listen but it had stopped. Still he waited. Another few seconds and it came again, this time louder. Thanks to the silence of the small house, the scratching noise echoed off the walls.

Maddie stirred. She reached for the comforter and pulled it up higher on her shoulder. "What's that noise?"

Outside. The sound originated there. Someone or something outside wanted in and Connor had no idea how close they were to being successful. The thought of that got him moving.

He threw back the covers and dropped his feet to the floor. Scrambling, he reached for the sweatpants he abandoned earlier and gave instructions as he stood up. "Call Ben."

She rolled onto her back and pushed the hair out of her eyes. "What?"

"The noise." He had pants on and a shirt half over his head that he tugged down while mumbling the explanation to her.

"It was probably an animal or—"

"No guessing." He refused to take that risk. "You heard me. Call."

"Where are you going?"

Halfway around the bed, he stopped and looked at her. Even in the darkness he could see her pushing the covers away and searching the floor for her clothes.

"I'm going to check it out." He snapped his fingers to get her to look at him. "You aren't."

"Do not even think of leaving this room without me."

His eyes adjusted enough to see the mix of fury and fear on her face. He hated that she had to deal with either emotion. "Get dressed and make the call."

"Connor!" When he glared at her she dropped her voice to a whisper. "Get back here."

"You heard me, Maddie."

He didn't stick around to see if she'd listened. Walking as quietly as possible, he stalked down the hall. Kept his back against the wall and stopped only long enough to grab a knife from the butcher block on the kitchen counter.

He squinted, trying to make out any shapes in the darkness of the living room. The porch light she kept on all night wasn't on. A second after he realized that, his gaze switched to the door. Still closed, but that didn't mean the person wasn't already inside.

At the sound of footsteps behind him, he spun around. The knife waved in front of him. He was pretty sure he'd lost half his life when Maddie appeared.

She blinked a few times. "What are you doing with that?"

"Protecting us."

"I called Ben—"

He held up a hand to quiet her and turned back to the door. The clicking and scratching had subsided but he could still make out noises that seemed out of place. The wind, yes. But not the swishing sound. His senses kept misfiring so he couldn't tell how close or far away the noise was from them.

She stood at his arm, practically on top of him. "There's nothing out here."

A dog barked and it sounded close.

"Something is out there," they said at the same time.

He grabbed her hands and put the knife in them. Curled her fingers around the handle. "I want you to—"

"Don't even think of separating from me." She shook her head. "That is not negotiable."

Reasonable but he didn't have a choice. They could be right on top of the one person they needed to catch. "I need to check outside."

"You're an engineer, not a self-defense expert. Wait for Ben."

She no sooner said the words than he heard a car door. Then another. He stepped closer to the window along the side of the door. Not an easy task since she was almost attached to him and trying to drag him backward, away from the glass.

He could see flashlights and make out two figures. When he recognized the steady gait of one of them, a wave of relief strong enough to threaten his balance hit him. "Ben's here."

"How do you know?"

"I can see him." Connor took the time to undo each lock and waited for Ben to come fully into view before opening the door. When he did, two men stood there.

Ben looked like he'd gotten dressed in the dark. His shirt was half unbuttoned and he didn't have a jacket despite the biting night cold. Evan wasn't much better. He yawned as he looked around the front area of the house.

"You two okay?" Ben asked as he looked at Connor and to Maddie behind his shoulder.

"Yeah." The way she grabbed on to Connor's arm and twisted suggested otherwise.

Ben raised a flashlight and scanned the room behind them. "Anyone get in?"

"Not that we can tell." Connor figured they'd already know if that happened, but so much of Whitaker was a mystery to him, so who knew?

Evan nodded. "I'll do a walk-around."

He took off around the side of the house before anyone could stop him. Connor didn't really want to. Right now he appreciated the law enforcement expertise that both Ben and Evan brought to the situation.

Ben looked from Connor to Maddie. "What's going on?"

"We heard noises." Maddie reached around Connor to flip on the lights. The living room filled with brightness but the porch light stayed off. "It was probably an animal. No big—"

"Wrong." Ben stepped inside but held the door open. He pointed to a spot along the edge of the door next to the knob. "It looks like someone tried to force the lock."

"What?" She stepped around Connor and bent down to study the damage.

"Look here." Ben outlined the area in question. "The cracked wood. Probably from a tool of some sort."

Connor wasn't any kind of expert but he could see the dent and the divot. It looked like someone gouged out a piece of the wood around the dead bolt, which explained the strange noises.

"It would have taken a lot to get through all of the locks." Maddie sounded calm but her chest rose and fell on harsh breaths.

Connor watched her demeanor change. All the effort tonight to relax her was wasted. Her shoulders tensed and her movements turned jerky.

Evan emerged out of the darkness at the side of the house. "Nothing."

"Maybe she just wanted to scare me," Maddie said, sounding doubtful of her own theory.

The unwanted island guest had tools and the will to get into Maddie's house even though she wasn't alone. That was good enough to convince Connor that this was more than a game to the woman. "That's not really the point."

"For once I agree with Connor." Evan holstered his weapon. "Daria isn't playing now. She's coming in hot, and you know what that means."

Maddie nibbled on her bottom lip. "This still feels wrong."

"What else has to happen before you stop taking chances?"

"That's enough." Ben sounded weary and exhausted and didn't look much better. "We are not having that argument again tonight, Evan. Stay focused."

"You know it's not safe for her." Evan looked from Maddie to Connor. "Hell, it's not safe for you either."

He was right and, for once, he hadn't flipped into full asshole mode. But Connor's patience was long gone and the sound of Evan's voice was enough to push him past what he could reasonably take. "Maybe if you put more effort into solving this and less into lecturing, she would be safe."

Evan's expression switched from neutral to furious. His cheeks flushed with rage but his voice remained deadly even. "Are you telling me how to do my job?"

"I'm out of the program. I'm not your job right now," Maddie said.

"That argument is asinine."

Ben took his cell out of his back pocket but not before shooting Connor and Maddie a quick look. "You should go to the Lodge."

"No." Maddie shook her head. "If danger is following me then I'm not spreading it around any more than I already have. Sylvia, the other people eating in the Lodge dining room. The people who live there. It's too dangerous for them."

"But not for you?" Connor asked because he really wanted to know the answer. For some reason she still viewed herself as immune to what could happen here.

Ben talked to someone in a low voice, then hung up and looked at the rest of the room. "I need to do some forensics on the door, but you two can head back in and try to get some sleep."

Evan's mouth dropped open. "You can't be serious."

"Yeah, that's not very likely." Connor wondered if he'd ever be able to sleep again. They were running out of houses and bedrooms.

Ben kept talking as if the room hadn't burst into chatter at his suggestion. "We'll regroup tomorrow morning."

"There's no reason to put this off. I'm going to work." Evan headed for the porch without saying another word.

"What does that mean?" Maddie asked.

Evan stopped just as he crossed the threshold to the outside. "Someone needs to investigate Daria, collect the evidence. I'll do it."

"You don't have jurisdiction here. Remember that and take the night off." Ben didn't sound as if he welcomed a fight. "I'll watch the house tonight. I have officers on patrol. We're covered without you."

Evan shook his head. "I guess I'll just hope that everyone will still be alive by morning."

"HE'S DRAMATIC TONIGHT." Connor watched the other man climb into his car and back out of the driveway. He didn't stop or even flick on his lights until he was well out of the residential area.

Ben continued to study the door. "I think hyperspeed is his only speed."

Maddie sighed. "You're not wrong."

"Neither are you." Ben's head popped up and he pinned Maddie with his stare. "This does feel wrong."

Every single piece of this. Every minute. Connor agreed. "That sounds like an understatement."

"If Daria hired Owen, why kill him? If she wants to come after you, why do it this way? You've been out in the open, around town. Your house is on a busier road than Connor's. There are streetlights." Ben shifted to the side and something crunched under his foot. "It looks like the person who wanted inside took care of the light first. Smart move."

"So, not an amateur." That was Connor's nightmare. He stood a chance at running down an amateur. They'd be on equal footing. But someone trained, someone who knew how to shoot more than a target at a range, that person would have an advantage he might not be able to overcome by pure adrenaline.

"She could have been planning this for a long time." Ben shrugged. "She might not be alone. We have to allow for that possibility."

Connor saw movement in the yard a few feet behind Ben. White and paws. A leash dragging along the grass. "Mr. Higginbotham."

The barking started again and Maddie smiled. "You can't tell that's him from his bark."

"No, there." Connor pointed at the spot where Mr. Higginbotham disappeared into a clump of trees to the left of the house. "By your neighbor's car."

The barking grew louder and the neighbor's kitchen light flicked on. Much more of this and the whole neighborhood would be up and roaming around, asking questions.

Ben must have sensed that danger as well because he rolled his eyes. "Oh, hell."

But the real problem hit Connor. The dog but no owner. That couldn't be good. "Where's Winnie?"

Ben was already out the door and headed for the yard. "At this time of night, Paul walks him."

Maddie gasped. "Then where's Paul?"

They all ran now. Ignoring the night and the quiet, they called out for the dog. Ben whistled and Mr. Higginbotham barked louder. Connor searched the ground for the stray leash. He finally found it right as the sound of the barking cut off.

The return to quiet had Connor running. He reached for the leash, thinking the dog could bolt and send them all on another chase. He didn't have to waste the energy. Mr. Higginbotham was sitting down now, staring at something and not making a sound.

Connor bent down to pick him up when he saw the slipper. "Shit."

"Don't touch anything but the dog." Ben shifted past Connor.

Maddie caught up a second later. "Paul!"

Ben reached for his radio but he didn't have it on him. Next, he pulled out the cell. The whole time he kept moving, checking for a pulse and searching the ground around the body.

His voice broke into the relative silence as a few neighbors filed out of their houses and hovered nearby. "I need an ambulance."

CHAPTER 27

An hour later they crowded around the reception area in Doc Lela's clinic. Maddie said every prayer she'd learned as a kid and half forgot long ago. She wasn't a religious person but she would do anything—ask for anything—if it meant Paul would be okay. If it saved everyone else on Whitaker from her messed-up past.

Her life swept through town, taking out everyone in its wake.

How could anyone hurt Paul? That was the question she kept asking herself. He was a nice old man. A little bossy and nosy even though he claimed not to care about what other people did. He loved the dog and felt something for Winnie, though Maddie didn't try to put a name on it because it wasn't her business.

They were cute together, always meeting in groups and rarely seen in public, just the two of them, unless it was to walk Mr. Higginbotham. It was as if they tried to hide their relationship. Forget that everyone rooted for them. They wanted privacy and their fellow residents let them have it, pretend though it was.

She blew out a long breath, trying to shut down all the questions bombarding her brain. All the *what-if*s and possibilities about what to do next. Evan's orders. That talk with Connor.

She sat next to Connor, holding his hand, but even that didn't calm her mental frenzy this time. Standing up, she started to pace. She'd burn the energy off however she could.

It was the two of them in the room and Ben by the door. Evan had stayed behind to secure the scene with one of Ben's volunteer assistants. An older couple waited in the chairs by the window. Maddie couldn't remember their names but the man's hacking cough had been steady since they arrived.

The building buzzed with activity, which seemed wrong for the time of day and where they were. An early-morning car accident kept all of the medical personnel jumping. Ben reported everyone was fine but a pregnant woman was in one of the cars on the way to deliver, so everyone rushed in—family and friends—to check on her. She and her baby boy were now resting somewhere in the building along with the usual variety of broken bones from the accident and respiratory infections from the weather.

Poor Captain Rogers, the fire chief, ran around checking on people. More than once he stepped into the room to talk with Ben then left again. The captain did double duty, racing to help whenever needed. This morning he handled the emergency baby delivery.

He and Ben worked well together, but nothing prepared anyone for seeing Paul wheeled in. He hadn't woken up since they found him.

When the captain left the room again, Ben seemed to relax. "He's going to check on Winnie and bring her in. Everyone agrees Paul would want her here and no one wants her to be alone."

Maddie felt sick. It didn't dawn on her that Winnie should be here. Grand love affair or not, and Maddie suspected it was, Winnie cared about Paul and deserved to be by his side. But then other thoughts entered Maddie's mind. Horrible ones. "She has to be okay."

Ben shook his head. "There's no reason to think she isn't."

Maddie didn't agree with that. She could be hurt or worse. Mr. Higginbotham went wild for a reason.

Connor stood up right as Doc Lela walked in. She looked rushed and harried but totally in control, as usual. A nurse raced in beside her, handing her a form of some sort to sign.

When she finished with the administrative stuff, the doc looked up. "Paul is okay."

The relief sweeping through Maddie almost dropped her to her knees. She forced her lungs to inhale. "What happened?"

"A serious contusion. Looks like someone hit him in the head."

Connor shot Maddie an unreadable look.

"Paul took a harder whack than you did, Connor. He has a concussion. He'll be staying." She tucked her pen in the pocket of her coat. "Has anyone gotten in touch with Winnie?"

"Captain Rogers is getting her," Connor said.

"And Mr. Higginbotham?"

Maddie hadn't even thought about the poor dog until Lela mentioned his name. The loyal pup's bark had tipped them off to trouble. Paul could have been there for hours, at least until the sun came up and people started moving around, before anyone found him. Maddie didn't want to think about that. She concentrated on Mr. Higginbotham instead. He deserved nonstop treats for life.

"Evan put him in Maddie's house for now," Ben said.

That was news to her. "My house?"

"The good news is the rest of you can go home and catch some sleep." The doc looked at her watch. "But I'd hurry because people will be moving around soon. Once they do, they'll want answers."

"We don't have many."

She frowned at Connor over his comment. "Then you're about to have a long morning."

WATCHING BEN TALK to the residents of Whitaker about possible danger was like watching a person walk into fire. He stood in the middle of the packed Lodge dining room and fielded questions about Paul and then about Owen. He never tied either to her, but Maddie felt the angry heat of every gaze in the room.

Lin, the island's one reporter and the owner of the local newspaper, took notes. "Is there any connection between Owen Pritchard, the dead man, and anyone on the island?"

What felt like a hundred sets of eyes turned to her.

"We don't have anything to share on that at this time. We're still collecting information, but we do have a few leads," Ben said, then quickly moved on to the next person when Lin tried to follow up.

Maddie watched the whole thing while holding her breath. Having Connor right behind her helped. His hand on the small of her back kept her standing. She feared she'd turn into a big pile of useless goo without his support.

Evan hovered in the background and Jenna stood with Sylvia behind the bar. The addition of those two was a lot of new people for a small, insular island. The room was awash with head-shaking and harsh whispering.

The guy who ran the grocery store, the same one she stayed away from because his nervousness around women was legendary. He shook and stumbled over his words. She didn't want to add to his distress now, so she tried not to stare.

He raised his hand. "One thing, if you could clarify."

Ben waited for him to continue and when he didn't Ben dropped a hint. "Go ahead."

"Who are all these people?" He glanced around and his gaze fell on each newcomer as he went.

Maddie was relieved that, for once, no one seemed to be talking about her.

Ben didn't waste time on details. Instead, he pointed as he went around the room. "Evan. Jenna, and you know Sylvia."

"Risky answer." Connor whispered the insight loud enough for only her to hear.

"Look." Ben's voice vibrated through the room. "We've had a series of incidents on the island. Paul is going to be fine and he might be able to give us some insight into what happened—"

"Winnie said he's still asleep." The comment came from the back of the room.

"That's true, but Doc Lela says he'll be fine." The low level of grumbling continued but that answer seemed to satisfy most. "The bigger issue is Owen Pritchard. He was visiting, came on and off the island a few times according to Dom."

"Don't suck me into this," Dom yelled from his seat at the bar.

Ben kept on talking. "Owen is dead."

The harsh words rang out. Maddie felt the surge of tension. A wild energy spun around the room. Something about hearing the truth, even when the man's death had been revealed in Lin's newspaper, made it more real.

"We don't know exactly what he was doing on Whitaker. We're not sure who he talked to or where he was staying." Ben glanced at Dom, who remained quiet. "But we know someone stabbed him."

The mumbling started again. Maddie heard a lot of

sympathetic noises. When she looked at Dom she saw something else. He watched her, not spilling what he knew and her ties to all of this, but his expression said he might do so later.

Great. Something new to worry about.

"On the tables and on the papers being passed around is a photo of a woman named Daria."

"Who's she?" Someone called out the question and a few others repeated it.

Another person said something about her being pretty. Dom passed the flyers without taking one.

"It's possible she came onto the island with Owen," Ben explained.

Dom crossed his arms over his chest. "She did."

Maddie felt Connor's hand brush against hers before he whispered in her ear, "This is ten seconds away from turning into a yelling riot."

"No kidding." That was exactly her fear.

When the voices grew louder, so did Ben's. "So, I want to talk with her."

"Did she stab the guy?" one of the yarn shop ladies asked.

"She is not a suspect right now. In fact, I want to make sure she's safe."

"How does he stay so calm when he does this? I'd tell everyone to be quiet and leave." Connor kept his voice low enough that only she could hear.

She wondered the same thing. Gossip churned in the room. People whispered and nodded. Some talked loud enough for everyone to hear and didn't care who did. More than one person gawked at her. A few pointed.

Panic. She understood. Their orderly lives had been spun upside down. Again. The fear and frustration from last summer spilled over into winter and they didn't like it. They wanted their quiet island back, or most did. So did she.

"I need two more minutes of your attention." Ben held up two fingers. "If you see the woman on the flyer, call me. Don't be a hero. Don't try to trick her." Ben looked at the librarian. "I'm specifically talking to you, Mary. This is not a cozy mystery. It's real life."

"I bet I could solve it," the woman said in a voice filled with indignation.

Ben smiled. "You probably could, but let me try first."

"What does this have to do with you?" Dom asked Connor directly.

Maddie felt her blood pressure rise. It ticked up and her brain scrambled to come up with a sharp answer.

Connor beat her to it. "Not a damn thing."

"And you?" Mary looked at Jenna. "Who are you?"

Then the whole room turned to Jenna.

Maddie waited to see what the woman would do. She owned the island. She could tell them all to swim to Seattle. Instead, she shook her head. "I don't know Owen or the woman. I'm here visiting Sylvia for a few days." She glanced at Ben. "Maybe longer."

A chorus of "oh" sounded around the room. A few people smiled. No one asked a follow-up.

"What just happened?" Connor asked Maddie in a low voice.

"They probably assume Jenna is Sylvia's new girl-friend."

"Oh."

Maddie wished that's exactly who Jenna was. That would make sense and erase any doubts about her motives. But her showing up when she did and not offering much in the way of an explanation still didn't sit right with Maddie. Jenna could come and go as she pleased, but she didn't. That was the point. No one knew her and she didn't stop by for tea—ever.

Maddie met Jenna's gaze across the room and nodded.

There were other things that didn't add up. Jenna couldn't be more than thirty-two or -three. The idea that she owned all of this had Maddie shaking her head.

"Ben?"

He sighed before plastering a smile on his face. Maddie knew the difference between the real one and the one he wore as part of the job. This was the my-tolerance-is-running-low smile.

He nodded in her direction. "Yes, Mary."

"There she is."

He frowned. "Excuse me?"

"You wanted us to watch out for this woman." Mary shook the flyer in the air, then pointed at the doorway into the dining room. "I did and she's right there."

Almost every head in the room turned.

Daria stood there in black pants and a slim-fitting lightweight down jacket. She now wore her black hair in a bob. The style flattered her face. Made her look younger than thirty-five. She'd been young when she met Ned. He strung her along as a girlfriend for years, insisting he couldn't marry until his multimillion-dollar company was more stable.

The brighter skin and lightness around her suggested she might be happier now.

That only made Maddie more confused about how and why Daria found her way to Whitaker.

Once she had all their attention, Daria smiled. "Hello, everyone."

"You're this lady." Mary pointed at the flyer.

"Yes." Daria stared at Ben. "I think you're looking for me."

CHAPTER 28

The uproar in the room took another fifteen minutes to calm down. People fired questions at Daria. Someone offered to tie her up so Ben could interrogate her. Daria stood there, taking it all in, with her gaze locked on Maddie. Connor noticed because it was hard not to notice. He also managed not to frisk the woman for weapons, though he was tempted.

Sylvia had cleared the dining room and shut the large double door entry. Connor couldn't remember ever seeing the doors shut since he got to the island . . . which now felt like years ago.

Connor and Maddie lingered because there was no way they were missing the explanation after trying to reason this situation out for days. Sylvia waited behind the bar.

Jenna, the wild card in all of this, insisted on staying. Ben couldn't exactly say no to his boss, so he didn't try. But he did take the lead in questioning Daria after he conducted a brisk pat down.

She sat in a chair at a table by herself. Every now and then her gaze would wander around the room, taking in every photograph on the wall and person hovering around her.

Ben waited until the people cleared out and the room slipped into silence to pull out a chair and sit across from their newest guest. "Daria Jones."

"Before you ask, it's my real name."

He hadn't tied her to the chair. The questioning struck Connor as informal, which was likely the right answer. It matched the island vibe and she could shut down if prodded. They needed her talking.

Maddie didn't wait for more. She jumped right in. "Why are you here?"

"Maddie." It was hard to miss the warning in Ben's tone.

"I've been looking for you."

What she said sounded pretty creepy. The way she said it didn't. Connor wasn't sure what to think.

Daria's dark eyes didn't blink. "Ned was killed in prison."

Maddie nodded. "I know."

"Of course you do." Daria broke eye contact with Maddie and looked at Ben again. "You had questions?"

It was a gutsy call to come out swinging. Connor admired the courage but doubted the strategy would work for her. Every person in the room, except for maybe Jenna, had run through their patience and now wanted answers, not games.

"What are you doing on Whitaker?" Ben asked.

She barely let him finish the question before she shot back an answer. "Is it illegal to come here?"

It was going to be one of those conversations. This woman might make Dom look easy to crack. Connor didn't envy Ben but the person he felt most for was Maddie. Having her past burst through the door couldn't have been easy.

"It is if you came here to hurt someone."

Daria waved off Ben's comment. "Just a tourist."

"You're saying it's a coincidence that you ended up on the same island as Maddie."

Daria shrugged. "It happens."

Which brought up the issue of where she was staying. Connor was about to ask when he saw Ben move. His chest lifted and fell on a heavy exhale. "Maybe it would help if I let you know we found Owen Pritchard."

"The man who was murdered on the island. I read about that in the island newspaper." She continued to pretend, putting distance between her and the PI.

"The man you hired," Ben answered without missing a beat.

Her strategy was transparent. They knew too much of the background. Connor wondered how long it would take Daria to realize that. Because tough-guy acts tended to get exhausting very fast.

"You've done your homework." Daria looked at Maddie. "Did you fill them in on everything?"

Maddie stared back with a blank expression on her face. "Why did you hire a PI to follow me?"

"I needed answers."

Maddie shook her head. "To what?"

"What really happened that night."

"What are you talking about?"

Daria's gaze lingered on Maddie for a few seconds before traveling around the room. "Do they know about the fraud and the bribery? About the rumors and your deal with the prosecutors?"

"Yes."

Whatever big reveal Daria was going for here wasn't working. Maddie had spilled all of this days ago. Connor could go online and search for the details if he wanted to. He didn't because Maddie back then didn't interest him nearly as much as Maddie now. The facts might fill in the holes and help him understand why she was so self-protective and spooked. But he'd rather hear what he needed to know directly from her.

"You're the one who convinced the prosecutor I didn't know what was going on in that office." Maddie's voice sounded hollow and confused. "We were friends."

Daria shrugged. "I thought so."

Silence pounded through the room. The tension ratcheted up with each verbal volley and now it crushed in on them.

"Let's back up," Ben said, breaking through the suffocating quiet. "You admit you hired Owen Pritchard to follow Maddie."

"I knew her as Ellen, but yes."

Connor saw Jenna look at Sylvia. The two of them didn't say a word but they watched and listened. He got the impression neither woman missed a thing. Jenna seemed to be assessing the situation and Ben at the same time. Her employee. The one who might be able to break through to Daria and end this.

"Did you know she was in witness protection?" Connor asked because that point pricked at him. It couldn't have been easy to find someone who didn't want to be found. Not when she'd had the full force of WITSEC behind her until very recently.

Daria's dark gaze landed on him. "As she just pointed out, I helped get her in."

"Which makes me wonder why you needed the PI." Ben didn't ask. He made a statement.

"She disappeared. The questions I had didn't."

A cryptic answer. It was on purpose and that's the piece Connor couldn't figure out. He assumed Maddie held back pieces when she'd told the story of that night in her old office. The story sounded too neat. With all those bullets flying the ending turned out too clean.

"What were your orders to Owen?" Ben asked.

"Track Maddie . . ." Daria smiled. "Is that what I should call you? Do you have a lot of different names now?"

The snide edge to her tone ticked Connor off. "Track her? Once he saw her, why not call you? We have phones here."

"She didn't want to be found. It took time to hunt her down and when I did I had to figure out how to approach because she had a new life now." Daria's gaze traveled over Connor. Up and down, not giving anything away. "And recently added you to the mix."

"You decided to sneak on the island and follow her instead of having a talk," Ben said.

"Owen found her. He told me and I came with him. That's when I saw Maddie for the first time. She was having breakfast in this dining room."

Maddie sat forward in her chair. "When was this?"

"Months ago."

Maddie visibly tensed. Her whole body stiffened. "After summer."

The pieces made sense. Connor didn't know all the facts and he could put them together. "When the notes started."

Daria frowned. "What notes?"

Ben's frown matched hers. "How long have you been on Whitaker?"

"A few days."

"And you didn't call Maddie or talk with anyone other than Owen?"

"I got here and wanted to . . . watch her." Daria waved her hand in the air. "I didn't have a solid plan. It was about collecting information and seeing what Owen was seeing."

Connor scoffed. "Because that's not creepy."

"I'm going to need specifics from you and an official statement, but let's go back to Owen. What else was he supposed to do for you?" Ben asked.

"That's it." Daria threw up her hands. "Find her. End of my story and how I got here."

"Then why is Owen dead?"

Daria slowly lowered her hands. The sarcastic edge to her questions and replies vanished. "I was hoping Maddie could answer that. Needless to say, when that happened I became less inclined to knock on her door. I've been hiding in the house we rented, trying to figure out what to do next."

Ben sighed. "You should have come to me."

"I don't exactly trust police and investigators right now."

Connor understood that reaction. The rest of the situation and all the facts and questions spinning around were harder to track.

"I didn't touch him." Maddie shook her head. "I didn't even know who he was or that he was connected to you."

Ben exhaled before diving in again. "What do you think is happening here? Spell it out for us so we can see your side of this."

"Maddie pulled off a pretty spectacular scam back home. Now she's willing to do anything to protect the secrets she has." Daria's body language shut down. She went from lounging in her chair, crossed legs with her foot bobbing up and down, to still. Both feet dropped to the floor and she sat up straighter. Her hands balled into fists on her lap.

"Scam?" Maddie sounded stunned at the accusation.

"I'm no longer convinced you're as innocent as you claimed."

"Why would you think that?" Connor asked, because it was the question that wouldn't leave him. It felt like Maddie held something back, something big. Maybe Daria sensed that, too.

But Daria kept her gaze locked on Maddie. "Who really killed Owen? I know it wasn't me and you're the only one with big secrets."

"You're clearly unfamiliar with the people who live on Whitaker," Jenna said in a hushed tone just loud enough for everyone to hear.

"I hired Owen. Killing him didn't help me." Daria hesitated for a few seconds before dropping her last bomb. "And of the two of us, Maddie, I'm the one with nothing to hide."

"Okay, we're done here." Ben stood up and gestured for Daria to do the same. "We're going to my office for formal questioning."

Maddie scrambled out of her chair. "Ben, no."

"I don't know what's going on between the two of you. Don't really care. I do care about threatening notes and attempted break-ins and assaults and a murder. All of those happened recently and all of it leads back to you." Ben pointed between Maddie and Daria. "The two of you."

Daria stood up and walked over to Ben. Didn't try to get out of the questioning or walk away. "Ask me anything. I tell the truth."

I TELL THE truth.

The words still rang in Maddie's head a half hour later. Sylvia had suggested she and Connor stay and have coffee. Maddie wanted out of there. Out of the Lodge. Off Whitaker. So, they left and went back to Maddie's house.

Her past caught up with her and delivered a smashing blow. The urge to run overwhelmed her.

Daria leveled accusations. Put them out there for the whole room to hear. They couldn't be stuffed back and hidden away again. The whispers would start. On top of being on the run and exhausted she would need to deal with everyone's doubts.

She couldn't live like that again.

She paced around the small area between her couch and the coffee table. "Any word from Ben?"

"Still no."

She glanced over at Connor. He bent over the kitchen island, balancing on his elbows while he studied something on his phone. His neutral look suggested he was relaxed and unconcerned but she knew better. A quiet Connor in the car was a thinking Connor. He likely turned over every word Daria said, searching for an underlying meaning. He could be searching for more information on his cell right now.

"How could he believe her?" She referred to Ben, but the *he* could stand for anyone in the room who listened to Daria's comments.

Connor finally set the cell aside and looked at her. "I don't think he knew what to believe."

"Did you?" she asked, then held her breath, waiting for the answer.

He hesitated, not diving right in. For a few seconds he studied her. His gaze roamed her face. "What was she talking about?"

Pain exploded inside her but she refused to let it show. She forced her knees to lock so she could stay on her feet and not drop to the couch. "You can't be serious. She convinced you not to trust me after a few minutes of questions?"

"I didn't say that."

The room spun on her but she blinked a few times to bring it back into focus. She fell back on denial. Tried to push the conversation there to keep it from going anywhere else. "It feels like it. The judging. The questions."

"For the record, you're a bit too defensive. You might want to bring it down a bit if you hope to sell this act."

A shocked sound escaped her. But the truth was bigger. He saw through her and she hated that. Being able to trick people, convince them, served her for so long. With him those old standards didn't work.

The realization made her retreat even further behind her emotional safety wall. "I don't—"

"Listen to me." He straightened up and walked over to her. "I don't care what happened back then. I know you now and what I see is a survivor. That appeals to me."

He said that but there was always a *but*. Those were the right words. The ones you said when you didn't want the sex to end. "I didn't scam anyone."

"Never thought you did."

The closer he got, the harder it became for her to mentally retreat. Her breath came in pants now. She couldn't wrestle it back under control no matter how many times she counted to ten in her head. "Then what are you saying?"

"You can tell me anything. If you need to say it, I'll listen."

His soothing voice had a hypnotic quality. The kind that could lull a person into divulging things they shouldn't. She felt his inner strength pull and tug at her, enticing her to let the last wall fall.

Her mind rebelled and she came out verbally swinging. "You haven't dealt with your sister's death and you think you can handle my past?"

She tensed, waiting for him to fight back. That's what she hoped for. A reaction that would shift the conversation in a way that made it impossible for them to double back to it without remembering the carnage.

But his anger didn't rise. He didn't give one hint that the blow landed.

He shook his head. "Trying to piss me off won't work."

Full-scale flailing started inside of her. Anxiety welled and formed this hard ball that bounced around in her stomach. "I'm being serious."

"So am I. Whatever this is, whatever is eating away at you that you've buried and hope will never see the light again, it won't change anything." He didn't touch her. Didn't move to close the gap between them.

He stood there and took it. Offered a lifeline and waited for her to grab on.

The last of the air left her lungs. A crushing sensation pushed down on her. "You don't know that."

"If you did things—"

No, no, no. "I didn't."

"Hypothetically, if you were stuck in a terrible situation or in danger or panicked." His voice grew softer, sweeter, the more he talked. "None of it matters to me."

Temptation swirled through her. He offered hope and forgiveness—a sort of catharsis she didn't deserve. And once he realized how misplaced his trust in her had been . . . "What if, hypothetically, you can't handle what I say?"

"I can." A small smile formed on his lips. It appeared then left again in a flash. "And don't get defensive and start talking about my sister. You don't need to derail the conversation to get through it."

"When do we talk about you?" She ignored everything he said about shifting topics and derailing and tried one last time to do both.

"This is about you." He broke the invisible barrier between them. His hands brushed up and down her arms.

The simple touch calmed the churning in her stomach. "I want all of this to be over."

"I know." He nodded. "Just say it."

He couldn't know. No one could know. "You . . . this . . ."

"Maddie."

His voice swept over her like a soft caress and shifted something in her. The dam holding back the memories broke and the words came spilling out. "I should have gone to the police. Instead, I went to Allison. That led to Grant's death."

"You didn't kill him." Connor repeated the phrase more than once.

The absolute sincerity he forged into every word humbled her. She wanted to believe when the smoke cleared and her ego lay shattered on the floor that he would still comfort her like this. That he wouldn't run to Ben, then get the first ferry off the island.

"That's not how guilt works." She whispered the words more to herself than to him.

"What happened in that office, Maddie?" His hands continued to sweep over her, reassure her. "You can say it."

The gentle words shattered the last of her resistance. She leaned in, letting him take some of her weight as the pain tumbled out. "I didn't mean for it to happen."

"Tell me."

"I picked up the gun just in case." She wiped away the start of tears and swallowed through the clog in her throat. "Grant kept it in the office safe and it would have been in the safe if I hadn't moved it."

She waited for Connor to tense and back away. For that bright light in his eyes to dim.

But he stayed right there. Touching her. Wiping a finger across her cheek. "You had it when you confronted him."

"Just in case, you know?" She looked up at him, silently begging for confirmation. She got it when he nodded. "If things went sideways, I thought I should have it. Be able to wave it around and calm things down again. That's how I thought the gun would work." Such naive thinking. She closed her eyes, trying to believe she once thought that lie was true. "Back then I didn't even know how to shoot. It was about holding it. The security."

"But something went wrong."

She closed her eyes and relived each horrifying moment in slow motion. The footsteps as Allison walked in. All the yelling. "I didn't expect her. Allison. The affair. The double-cross. Brother against brother."

"You took out the gun."

Grant exploded. His rage was thunderous. The walls shook from it. The louder he got, the more she'd mentally retreated. It was a family thing and she'd dropped herself right in the middle of it.

She'd frozen, unsure what was happening. Thinking the argument was about money until she realized it went so much deeper and tangled up with love and marriage. Jealousy and revenge. "Ned grabbed the gun from me and then Grant was on the floor in all this blood."

Connor gave her arms a gentle squeeze. "You didn't shoot him."

But she was lost in the horrible reenactment playing in her mind. "Allison kept screaming. She said that wasn't the plan and then Ned shot her, too."

The shock on Allison's face. That moment when it registered that Ned was turning on her. Maddie witnessed every terrible second.

She blinked, transporting her mind back to the present. She blew out a long breath, trying to ease the pain wrapping around her heart. "I didn't hit the alarm, as I said the other day. I didn't think to do it. The cleaning crew heard the shouting and called security. They ran in but by then . . ."

"It was too late for Grant and Allison."

She wiped away the tears. "At first Grant, but Allison died in the ambulance on the way to the hospital."

"Maddie."

"I put that gun in that room. Without it there they would have only argued, and security would have calmed them down." Her voice broke but she kept talking. "I escalated. I took the fight to the level where it became murder. A double murder."

"Come here." He wrapped her in a hug as he said the words.

"It was me."

All those years of tucking that away, of letting it fester, rolled out of her. She cried and held on. Grabbed on to his waist and pulled tight, not letting an inch of light between their bodies. In that moment he was the one sure thing in her world. Secure, calm, decent, and kind.

She let the tears fall for Allison and Grant, for their mistakes and their terrible loss. For her wrong turns and all she'd given up just to survive.

Through it all, Connor stood there. He took the emotional battering. Gently coaxed the truth out and stood with her, knee-deep in the aftermath.

She cried for minutes or hours, she didn't even know. It felt like forever and nothing at the same time.

"You didn't know, Maddie. You could never have known."

"That doesn't change what happened."

"That's how life works." He kissed her hair. "You make choices and those choices spin into consequences and the rampage begins."

"Two people died because of me."

He separated their bodies and looked down at her. "Ned killed them."

"I helped."

"No, Maddie. You didn't. You were a witness and a victim, not a participant." He wiped the tears away with his thumb. "And that makes all the difference."

She wanted to believe. She ached to believe. "Are you sure that's not an excuse?"

"I'm sure that the woman in front of me, regardless of what name she uses or what she does for a living, would not kill anyone. You'd protect and defend. You'd never launch an offensive strike."

Some of the heaviness around her heart eased. The pounding in her chest stopped. "You forget that I hit you with a stick."

"Best first meeting ever."

She felt him smile and lifted her head to see that beautiful face. "McHottiePants."

That sexy smile widened. "Excuse me?"

"It's a compliment."

"Then I'll take it."

The coaxing of his lips against hers wiped away the last of her fears. The kiss, gentle and reassuring, packed just enough heat to steal her breath.

She said the first thing that came into her head. "You're the only one who knows."

He dropped a quick kiss on the tip of her nose. "Your secret is my secret."

She believed him.

CHAPTER 29

The crying turned into an hour of sitting on the couch, holding her. Connor didn't regret any part except when she had to relive all that pain.

Now she rested against him with her legs curled underneath her on the couch. She wove her fingers through his. Watched their joined hands as if mesmerized.

They should get up and find something to eat. A part of him wanted to carry her to bed. He ignored every impulse and sat there with her. Let her set the tempo and decide what happened next.

He meant what he said to her. Everything that happened, the horrible cascade of events that changed her life forever, was out of her control. She didn't bring that gun into the room thinking the evening would end with a shooting. She held it for protection and leverage. That's what a smart person would do and he didn't blame her.

A hundred little things could have happened to change the result. She could have been one of the victims bleeding out on the floor. Realizing that sent a slicing pain through him. Made him hold her a little tighter. Had him rethinking how long he would spend on Whitaker and how hard it would be to leave her. He wasn't a long-distance guy. For years he hadn't been a relationship-of-any-type guy. He had no intention of changing that . . . Then he met her.

She lifted her head and he kissed her. A slow brushing kiss that burned him from the inside out. One led to another. Then to a third. Their mouths traveled over each other, heated and full of need.

That fast, he morphed from wanting to give comfort to wanting her naked. His hands skimmed up her back, over her shirt. He might have pulled back and taken a break tonight, but her fingers danced over his face to the back of his neck.

When she pulled him in tighter, he gasped.

When she crawled on top of him and straddled his hips, he almost lost it.

Her tongue traced over his ear as she whispered, "Bedroom."

Heat surged through him at the suggestion but he'd never make it that far. He was too primed. Too caught up in wanting her. "Couch."

"Excellent suggestion." Excitement shone in her eyes.

One hand slipped down to her ass and pulled her body tighter against his. The snug fit of his growing bulge between her thighs had his head spinning in the best possible way.

"You have too much clothing on," she said as she tugged at the bottom of his sweater.

"We should fix that."

With each yank, she kissed him. She'd pull, then lean down and press her mouth against his. Let him feel the excitement thrumming through her. She kept bunching and pulling until she exposed his stomach and chest. The kissing changed then. The mood shifted and the touching became less controlled.

Her tongue licked against his nipple, then traveled lower. Just as his head fell back against the couch cushion, her doorbell buzzed.

Fuck no.

"Ugh. Not now." She collapsed against him.

"Ignore it." He heard the desperation in his voice and didn't care.

"It could be Ben."

"Definitely ignore it."

Knocking started next. He felt her shift to the side and knew he'd lost this round. "The person on the other side of that door better be holding apology cake."

She lifted off him and straightened her clothing. "It was pie."

"It worked."

She smiled at him over her shoulder as she walked to the door. "Apparently. Fix your shirt."

He could admit defeat. "Fine."

She glanced out the peephole. When she looked his way again, she winced.

"You are not going to like this." She had the locks open and was ushering Evan in the door before Connor got off the couch.

Evan's smile faded as soon as his gaze traveled from Connor to Maddie and back again. "Well, shit."

Connor didn't hide his annoyance. "Yep."

"Sorry to come over without warning." Evan's expression suggested he was telling the truth.

"This is new." Connor's comment earned him a look from Maddie that said to be careful, which he promptly ignored. "The apology thing."

Evan laughed. "Well, yeah, I think we're all a little calmer now that Daria has been caught."

Connor wasn't ready to admit that or to trust the guy. He held on to his dislike, ready to whip it out if needed. "Technically, she walked up and introduced herself."

"It's only a matter of time. There are limits on where someone can hide on an island."

Maddie laughed. "You'd think that, but no."

"You had a good teacher," Evan said before immediately jumping back into the previous topic. "The threatening note in Owen's file gives us the connection we need. That settles this and lets us wrap it up for good."

Maddie gestured for Evan to come further into the living room. She shut the door behind him but didn't throw the locks. That was new, too. Connor didn't know if it was relief over finding Daria or over finally telling someone about the guilt she'd been harboring for years. Either way he saw it as a step into the future.

"But that would mean the PI was involved in the threats. Was he the one who left the notes?" she asked.

"People will do anything for money, as you know." Evan's gaze switched from her back to Connor. "That's actually how all of this started. Maddie's then-boss and his brother."

He didn't need the explanation since he likely knew more about what happened that night than Evan. But Connor settled for agreeing rather than winning the argument. No need to stomp around and prove he was closer to Maddie. He knew and so did she, and that's all that mattered. "True."

Maddie leaned against the barstool. "What do the people in your office think?"

Evan's expression went blank. "About what?"

Connor understood the question even if Evan didn't. "With the threat gone, I'm guessing all talk of Maddie going back into the program can end."

Evan made an odd sound. "Not necessarily."

Maddie's groan outdid Evan's. "It's over. Give it up."

For the second time in a few minutes, Evan laughed. "Fine. I concede."

The surprises kept coming. Between the lighter tone and willingness to back off Maddie, it sounded as if Evan was a new man. That was probably good since Connor couldn't stand the old one. "Never thought that would happen."

Evan shrugged. "Me either. Look, the protective streak is ingrained. My job is to overreact and over-prepare. I know it can come off as too much."

Connor pretended that was an apology. "Understood."

"You taught me how to fight and how to hide. To listen when my instincts screamed for me to run." The soft look she gave Evan spoke to her sincerity. "We both know some of those lessons, the repeated practices and drills, weren't in any WITSEC hand-book. You prepared me for things I hope I never have to face."

"Then my job is done." Evan gave her another smile then glanced at Connor. "Do you mind if we—"

"Yeah, of course." Connor got it. If Evan could con-cede, so could he. There were still a lot of loose ends and open questions, but Evan being here and acting like this was a huge step forward. "You two probably have some things to wrap up. I can head over to the Lodge."

"I'll drive her over in a few minutes." After a bit of hesitation, Evan held out a hand. "Thanks."

"For what?" But Connor met the other man halfway and shook his hand.

"Watching over her."

Statements like that showed that Evan didn't know her as well as he thought he did. The watching over part was mutual.

Connor winked at her. "My pleasure."

"All right." Evan dropped his hand. "That's more information than I need."

He sounded amused and a bit fatherly. As if he were coming to terms with Maddie moving out of his house to go to college. Connor didn't understand the dynamic but it worked for them.

He grabbed his coat and gave Maddie a quick kiss on the cheek. That was probably more affection than Evan wanted to see but the kiss wasn't about him. Nothing would be from now on.

CONNOR MET UP with Ben outside of Lela's clinic. He only knew to come here because he stopped at the Lodge first and Sylvia said he'd just left. The conversation with Evan should have resolved his concerns. The guy he hated had one foot off the island. Great news, but Connor couldn't help but think he was missing something. The Daria piece was muddled in his head. He had no idea why it was so clear for Evan and hoped Ben could help.

"What are you doing here?" Ben asked as he opened the clinic's outer doors and motioned for Connor to go first.

"I was out walking and saw you, so I followed."

"That's quite the story." Ben laughed. "Not believable at all."

"Evan is leaving." The words still sounded good in Connor's head but every time they passed through there, he heard a faint alarm bell.

Ben stopped walking and faced him. "Shouldn't you be celebrating?"

"He's with Maddie now. They're saying their good-byes."

"That's . . . unexpected."

No kidding. "He said with Daria caught he wasn't needed."

Ben frowned. "Really?"

This was why he liked Ben. He *got* things. He might look laid-back but his mind never stopped. He assessed and reassessed, always working. He just hid it well.

"It was a surprise to me, too. I thought he'd stick around until the end and I'd have to pry his hands from the dock to put him on a ferry." He tried to sound light and not worried but anxiety built inside him. The longer he was away from Maddie the more he hated the separation.

Ben started walking again. "You don't actually believe Daria about the scam, do you?"

"What? No. Of course not."

"Because I asked her a million questions and it was clear to me she got bad information. She admits most of it came from anonymous sources and rumors. The steady drip—the emails and copies of financial records—wore her down and had her doubting."

Someone set Daria up. And why implicate Maddie unless she was the ultimate target? "Who?"

"Not sure yet."

This time Connor was the one who stopped walking. They'd almost reached the last turn in the hallway and he felt the pull to head back to Maddie's place.

"You don't think Daria killed Owen." But Connor knew the answer before he asked. He didn't believe it. He doubted Ben did.

"I can't see a motive."

The anxiety threatened to burst into panic. He reached for his cell. "I'm calling Maddie."

"Do it."

MADDIE DIDN'T ANSWER the first or second time he called. Every second without contact made him more nervous. After three minutes, Connor went looking for Ben but he kept glancing at his phone waiting for her follow-up text. Nothing.

At minute four, Connor nearly yelled the building down when they had to wait for Doc Lela to come out of Paul's room after her exam. He didn't remember the exchange of pleasantries. All he needed was to be in that room.

Paul sat up as they entered. "About time you got here. Both of you."

"How are you feeling?" Ben asked.

Connor knew it was polite and the right thing to do. The poor man had been hit and the result could have been so much worse. But worry ate away inside him. He needed to get to the part about Maddie.

Paul skipped answering and scowled at both of them. "Did you get him?"

Connor felt everything inside him freeze. "Who?"

"The bastard who hit me."

That answered one question. Connor had more, but he wanted to be sure. "It was a man?"

"The one who doesn't like you."

A list of questions flooded Connor's brain but Ben stopped him and took over. "What are you talking about, Paul?"

"The new guy."

"Paul, start at the beginning."

Paul took his time getting settled in the stack of pillows behind him. Raised and lowered the bed twice before he found the right spot. "I was dog sitting for Winnie and Mr. Higginbotham needed a walk." He stopped as if waiting for someone to question that. "We went out by Maddie's place and I saw him."

Connor didn't care about protocol or evidence. He wanted an answer. "Evan?"

"I don't know his name." Paul waved a hand in the air. "Tall and serious, always frowning at you when you get near Maddie."

"That's Evan," Ben mumbled. "What was he doing?"

"Messing with her front door. It was late, too. Didn't see any lights on in her house." He reached for the remote for the bed again and Connor put his hand over it. That seemed to send the message because Paul picked up speed with his storytelling. "I backed away and pretended not to see him, but Mr. Higginbotham barked. The next thing I knew I woke up in here."

"Evan." That fucking asshole.

"Right." Paul nodded before glaring at Ben again. "Did you arrest him?"

"Not yet."

"Well, Winnie is off getting some clean clothes for me." Paul shooed Connor's hand from the remote. The steady buzzing of the motor hummed through the private room as he shifted the mattress to get up. "I'll come along and help you."

Connor put a hand on the older man's shoulder. "Whoa."

"Stay in bed," Ben ordered.

"Someone has to watch over Maddie."

"I will." And that was a vow to Connor. No more trusting marshals or ignoring his instincts. That mistake could cost Maddie everything.

Paul put a hand to the bandage on his head. "He's bad news. You get rid of that guy or I will."

"I'll do that, too." No matter what it took.

CHAPTER 30

Maddie watched the door shut behind Connor. Heard the crunch of his boots on the stones outside. Happiness rushed through her. She smiled because she couldn't *not* smile. He made life better. Bigger than that, he made her want to have a life again. Not hiding in shadows. Not wondering what would happen next or if she would make a mistake that sent him running.

He was solid and sexy. A little grumpy, which she loved, but so in tune with her. If she had to travel through the last three years of hell to get to him, it was worth it.

But before she leaped headfirst into a relationship with Connor she needed to be grateful for the one that saved her. She turned around and looked at Evan. He stood a few feet away, gazing around her house and not really paying attention to her.

She thought about his joking. "This is a different side of you."

"Sure."

His voice changed from earlier. She reached over and touched his arm to get him to look at her. "Evan?"

He lifted his head and pinned her with a furious gaze. "That asshole doesn't leave you alone for a second."

She stepped back. "What?"

"You heard me."

She saw a flash as Evan turned something over in his hand. It took her a second to recognize that he held her phone. "May I have that?"

Evan's gaze followed hers to his fingers. His hands tightened around the cell. "No."

She thought about her gun in the safe. It sat in another room and she'd never get the lock open. He'd be on her, and if he wasn't, if this was her imagination, he'd likely still stop her from taking it out on principle, then insist she'd somehow had a break from reality.

No, she wouldn't have a weapon for whatever was happening here. She needed to depend on her smarts. "I don't understand what's—"

"The whole protective guard thing got old fast." He grabbed her arm in a grip that cut off her circulation. "Not sure why you thought bringing him into this made sense. Why settle for an amateur when you had an expert?"

"What are you talking about?" She pushed and shifted, trying to break his hold.

"Get a bag or not, it's your choice. Either way, we're leaving."

"But you just said—"

"No questions." He yanked on her arm, dragging her even closer. "Don't make me tell you again."

But she had a million of them. "What changed?"

"My strategy. I tried to be reasonable and your boyfriend fucked that up. So now you come with me. We get off this floating piece of crap, or Connor is the next one I kill."

ON THE WAY out of the clinic, Connor nearly broke into a run. Ben stopped him. "One second."

"What are you doing?" Connor yelled the question.

"Making a few more calls." Ben nodded toward the cell in Connor's hand. "Try her again while I check on one thing and get some reinforcements."

Screw that. He wanted to *get* to Maddie. "She's with him."

"He doesn't know Paul is awake. We have the advantage here."

That news was the only thing that kept Connor together. He'd never wanted to beat on another person like he did on Evan. He'd terrorized her. And why?

Paul being awake started some sort of timer. If he thought the older man saw him and might wake up and talk, he'd need to make a move. Whatever move he came there to make.

Connor hit her contact and listened for her voice. Again, the call went to voice mail. So did the next one. That made four unanswered calls. She'd never *not* picked up before.

He debated trying another text, but if Evan was there and saw the screen . . . no. He needed to see her or hear her voice. Now.

He turned to Ben, ready to dump his ass and leave him behind, gun or no gun. "What is so important?"

Ben hung up. The strained look on his face suggested the news he received wasn't good. "I called yesterday to check on Evan's status."

Connor didn't have time for a play-by-play. He was too busy plotting out the next ten minutes and trying to figure out how fast Ben's car could go.

They sprinted to the vehicle. Connor asked his question on the way. "Status of what?"

They slipped in and Ben had his keys out. "I couldn't figure out how he could be here unless he was taking vacation to come see Maddie."

"And?"

Ben started the car. "He's been on administrative leave for four months."

Connor heard a thunking sound in his brain. Too late. He'd messed up last time and this looked like a repeat.

He forced his brain to focus. "What? Why?"

"No one will say but whatever he's doing here, it's not for WITSEC." Ben backed out and entered Whitaker's version of traffic, gliding in and out of the few other cars on the road. "We need to get to Maddie."

Only one word registered in Connor's head. "Now."

CHAPTER 31

Maddie waited for Evan to laugh after his weird comment . . . to do something. As far as jokes went, this one sucked. Her stomach dropped when she saw the anger in his face. Okay, yeah, she got it. He didn't like it when she didn't listen to him. But he's the one who said the danger had passed.

Since he dropped her arm, she backed up, trying to angle her way toward the butcher block. A knife was the closest weapon and, unlike the gun, not locked down. She really hoped she was overreacting and didn't need either.

The other weapon she had was her. She'd been trained to talk to attackers. Humanize. Stall. Do whatever was needed to gain the upper hand.

One problem. Evan had taught her all that.

She fell back on reason. Maybe they could talk this out. "Tell me what is going on."

"What's the fastest way off the island without being seen?"

"Water taxi." Even Dom would get a distress signal. She had to believe that.

He grabbed her again and pushed her against the edge of the kitchen island. Fingers dug into her arm and his expression, utterly without emotion, suggested she listen.

"Are you really going to risk your beloved Connor's life by lying to me?"

Guilt smacked into her. Evan would do it. He never hid his hatred for Connor. She didn't understand but she didn't have to. Hate could be irrational. And Evan could kill without blinking. He'd told her that a thousand times over the years. He believed she could kill the same way, but he was wrong.

When she didn't answer, his eyebrow lifted. She felt the challenge like a punch to the stomach. Part of him wanted her to test him. A sick part she'd never seen before, but she could see it now. Every line and every muscle pulled taut. He was ready to pounce and looking for a reason.

The one thing—only thing—she would not risk was Connor's life. Evan knew her and knew her weakness.

"Over by the prison." Even as she talked, a rough blueprint of the ruins flipped through her head. She mentally examined escape routes and places to hide. "I keep a small boat there. It will get us to Arnold Island. From there we can jump off to wherever you want to go."

All truthful. Every word of it. If this were a test, she'd pass.

A satisfied look crossed his lips before dying again. "That's my girl."

The words screeched across her brain. She wasn't *his* anything. "Evan, tell me what's going on."

"You just wouldn't stop." He tightened his grip and shook her.

She tried to pry his fingers off her bruised skin but he wouldn't budge. He weighed more, was taller. More lethal. She kept reminding herself of each one of those things when the need to flail and scream pummeled her.

He could kill her.

She forced her breathing to slow. She needed to stay sharp. "Stop what?"

"Fighting it."

She swallowed her cringe. "If this is some sort of unresolved love thing . . ."

"Don't be stupid." He shook her hard enough to snap her head back.

When he dropped her arm, she rubbed the thumping part he'd just squeezed bloodless.

She tried to keep the pain out of her voice. Not give him that satisfaction. "Then tell me."

"Not sure how it worked with your boy toy, but you don't give the orders." He grabbed her coat off the rack and threw it at her. "The opportunity to pack is closed. You'll wear what you have on."

"I'm trying to understand." She slid her shoes on before he dragged her outside without them. "We've known each other for years. We get each other. Please just talk to me."

"Appealing to my protective side." His smile was almost feral. "I taught you that."

She fought the urge to throw up. "That's the point, Evan. You saved me."

"And I have to keep on doing it."

None of this made sense. He'd been territorial and a jerk. But he'd never hurt her before. The menacing thing . . . if she didn't know better she'd think it was part of some new training. But she *did* know better. This was not a drill.

"Am I in danger?" She meant someone other than him but he was enough.

His face flushed and he clenched his teeth together. "You got messed up in a financial scheme that put powerful people in prison. Of course you're in danger."

He acted like he hated her. Like she disgusted him.

She stalled. "Have you heard about a threat?"

"I don't have to. I just know."

He sounded . . . deluded. "Do the other people in your office agree?"

"My judgment matters, not theirs." Evan shook his head. It was almost as if he was talking to himself and not her. "They don't understand. They think of this work as a job. It's so much more than that."

"You like helping people."

"I create survivors."

What the hell? The words sounded sick and twisted. Like she was more machine than human to him.

Her heart hammered in her ears. "I'm not a creation."

"You sure as hell are." He smiled as pride crept into his voice. "The way you conquered your fear of heights. All those drills. You learned to shoot despite watching people die in front of you in a hail of bullets." He held up a fist. "Nerves of steel."

"No." She shook her head. If he saw the truth maybe he would back down. "I'm a mess."

He got right in her face. "Because you've been away from me. Getting soft."

"I'm trying to have a life."

"You don't get to. You fucked up and your life was turned over to me."

He did hate her. She could hear it in the dismissive tone. As far as he was concerned she'd forfeited her life and now it belonged to him.

It was all so clear now. The way he treated everyone, including her. His immediate hatred of Connor and anyone who cared about her. The way he yanked her back for more training whenever she started to venture out and live. Made her log hours at the shooting range. Buried her in guilt. The emotional manipulation and all that talk about keeping to herself.

He'd shown Whitaker to her. She could disappear here. Live in the woods. All of his words came back to her. Slammed into her with enough force to knock her over.

A new wave of fear crashed over her. "Evan . . ."

"For once I am going to keep what's mine."

CONNOR COULD NOT stand still. They'd been to Maddie's house and his cabin. Now, he paced the small confines of Sylvia's office. He could feel Ben watching, along with Sylvia and Jenna. They gathered there to make plans. It would be at least an hour before reinforcements could get there. They expected snow showers today, which would only delay the assistance.

For now, the rescue was on them.

Jenna hung up the phone on the corner of Sylvia's desk. "I grounded Dom's water taxi. No planes can come in or out without Ben's permission, and the marinas are shut down. No boats in or out."

"I have my volunteers and the few officers we have split between searching and watching the obvious ways off the island," Ben said. "More officers are on the way, but we need to move now."

That sounded positive but Connor feared it wouldn't be enough. Despite being a small island, Whitaker had too much water and land to cover. Too much land where no one lived and other patches where people did but didn't take to strangers.

"Are we saying this marshal killed Owen?" Jenna asked.

Ben studied a map of the island they'd tacked up on Sylvia's wall. It wasn't recent but it could give them a lead. "We don't know that."

"We can assume." Connor didn't think it was a leap to get there.

Ben turned and faced the one other person in the room. Daria sat in the chair across the desk from Jenna. He brought her in because with everyone else out looking for Maddie and Evan, and warning residents, either they moved to babysitting duty or they dumped her in a jail cell. Connor preferred the latter but Ben insisted she might help.

"Someone has been feeding you information," Ben said to her. "That's why you started all of this. The PI, the case files, coming here. You believed Maddie until the moment you didn't, and someone wanted it that way."

"Yes. I started getting emails. They claimed to be from someone in the prosecutor's office and talked about Maddie being in on the financial scam. There were suggestions she was Grant's partner and played me. That she walked away with a pile of cash and her freedom." Her voice no longer held a defensive edge. The verbal battle she'd unleashed when she got to Whitaker was gone. She didn't talk about things Maddie had done or cast blame. She sat there looking as confused and unsure as the rest of them.

Those emotions were nothing compared to the battle waging inside of Connor. It took all of his energy not to let his mind wander to the worst-case scenario. He would not be too late this time. They would get to her and stop whatever Evan had planned. There was no other answer.

A part of Connor still hoped Evan's only need was escape. That he was using Maddie's knowledge of the island for passage and holding her as a shield. But that didn't explain the notes or trying to break into her house or Owen. No reasonable explanation covered all of those. And he refused to give the unreasonable reasons any space in his brain. Letting his mind go there spelled disaster.

"None of the stuff about Maddie being in on the financial scam is true. She was used just like you were. These brothers didn't care who they destroyed so long as they collected the cash." He needed her to know that. He needed everyone in the room to be clear on that.

"You're sure about Maddie's role? I mean, none of it matters now but, if true, it could point us in other directions. Maybe we should keep an open mind here." Jenna's voice sounded genuine rather than accusatory. "You haven't known her that long. Right?"

"Connor has been here almost two weeks, but I met her after she arrived here years ago." Sylvia looked at Ben as she spoke, then back to Jenna. "I agree with Connor. No way is she heading up some elaborate scheme and letting other people pay for her crimes. Not Maddie."

"The question is, who would benefit from feeding Daria false information?" Ben said, cutting right to the point.

Daria shrugged. "No one."

"Evan." All the confusion and frustration blocking Connor cleared. The truth stood out in its starkness. So clear that he wondered how they all missed it before. "Don't you see? He gets you enraged and doubting, Daria. Picks at the friendship and the doubts, but does it anonymously. Basically weaponizes you and then pretends Maddie is in trouble."

"Why?" Jenna asked.

Connor looked around the room to see if they were listening, getting it. "To give him the leverage he needs to convince Maddie to leave Whitaker and go with him."

"I thought she was his escape plan, but maybe there's more happening here," Jenna said.

Exactly. That was Connor's worry. He didn't expect Jenna to be an ally in the concern, but he welcomed any help. "Hell, he had Maddie feeling guilty and thinking about going back in days ago."

All that blackmail and manipulation. He found her weakness and pressed on it until she flinched. Connor vowed never to doubt his initial impression of a person again. When it came to Evan, Connor waded through bouts of unexpected jealousy. Let his past creep in and throw him off stride.

Never again.

Ben made a humming sound. "It's more likely he's using you as the bargaining chip."

That stopped every thought moving through Connor's brain. "Meaning?"

"The one way to get her to help him off the island is to threaten you."

"I agree," Sylvia said.

Jenna took over. "And he would have had access to the note. I mean, I'm assuming."

"No." Daria shook her head. "I told Ben I'd never seen that before."

"I understand. That's not the issue." Ben stopped there as if he wanted to reassure Daria there were no open questions about that. "Evan is the one who told me that his people saw it in Owen's file. Problem is he doesn't have people. He's on leave from WITSEC."

Sylvia closed her eyes. "Unbelievable."

Connor understood the feeling. He'd bought into that part about the note as well. They all had. It made sense. It tied up their suspicions in a neat way that made them easy to package and handle.

"He planted the note to frame me." Daria's voice gained strength as she spoke. By the end she sounded as furious as the rest of them for being duped.

"Possibly," Ben said.

Jenna snorted. "I'd say definitely."

They'd all arrived at the same place. Same conclusions and a shared belief Evan was the key to everything. That still didn't save Maddie and that's all Connor cared about. "We can run through all of this later. Where do we look now?"

Jenna walked up to the map and pointed out the known areas of access in and out for larger vessels. "We've blocked his access off the island but there are still small craft."

"Where would someone launch one?" Daria asked, fully engaged now.

Jenna sighed. "From any house with a dock. That's the problem. We live on water. It's all around us. The only thing that may help us here is the weather. Cold and snow. That makes water travel pretty prohibitive."

"Son of a bitch." The boat part. Connor knew that was the answer but hearing it made it real.

Adrenaline pinged around inside him. The need to get out there, yell her name in every corner of the island, swamped him.

"I have everyone—Dom, Captain Rogers, and some others—out on boats watching for that." Even Ben didn't sound convinced by his words.

"You can't blanket the entire island with a few volunteers on boats." Jenna picked up her cell again. "I can put a plane in the air to give us a better visual."

Still a long shot. They needed a shortcut. Connor joined her at the map. He scanned the edges, hoping something would jump out at him. Marinas and docks. Older greenhouses that hadn't been refurbished. Forest land and open tracts.

So many options and none of them good. There were too many places to cover. Too many miles of open water.

He glanced at the least populated piece of the island. The section without any landmarks but one. The black letters jumped out at him. "The prison."

"What?" Sylvia asked.

Of course. They were doing this backward, looking for loopholes in the obvious places. Evan needed seclusion. And no one knew the secluded parts of the island like Maddie did.

He turned around and faced the room. "You said he might convince her to help him leave the island." He glanced at Jenna. "Is there a way off near the prison?"

"It's rocky, but yes. It's actually the hardest part of the island to patrol and watch over."

Sylvia shook her head. "What am I missing?"

That had to be it. For the first time in the last hour Connor felt a bit of hope. "Evan trained her how to hide. Maddie staked out the island and picked the prison ruins as her ultimate hiding place. She knows that ground. If he has her there, she might have an advantage."

Ben opened the door. "Let's go."

CHAPTER 32

Snow fell as they drove through the center of town. Winter had held off but now set in, blanketing the sky in a soft gray. The unseasonably warm temperatures of a few weeks ago broke, and frigid air circled around them.

The car windows fogged and she used the side of her gloved hand to clear a patch for her to see through. Evan had locked the doors from the inside. But it didn't matter. She wasn't going to run. Not when he bargained with Connor's life.

As Whitaker passed outside the window she looked around for any familiar face. If she saw one, she didn't know what she could do. It's not like she would endanger someone else to save herself. She could try to convey a message but Evan sat next to her, watching every move as his gaze switched back and forth between her and the slick road.

The car ventured out of the more residential area and through the towering trees. Even without their leaves, the massive trunks blocked what little light managed to break through the clouds. Neither of them said another word for ten minutes.

With every mile they drove, her mind raced to come up with a plan. She was bringing him out here because it was the one place she knew better than others. And she'd talked about it with Connor. If he could work out that she was missing and in trouble, he might think about the prison and get Ben out there. But there were so many *if*s and *maybe*s, and really she just wanted to stall until a better plan popped into her head.

The one wild card sat next to her. She had no idea what Evan was thinking. She now knew that was always true.

"There." She pointed to the turnoff for the prison. The sign had been torn down long ago but locals knew. She found the place on a map and spent hours investigating.

"Excellent surveillance."

That's what she was to him, a mix of skills and training. A prize that he plucked out of danger and shined to his satisfaction.

The change in him still made no sense. He'd never been emotional or charming. He treated her as work and she never took it as an insult because that's exactly what she was. One of the people he watched over. He and a team, but she dealt almost exclusively with him. That was the point of the program—secrecy. For it to work, only a limited number of people could have the real details about her life.

"It's too cold to use the boat." Between the air and

the water kicking up the sides, they'd freeze. She doubted the small engine would even work. It would be useless and she needed him to know that.

"We've been through worse."

It had been eight months since they practiced any survival skills. Ned was killed in prison, stabbed while eating lunch in the dining hall when he refused to give up his seat. The news termed it as a turf war of some sort. An inside prison sort of thing. She always struggled to believe that was true because Ned wasn't the type to walk into the middle of a battle he knew he couldn't win. But she had no idea what the truth was and never would. One of her many fears—a new one she never expected—was that her end would become a big mystery like Ned's was.

"I haven't prepped the boat for winter." A few days ago she planned to show off her favorite place to Connor. Now she might die there.

Evan shot her a quick look while maneuvering through the overgrown path. "I doubt that you would be so careless with your life."

"I got complacent." That was the only explanation for her failure to see that Evan had unraveled. She noticed it all now. The lash in his voice and the underlying current of darkness that ran through him. It swirled around him, infecting everything from his walk to the way he snarled and snapped at people.

He'd changed. Some invisible switch clicked inside him. And for some reason, he aimed his obsession at her.

"You were lazy." He swerved to miss a stump lying half over the makeshift road.

The quick move sent her slamming into the door. Her head banged off the window. "Damn."

"You're fine."

She rested the injured spot against the cold glass, letting the icy slickness ease the throbbing. "If you say so."

"But those lazy days are over. You'll learn from this experience and not repeat it. We'll be more dedicated to your training. I can take the time and mold you."

There was nothing warm or genuine about his self-satisfied smile. It chilled her. So did his comment. More time with her meant more time away from his desk and the other people he watched over at work. WITSEC had black sites or the equivalent where he could help her get tougher, or whatever his ridiculous plan was.

"What about your job?"

"You are my job."

She feared that would be the answer. But she had so many other questions. Where would she live and how would he hide her? He couldn't think she would sit somewhere and stay quiet forever. Once she figured out how to protect Connor, she would scream the world down about Evan's new demeanor and cult-like need to be praised. She would dismantle him and make sure anyone who had ever heard of WITSEC knew about this rogue agent.

Then there was the issue of Daria and Owen. Poor Paul. He still hadn't woken up this morning before she left.

"Did you retire?"

"I made adjustments." The car skidded to a stop next to a fallen tree and he looked at her. "Life is about learning to shift priorities and keep moving forward."

"That's what I was trying to do."

"You. Were. Going. Backward." His yell bounced around the inside of the car.

Her instinct was to shrink back, make her body smaller, as she tried to come up with the safest exit. She forced her body to still. "It's my life."

He turned off the car. "Not anymore. Get out."

She scanned the area. The prison's side entrance sat about twenty feet in front of them through the woods and a gate. She knew where the fencing gave and they could squeeze through. Knew because she'd tracked every inch of the outlying area and structures for signs of weakness.

That gave her an advantage but even if she got there first and somehow broke free, he would still follow. She had no car or way back. Limited clothing and no weapon.

Evan got out and circled the car. He leaned in, putting his face close to hers. "Pretend your boyfriend's life depends on you complying, because it does."

Biding her time. That was the game here. Talk and act like she was complying until she could come up with a strategy that protected Connor and got her away from Evan. If she ran, he could grab Connor first, before she could get to him. If she left with Evan, then ran away from him later—the option that sounded the smartest right now—she still had to get word back to Connor first to ensure his safety.

Evan knew people and she no longer took for granted that he played by a certain set of rules. Nothing confined him or reined him in. He lived like a man with nothing left to lose. No job or family . . . just her.

He put a hand on his gun as he stood there. "I'm not asking again."

The weapon. That was the answer. Distract him, then shoot him. She'd vowed never to hold a gun with the thought of hurting a person again. She went along with the firing practice, knowing it would be a skill she never used. Now she wasn't so sure.

She got out of the car and wrapped her oversized jacket around her. Her footsteps slipped on the iced-over path. She stepped into the more wooded area to keep from falling.

Evan's steps mirrored hers. The crunch of their footsteps echoed through the woods. Snow made a distinctive sound as it hit the ground. If they'd been deeper into winter without the warm spell, the packed mud would be frozen and this area of Whitaker would be a wasteland.

They marched, ducking under bent branches and climbing over fallen limbs. With each step she calculated the risk if she grabbed his gun. The amount of damage and blood if she could get off a shot. The time it would take her to crawl to safety if the whole thing backfired and she got shot.

Then she thought about Connor. His smile. Watching him work in the kitchen. All those articles about the workaholic. The way he touched her when he peeled her clothing off. So many sides that made up the complex, flawed, beautiful picture. If he was her last breath of happiness on the earth she could live with that.

Wordless, they walked over the rocky and uneven path. Broken pieces of concrete and ruins littered the trail. Some walls still stood and time had preserved a labyrinth of rooms from the innermost collection of the cells.

The small prison had held maritime prisoners, caught for committing all sorts of crimes. But sometime fifty or so years ago someone decided it was cruel and unusual to house people in the path of frigid winds at the end of a secluded island. Interesting she should end up here.

They made their way to the far side of the compound, around walls overgrown with ivy. At this end the water lapped against the slim shoreline. The waves rushed in and out, leaving approximately five feet of rocky beach exposed.

The temperature dropped another ten degrees here. The snow had stopped but the sky threatened to let loose again.

She looked out over the pale blue water. Watched the waves and whitecaps dance in the distance. There was no way to survive out there. Her only chance was to get off a shot.

More stalling. "The temperature—"

"Don't fall in and you'll be fine." Evan looked around. "Where's this boat?"

Her mind zipped to the shed and to the preserved rooms. Which one gave her more of a chance?

"Do you think you can put this off? I've waited three years for you to hone your skills. That's enough."

"What's the plan here, Evan?" She crossed her arms over her chest. "Are we going to live together off the grid? Are you going to start a compound with other people in the program?"

"The place is picked out."

Her stomach heaved at the thought of how long he'd planned this. "Where?"

"Not something you need to worry about."

He had lost all touch with reality and he intended to drag her to that same mental place. To break her. "This is over, Evan. My case. The danger. There's no need for any of this. I need to be able to make my own choices, not live in fear."

"You forfeited that life. Now you will return to the program."

"You mean your program."

He ticked off the parameters. "Limited contacts, all preapproved by me. Work. Studying your craft. Practicing maneuvers."

"So, I'll be your servant."

"You'll be my greatest achievement." He managed to make the comment sound serious.

She felt like she was locked in a bad movie. "You've lost it. You're not even rational anymore."

"Then you shouldn't test me."

CONNOR HAD SEEN enough. He watched with Jenna, Ben, and Sylvia as Maddie and Evan talked. The distance gave them some protection. So did the remains of the two-story building they waited on. They lay on their stomachs. Among rocks and debris on the cold concrete.

He couldn't feel anything but the anxiety clenching in his gut. Adrenaline pumped through him. Whatever needed to be done he'd do, even if he had to go through Ben to do it.

The special glasses Jenna grabbed at her house let them see most of what was happening but not hear a thing. He had no idea what Evan was saying but he could see Maddie argue about something.

If he waited too long she might piss Evan off. Connor did not trust the man to be mentally steady enough not to open fire.

Connor started to get up. "I'm going."

"Do not move." Ben issued the order without taking his gaze off Maddie.

"She doesn't look like she's hurt," Sylvia said.

Jenna swore under her breath. "Yet."

Ben glared at Jenna before returning to surveillance. "We watch and wait. The police officers are on the way. We need numbers and firepower. Not you rushing in and getting hurt."

"We're not waiting." This time Connor got up.

Ducking and keeping low, he ran to the back of the floor and shifted behind a crumbling wall.

When he looked up, all three of them were standing there, staring at him. Sylvia stayed back a bit and watched the scene below them.

Ben's glare was the most heated. "He is trained and has a weapon. If bullets start flying the chances of Maddie getting hit are too high."

Ben's arguments made sense but nothing about Evan or his plans or what had happened over the last few weeks was logical. They needed to deploy a different strategy to keep up. "Then send me in without a gun. He hates me. The attention will be on me and you can get off a shot."

"Wait, doesn't that mean he'll shoot you?" Jenna asked.

Ben nodded. "Exactly."

There was no other choice. They all knew it, but for some reason only he wanted to face it. Maddie couldn't stall forever. No way would Evan fall for that.

Connor turned to Ben. "Your people are spread out on boats and across the island. Reinforcements are trying to fly in and ferry in, but the weather is messing with visibility. Even when they do land, they still have to get to this side of the island. There's no time left."

Ben shook his head during Connor's entire speech. "I'll move until I can get a clear shot."

"Just make sure you don't hit Maddie." Connor refused to let that happen. "You're the one who just made that point."

"I'm not sending a civilian in."

"I'm not asking, Ben. This is happening. I'm the decoy. I distract. You shoot."

"Okay, wait." Jenna stepped between them and looked at Connor. "One of those flying bullets could hit you, too. You're not immune."

Connor heard the pleading in Jenna's voice. Saw it in Sylvia's eyes. None of them got it.

He glared at Ben because he knew the history. Every sick detail of how his sister died and how neither he nor Hansen stopped it. One shove off a cliff by the man she was married to. A failure neither of them could live with. "Do you honestly think I am going to let another man kill a woman I care about?"

Ben closed his eyes for a second. When he opened them again they were filled with frustration. "Connor, come on."

"You would do the same thing."

Ben exhaled. "I'll be the decoy."

"You're a better shot than any of us." Connor had turned the facts upside down and examined them from every angle. This was the right answer. The only one. "There isn't a choice."

Ben stood there for a few seconds. He glanced over his shoulders in the direction of where Maddie stood when they last saw her. Then he unzipped his jacket.

Jenna held up a hand to stop him. "What are you doing?"

"He wears the vest." Ben had stripped down to a thin shirt and started working on the bulletproof vest's Velcro straps.

Sylvia shifted her weight from foot to foot. "Ben, is this a good idea?"

Jenna answered. "No, it's a terrible idea."

"It's the only idea we have. We can't wait and hope reinforcements arrive on time." Connor would keep saying it until they got the point. "And Evan isn't the type to be inclined to wait around and give us the chance to come up with something better."

Connor wrestled with the vest and got it on. Keeping low, they made their way back to the edge closest to Maddie's position. Whatever conversation they were having ended. Evan took her by the arm and shoved her inside an open doorway and out of sight.

The adrenaline pumped faster. His sole focus was on getting her out of there.

He'd seen enough to get him moving. "He's dragging her inside. You don't have a shot now. Decoy is the only option."

When he started for the stairs, Ben stopped him. "No games, Connor. Do not be a martyr. Maddie will fucking kill me if you get as much as a scratch on you."

"I'm not looking to be a hero." He was buying time. That's all. "You move in and fire. I'll grab her and duck."

Jenna made a face. "That's not a strategy."

"It's barely a plan," Sylvia said right after.

They were both right. "For Maddie's sake, let's hope this works."

Connor moved then. He jogged down the stairs, careful to dodge the crumbling parts and rusty screws sticking out at random places.

Ben caught up with him on the bottom level. "If there was another way or if I thought Evan had the sense to wait for the weather to clear we wouldn't be doing this."

"I know." Connor checked to make sure Jenna and Sylvia weren't standing right there. "Look, one thing we need to agree on."

"I'm going to hate whatever you say next."

Maybe, but it had to be said. Connor needed this to be clear. "If you can save one of us, you pick her."

Ben shook his head. "We're not having this conversation."

"Promise me."

"Connor."

He stood there wasting precious seconds Maddie didn't have. That's how much this point mattered. "Do it, Ben."

"Done."

CHAPTER 33

The **rough** edge of the boat frame dug into Maddie's palms. She struggled to drag the unwieldy mass out of its hiding place. It was awkward to carry. Her shoulders slumped under its weight.

The scrape of the metal against the rocky ground made for a bumpy ride and a loud one. She just needed this done, so she carried it the last few feet into the open air. Alone. Evan was smart enough to leave his gun hand free and make her do all the work.

She held on for the last few steps, heaving the front end of the boat higher on her hip as she maneuvered it through the patchwork of leftover walls and fallen rocks. They barely cleared the building when her anger swamped her. At him. At the situation. At her luck.

"This is a terrible plan." She meant to think the words and not say them but they tumbled out of her. The longer this day dragged on, the less of a filter she possessed.

"It will work." He barked out the assessment as he slammed the door shut behind them.

"Once the storm passes, maybe." She hitched the side of the boat higher on her hip. Let it dig into her side. "Until then it's a suicide mission."

"That's enough whining."

She wasn't nearly done. There was a lot left inside her. "We don't even know if this will float."

"We will test it. Case closed." He sounded exasperated now.

She shut her eyes, trying to think this situation through. She would not drown today. "What if we—"

"I'll decide what we do and . . ." Pebbles crunched under Evan's feet as he came to a stop. "You. I wouldn't have said you had it in you."

She opened her eyes. Connor stood there, wearing a protective vest and holding his hands in the air. He practically begged to get shot.

"No!" She dropped the boat with a crack and lunged for him.

"Stop right there."

Evan grabbed her arm, wrenching it behind her as he yanked her to his side. He took a few steps back, bringing them under the framework of an old doorway. Connor stood out in the open. Evan didn't have that risk.

Icy pain raced up her arm and tears sprang into her eyes. She didn't care. He could pull her arm off so long as Connor got out of there.

What the hell was he doing?

"Run!" She screamed the word and heard it bounce off the walls and trees around them.

Evan wrapped an arm around her waist and squeezed. "That's enough helping."

The vise-like grip choked off her breath. She gasped, trying to drag in air as she pounded her fists against the arm banded across her middle.

"Connor." His name came out on a harsh whisper. She didn't have the strength to break Evan's hold or loosen the constriction.

Connor glanced at her face and held her gaze for a few seconds before he looked behind her to Evan. "There's no way off this island. You're a smart man. You have to know that."

Evan just laughed. "Says the businessman who doesn't know shit about survival. Though I am impressed with your attempt to compliment me. That's Negotiation Tactics 101."

"You'd be surprised about the things I know."

"You think you're an expert on survival because you're upset about your dead sister." Evan pointed the gun at Maddie's head. "How about her? Do you want another death on your conscience?"

A gasp escaped her throat when the cold metal made contact with her skin. She shifted and squirmed to get away from the barrel but his grip did not ease.

"Tell me why I shouldn't shoot you in the head." Evan pointed the gun at Connor, then back at her. "Or Maddie."

"Shoot me, and Ben or one of his men will shoot you." His firm voice made it hard to ignore him.

She was so proud of his bravery. Any other circumstance and she would have been charmed. But right now she was ticked off that he walked into this danger. That Ben let him. She would clunk their heads together if they survived this.

"Men?" Evan looked around but didn't seem impressed. "If you're going to lie you should make sure there isn't an island website that talks about the one—single—lawman on the island."

Connor shook his head. "That was before."

"Don't try—"

"You think after the murders here last summer there's still just one? The Board fixed that mistake immediately." The lies bubbled out of her. She let them spill even though he hated to be interrupted.

Connor had to be the decoy. Ben needed to get into position and do it fast.

Evan shrugged. "You forget I've spent time with the island's lawman. Decent enough, probably a good shot, but I'm better."

The pressure from his arm made her dizzy. He didn't allow any space between their bodies. She was his shield. His guarantee no one would take a shot at him. He even ducked a bit, probably in an attempt to ensure his head didn't stick up higher than hers.

"People come in from Arnold. Then there's a crew he has at his disposal on the island. All trained." She was just making stuff up now. Throwing in a fact or two as she stalled to give Ben time to make his move.

"You talk a good game, but no." Evan pressed his cheek against her hair. "He wouldn't take the risk of accidentally shooting Maddie."

"He'll save her," Connor said without missing a beat.

The confidence in his voice tore at her. Ripped and shredded until she thought her stomach might split open right there. "What did you do?"

"Doesn't matter because we've stalled enough." Evan pointed the gun at Connor. "You, move the boat. Now."

He would shoot Connor in the back as a scare tactic to keep her in line. To break her down. She could feel it. "Don't do it."

"He'll do it or he'll see you bleed out on the shoreline."

Connor shook his head. "You won't hurt her."

"Don't be so sure."

"You planted evidence to frame Daria. You killed Owen." Connor's eyes narrowed. "What did he do? I'm guessing he tried to warn Maddie instead of hunt her down. Yes?"

The gun didn't waver as Evan moved his finger to the trigger and kept it trained on Connor. "You should stop talking."

A new wave of dizziness swept over her. She couldn't let this happen. There was no way she could watch Connor get shot and survive it.

"Connor, please." She didn't know what she was begging for other than his safety and he'd already forfeited that.

He treated her to a small smile that didn't reach his eyes. "I have no regrets."

No! He was going to die for her.

Her knees buckled. "Please don't do this."

"You're worth it." He talked right to her now. "I didn't know the you *back then* but the you *now*—the one in front of me—deserves everything."

Forget Evan and the freezing cold. He stood there, making himself a target, for her.

Her breath hitched and her energy drained away, leaving nothing but sadness behind. "Please run."

"I'll shoot him in the back." Evan continued to aim at Connor as he let her body sag against his. "Pick up the boat."

He would die. She knew that much. "Don't."

Evan swore under his breath. "That's enough. We'll do it without you."

His hand shifted a bit, no more than an inch, and she reacted. She threw her body to the side, aiming all her weight against that outstretched arm. She caught him off balance and his arm swung wide.

She saw a blur in front of her and heard shouting in the distance. It all blended together but she didn't lose focus. She slammed into that arm a second time and kicked back at his shin. The double hit had him stumbling.

Connor smashed into them and they all went down. The hit against the hard ground made her teeth rattle. It took a second for her to get her bearings and move again.

While Connor and Evan traded punches, she scrambled, climbing over their bodies. Kicking and fighting. A hand slipped into her hair and yanked hard enough for her vision to blink out. Fingers wrapped around hers and her wrist ached from where Evan pounded on it.

"Maddie, no."

Connor's voice rang out but all she could see was the gun. It dangled from Evan's fingers as he kicked out against Connor's shoulder. She gave him an extra shove and the weapon landed on the ground. She dove across Evan's thighs to get it.

Her fingernails dug into the dirt. Someone landed a kick to the back of her knee that made her gasp. Aches and pains thumped on every inch of her body. She groaned when the men battling above her rolled on top of her, pinning her thighs down for a second before rolling off again.

With all the patting, she crawled and reached out and her fingertips finally hit metal. Flipping to her stomach, she watched the fight rage above and beside her. She held the gun steady. She could not miss, but she could not wait for a better angle either.

Her lungs compressed and her chest tightened. She rolled fully onto her back and followed their movements, trying to track each body and mentally separate one from another. She saw a window and took the shot.

The second after the bang rang out, blood ran and pooled on the ground. Making a rough noise, Connor rolled onto his back until he lay next to her.

She could see his chest rise and fall but those beautiful dark eyes drifted shut. "No!"

She scrambled to sit up. Footsteps pounded around her. Ben came into view, then Sylvia. Evan and Connor hadn't moved again.

"Connor!"

She'd shot him. The sentence played over and over in her head.

He panted and lifted his head. "Not me."

She ran her hands over him. Realizing she still held the gun, she dropped it, freeing up her arms to cradle him. "There's blood."

He looked at the red covering his hands and wiped a splotch off his cheek. The whole time he shook his head. "Not my blood."

He had to be in shock.

"Maddie, move!" Ben yelled the order.

She saw his arm come up, and Connor rolled on top of her. Darkness blanketed her and she struggled to breathe. He could not be her shield. She shoved and fought, trying to lower his body. Somehow make it smaller.

A whooshing sound echoed in her ears. When she opened her eyes again, Connor still lay on top of her with Evan sprawled next to them. The silence only lasted a few seconds before Connor shifted off her and went to Evan's side. Working quickly, he grabbed the jacket Jenna handed him and pressed it against Evan's wound.

Evan jackknifed and his eyes grew wide. Connor gagged but he held on.

She couldn't make her brain digest any of it.

Ben and Jenna moved around, bringing Connor more material to press against Evan's seeping wounds. Sylvia talked with someone on the phone.

Maddie sat motionless with her bloodstained hands on her lap.

Not his. All that blood but none of it was hers or Connor's. All that training, everything Evan taught her paid off . . . and she used it against him.

Ben and Connor shouted directions at each other. Maddie tried to get her legs to move. To get up and hold something or pass something.

Evan lifted his hand but it dropped again. Whatever strength he had was gone. All the threats extinguished.

On Evan's second try his hand landed on Connor's arm. "She belongs to me."

That she heard.

She sat back on her knees, refusing to get closer. Also refusing to give in. "Never."

Connor shot her a glance then nodded. "Never."

CHAPTER 34

The nightmare of the last twenty-four hours wouldn't leave Connor's head. He stood in front of Maddie's floor-to-ceiling windows and stared out over the water. Her view put his at the cabin to shame. Miles of water. Today the sky was blue but the gray would soon return. He half wondered if that was a metaphor for something.

He didn't have the energy to work through any problem at the moment. He wore his lounge pants and vowed not to get any dressier for days.

They had been questioned and requestioned. Every agency sent a representative and ran through a list of questions. When a federal law enforcement official—on leave or not—was involved in a shooting, a lot of people showed up to lock the story down. Ben. Police from Seattle. The FBI. Representatives from the Marshals Service. Each wanted a piece of them and almost no one looked like they believed the whole story.

Of course, it wasn't the entire story. They strategically and by silent agreement left Maddie's secret piece out. The two of them shared that information and no one else needed to know. That was the unspoken deal.

Daria returned home. Maddie commented that she looked more broken than she had when Ned went to prison. Connor had trouble mustering any sympathy. She'd bought into the stories about Maddie. Sure, Evan used her, too, but Daria struck him as someone who wanted to believe the worst. It was likely the only way she could cope with the series of disasters in her life. That part he got.

"You've been staring out the window for hours."

The exaggeration made him smile. "It's amazing what almost dying will do to you."

She groaned. "Don't joke about that."

He turned to see her sitting on the couch. She had thrown on her pajamas but that was it. Even though it was noon, they'd only rolled out of bed an hour ago and he was fine to jump right back in. All she had to do was give him a signal. Any signal.

"It's over." More than a little relief came with saying those words. From the notes to Owen's death to the attack on Paul, they were able to tie it all back to Evan and his delusions.

"Is it?"

And like that she ruined his good mood. "Do you know something I don't know?"

If Ben found more clues that took him in some new direction, Connor gave up. The twists and turns exhausted him. The hour-long phone call with Hansen hadn't helped. His big brother was pissed about Connor's supposed vacation and all the danger. He'd flipped into overprotective mode and refused to stop lecturing until Connor took him off track by mentioning Maddie.

After only a little time on Whitaker, Hansen loved gossip as much as any resident.

Connor watched Maddie sip her coffee and decided Whitaker wasn't so bad after all.

She caught him staring at her. "Are you okay?"

He'd lost the string of the conversation. Something about more evidence . . . or not. He couldn't remember. "All I did was dive on Evan. I'm fine."

Evan wasn't. He'd survived the two shots, but he would be in the hospital for a long time. There was a fear of infections and secondary problems. Connor didn't understand all of it, but he did get that Evan's life would never be the same.

From the hospital he would go to a series of hearings and, Connor hoped, eventually prison. All signs pointed that way. He wasn't denying what he did to Maddie. He wore it as a badge of honor. Even suggested his old office adopt his training program as standard procedure.

The general view, or at least the one Evan's old boss was willing to share, was that Evan had some sort of break. He'd always been too focused on Maddie and had been disciplined for that. The last round landed him on administrative leave and that's when his reality seemed to splinter.

He bragged about disciplining her and talked about teaching others his techniques. It scared the hell out of his bosses . . . and so did meeting Maddie. She made it clear she blamed them for not exercising oversight over Evan. Connor knew she was prepared to negotiate to get Evan specialized help for his break from reality, if he would take it.

Connor couldn't be that generous. Maybe one day when he no longer closed his eyes and saw Evan pointing the gun at her head, but probably not. He stayed up most of last night thinking about that.

But since he couldn't remember if he'd answered her question, he tried now. "I'm just tired."

She set her mug on the coffee table. "Of?"

He needed more sleep to keep up with this conversation. "What does that mean?"

"You're still running."

He groaned inside. "Maddie, don't."

"Evan tried to kill you."

"And you." She kept jumping over that horrifying point but he couldn't.

"Why did you insist you be the one to walk in there? You were so vulnerable. A pure target since Evan hated you so much. Even more than he hated me." She dropped her feet to the floor but didn't stand up. "Ben told me you didn't give him much of a choice about the plan."

"It felt like time was running out. If Evan was willing to grab you during the day like that, risk having us all track you down, I knew he'd lost perspective and feared he thought he had nothing left to lose."

She stood up and hovered by the couch. "You didn't answer my question. Why you? There were law enforcement people on the island, even more than usual. You went in. Why?"

"Could we do this another time?" Preferably when he was on his game.

She wanted him to unload. He got it. But he was the wrong guy for that. That sort of emotional response was burned out of him when Alexis died. He thought all of his feelings died that day, but knowing Maddie taught him differently. There were pieces and fragments left. For her, he'd try to pull them together and be as close to whole as possible.

She tilted her head as she stared at him. "What do you see when you look at me?"

This felt like a trap. Any answer could lead them down a dangerous path.

He didn't know what she was digging for, so he went with the truth. "A beautiful survivor. Someone who cares about others even though she is desperate not to."

She smiled but didn't say anything.

That reminded him of his favorite part of her. "You have this smile, which you hide most of the time. But when you show it, it's blinding." She didn't move, so he didn't stop. "Your oversized coats make me laugh and your body makes me weak."

"Sweet talker."

"I can be whatever you want me to be." He would turn himself inside out to please her. Step in front of a bullet to save her.

Other than for family, he'd never really felt this level of connection before. He hadn't made time for deep relationships and before Alexis died didn't think he was ready.

She frowned at him. "How about honest?"

"What does that mean?" He searched his mind for a single time when he'd lied to her and came up empty.

"Saving me—"

"You saved yourself, Maddie." He knew because he'd relived the scene in slow motion every time he closed his eyes last night. "You shot Evan and made sure I wasn't in the firing line."

"Do you feel anything for me?"

What the fuck was this about? "Everything."

"What?"

They stood on opposite sides of the room and right now it felt like different corners of the state. She searched and poked and looked for the right answer. He wished he knew what it was.

"I feel everything and it scares the shit out of me." Had him panicking and making excuses for why he should cut out early before this relationship grew into love and took a piece of him. The games running through his head to protect the heart he thought he no longer had surprised even him.

"I feel like you hold back." She glanced at the floor before looking back up at him. "I mean, I know what's between us is new, and it happened under odd circumstances, but it feels real. At least to me."

The truth hit him. This was the relationship talk.

She wanted to know where they stood, which was fair. He was still working that out himself. "I don't want to leave you. This might be new to both of us, but I want to explore it."

She made a humming sound. "Okay."

"That's it?" For some reason he didn't feel as if he dodged a bullet.

"I guess that's enough."

LATER THAT NIGHT he pushed into her for the last time and let the orgasm overtake him. As the last of the pulses hammered him, he let his body fall heavy against hers. Let the smell and taste of her wash through him.

Her softness lured him in every time. Tonight started in the shower and continued on the sheets. Even now, damp piles were trapped underneath him. She had her legs wrapped around his waist and her fingers plunged into his hair. She held him close and kissed his neck.

The lovemaking mirrored every other time they had fallen into bed. A wild frenzy of need that slowed and sped up as their moods changed. A space where they were free to do what they wanted, ask for what they needed.

He loved that about her. The way she owned her pleasure. She didn't hide from it. She pushed him to do the same.

In such a short time, they'd bonded and connected. In here and out there.

"We're going to need another shower."

Her words broke through his mental wanderings. He wasn't even sure why his mind had taken off. He usually stayed in the moment with her. Steadied his breathing and calculated how long it would be before he could be inside of her again.

"I'm happy to shower as many times as needed." He had to force the words. They didn't flow naturally like they usually did. He wasn't even sure they made sense in context.

But she didn't complain. She'd barely said anything tonight. Her consent was clear. He asked for it because that's what he did. They both needed to be in the mood for him to want it. He wasn't a sex-for-the-sake-of-sex guy. The days of quick hookups for relief were far in his past.

His mind refused to shut off. Something bugged him but he couldn't tell what it was. It pricked at the back of his mind, just out of reach. He tried to assess and analyze but those skills abandoned him as well.

That was annoying as hell.

Every piece of tonight had been good but not mind-blowingly great. He wanted to blame exhaustion and all they'd seen and been through over the last few days. Switching houses, worry, panic. A shooting. The list of horrible examples stretched out pretty long.

He rolled off her onto his back and stared at the ceiling. He didn't go far and still held her hand.

This was the part where they talked. Curled around each other in the darkness and laughed. Told a joke or a story. Relived something that happened that day. It was their ritual. An intimacy shared in the darkness that went beyond sex. Those moments were about connecting, about learning things about her other than how to give her pleasure.

In those quiet minutes of understanding she started to mean more to him than he'd planned. The vacation fling he thought they both expected blossomed into something deeper. They practically lived together—they actually had for two weeks—but this was the first time he felt a chasm stretching between them.

There was an easy argument about the danger working as an aphrodisiac. He discounted that as soon as he thought it.

He was overreacting. A tired body and a frazzled mind. That explained their last few days. No wonder the mood felt . . . off.

He rolled over, thinking to wrap an arm around her and drag her close to his side. Just as he did, she turned. Away from him. She didn't inch to the edge but she didn't rest against him either.

The closeness he'd come to expect vanished.

He hoped it was just for one night.

MADDIE WAITED UNTIL Connor's breathing grew heavy to ease out of bed. The mattress dipped under her but when she turned to look at him, his eyes stayed closed.

She made it to the bathroom before letting go of the breath she'd been holding.

The night hadn't gone as she'd hoped, but it was about what she'd expected. He'd shut down the emotional side of her right after he made that declaration at the prison. For a few seconds she caught a peek of who he was underneath. Before Alexis died. It had been mixed in with the terror of the moment when she'd been so sure and stunned by the idea that Evan might kill Connor.

She rested her palms against the marble countertop and stared at her reflection in the mirror. She could only hold it for a few seconds before her gaze dropped. She was naked but no part of her felt exposed. He closed down rather than opened up. When the communication ceased, they fell back on sex. Good sex but sex with a piece missing. She never knew how important it was until they lost it.

She looked at him and saw a future. It was too early for love declarations but the words hung there. So close. All of that shut down when he pushed her away. Not physically but with every other part of him.

Again.

She wanted all the pieces. Every last one, ugly or not. She hoped to help him carefully step through the emotional battlefield left by Alexis's death. Let him grieve and grow and realize they had something precious. Something they would need to cultivate and feed.

It was a grown-up conversation, and he wasn't ready to have it.

She wanted all of him and he wanted a bed partner.

That reality filled her with a dragging sadness she couldn't kick. It leaked over into the bedroom. Now it would kill everything else.

CHAPTER 35

The next night Maddie skipped their usual dinner together. She decided to go out with Sylvia and spend more time getting to know Jenna. The three of them had taken off for a Girls' Night that left Connor alone.

He liked that she was learning to reach out and make friends. That gift had been stolen from her for so long. The first bit of excitement he'd seen in her all day spiked as she rooted through her closet looking for the right thing to wear.

Connor felt like a spy watching the going-out ritual happen. When she twisted her hair up in an intricate knot he almost asked her to take it down and do it again. The way her hands moved and her fingers slipped through the strands. It was such an intimate peek into who she was and the part of her that she'd buried in favor of safety.

But now he was by himself and looking for food. That led him to the Lodge. Sylvia, Jenna, and Maddie might not be there, but he could go in. That wasn't weird. Men ate alone. He'd done that plenty of times before he found her.

He kept telling himself it meant nothing. Nothing at all. It wasn't a reflection on him or them as a couple. One night apart was normal, even. Others did it. He could adjust and get used to it.

The first person he spied was the guy who ran the market. He sat with two other men at a table by the window. Then he saw Ben. He sat at the counter, nursing a beer. No one bothered him. All that crime solving had earned him some downtime but Connor was half surprised that the residents of Whitaker respected that. Probably had something to do with the don't-bother-me vibe Ben gave off.

If the last day hadn't dragged and had his sense of security flipping upside down, he would have left the man alone. He'd probably also be with Maddie right now, but that was beside the point.

He slid onto the barstool next to Ben's and immediately started playing with the napkin the bartender on duty for Sylvia slid in front of him. He folded and unfolded the edge. Ran his finger along the seam as he ordered a club soda.

He didn't drink in support of his father's abstaining, and he didn't miss it, except for the ritual of it. Holding a drink always made it easier to stand around and talk. Not that he was a big talker.

Ben watched him, his gaze switching from Connor's face to his fingers. "What did you do?"

Connor's hand froze. "I just walked in the door."

"It's snowing. You just survived a dangerous situation. You're sharing a house and bed with Maddie. And you're here like a dumbass instead of there." Ben took a long drink. "That can't possibly be your choice. Please tell me you're smarter than that or I'll regret not letting Evan shoot you."

"Maybe it is my choice. It's not weird to want some alone time."

"In a bar." Ben glanced over his shoulder. "With other people."

His plans for tonight included a movie and another try at sex. He had to believe the *off* feeling he got last night and the fact it was only that one time was an aberration. Now that he'd had more sleep, he expected their mojo to be back in full force.

"See, I'm thinking you fucked up." Ben delivered the assessment, then shoved the half-empty beer glass away from him. "Am I close?"

That made Connor's defenses rise. "Maybe it was her."

"It's never them."

"You don't believe that."

"Your life will be easier if you pretend to get that." Ben dragged out his phone and typed something in. Then he turned the screen around to face Connor. "There's a betting pool and I have next Wednesday as the day you blow it and come hunting for advice. Any chance you can keep it together until then?"

Connor refrained from taking a look. Seeing a spreadsheet or whatever was on there would only tick him off. "Why do I like you?"

"It's a mystery."

"Thank you for your faith in me, by the way. Blaming me if we had an issue, which we don't." He needed to make that clear. He'd decided on the word *aberration*. It's the one that kept kicking around in his head.

"Being the law around here is a full-service job. You'd be amazed what nonsense I have to listen to just to have a beer."

Yeah, he should have gone to the takeout pizza place. He didn't really need company. "I wonder what Jenna, Sylvia, and Maddie are doing right now. Probably not this."

"Admittedly, I'm not an expert on marriage."

How did they jump to that? "I'm not married. Not looking to be either. You've got the wrong Rye brother."

Ben switched out beer for water. He sounded and acted sober. He probably limited himself to half a beer even off duty. A sensible move. Far more sensible than a marriage talk.

"Maybe you're not now, but this advice will be helpful despite the fact I only managed to make mine last for a short time."

"You were married?" That was news. No one talked about that on Whitaker, which made Connor think the relationship was far in Ben's past where residents were hesitant to go or at least ask about.

"Speaking of the Rye brothers. Why do you two have trouble imagining me married?"

"I wonder. You seem so stable and all."

Ben waved that off. He also waved to the couple in the corner who were smiling at him. "I'm going to pretend you mean that."

"Let's."

They didn't say anything for a full minute. They both pretended to watch the television over the bar. Two talking heads argued about something football-related. Connor loved the sport but that's not where his mind was right now.

Before he could come up with a safe topic that didn't involve wedding bands, Ben started talking again. "But I do think the key is sharing."

"For relationships?" Maybe he would prefer to talk about football. Football seemed safe and didn't involve Maddie.

Ben frowned. "Isn't that what we're talking about?"

"I have no idea. But, for the record, we almost died together out at the prison. That's sharing."

The frown turned into a scoff. "That's not what I mean, dumbass."

This was really a great night. Connor needed to re-member to pencil in another one of these very soon. "Enlighten me."

"She wants to know you."

She'd seen every inch of him. Literally. "We've been informally living together."

"Uh-huh."

At least he didn't throw out the *dumbass* tag again. That might amount to progress. "Is that the sum total of your advice?"

Ben shifted in his chair to face Connor. "Okay. Ready?"

"Nope." Because he wasn't a total jackass.

Ben kept talking anyway. "What have you risked?" He held up a hand before Connor could answer. "And don't talk about the shootout. I mean emotionally. With her."

"Why do I have to risk anything?" People made relationships too hard. They sliced open their skin and let their hearts drop on the table. It was ridiculous to him. There was no need to go that deep or be that vulnerable.

"Because that's how it works, Connor." Ben rolled his eyes. "She shares . . . and she has, right? You think I don't know that office story of hers is bullshit?"

Talking about that would be a violation of trust. Connor was not going to add that to his list of sins . . . and he was starting to believe maybe he did have such a list where she was concerned. He thought he'd been doing okay. Keeping his head up and not being a demanding jerk. "No comment."

Ben went off on this forbidden tangent anyway. "She laid it out there. Took the risk you would hate what you saw in her and walk away."

"Yeah." He didn't take that piece for granted. He could see how difficult it was for her to open up about what happened. She'd had tears in her eyes and a determination in her voice that said she expected to be batted down. As if he would ever do that to her.

"Your turn. Or not." Ben picked up his water glass and drained it. "Your choice."

"That's helpful."

"Oh, you can keep doing this." Ben gestured around the bar area. "Just be prepared to lose her."

The thought made him clench his teeth together. "I'm not."

Ben nodded. "Then risk something."

CONNOR WENT THROUGH most of the next day without seeing Maddie. It was on purpose. He did busy work. Helped with some odd jobs at Paul's house and walked Mr. Higginbotham twice.

He still didn't want to talk about the walks.

He needed to clear his head and think about Ben's advice. His initial instinct was to discount it. What did Ben know about women? But the hours ticked by and Connor's resistance weakened. Staying away from Maddie turned out to be a bigger job than anticipated since everyone on the island asked where she was. And he didn't like going hours without seeing or talking to her.

Jesus, he had it bad for her.

That meant listening to Ben, or at least trying out his suggestion. Easier said than done because the potential downside to spilling his guts could be huge. He was not that guy. He'd never been that guy but now he *really* wasn't him.

When he walked in the house before five, which was as late as he could push it before people started staring at him for sitting around doing nothing at the Lodge, Maddie passed right in front of him on her way to the barstool. Now she sat with her hair up and was reading a book. She didn't even look up from the pages. No kiss. No warm smile.

Yeah, he'd screwed this up. Big.

He wasn't a hundred percent sure how to fix his mess but the dragging sadness needed to go. Seeing her, being with her, made him feel lighter and he wanted that sensation back.

"Interested in dinner?" she asked as she turned a page.

"No."

Something in his tone must have grabbed her attention because her head shot up. "What's wrong?"

He debated going halfway in. Leaving enough of him outside of her reach to stay whole but letting her have a peek. But then he saw the worry in her eyes and the tension pulling around her mouth. Part of that expression belonged to him. He'd sucked the life out of her and now he had to figure out a way to give it back to her.

He dove in, hoping he found a soft landing. "You're not Alexis. I get that."

She closed the book and set it on the kitchen island. "Okay."

Every part of his brain screamed for him to back out now. Going deep meant going under. He'd experienced that choking feeling. He plowed over it by being in the office when other people were out experiencing life.

"That conversation we had about hiding places? I knew you were at the prison. That you would lead Evan there." For some reason he needed her to know that he'd gotten the message. That he'd listened and the connection between them had made a difference.

"I actually worried you would come there with a misguided idea of rescuing me and walk straight into danger." She rolled her eyes. "And you did exactly that."

The flatness of her voice told him what she thought of that risk. But it was a calculated one. "Ben was there."

"Are we pretending you don't have a death wish?"

He didn't understand the way she saw him. She said things about his life and his reactions that made him think she was looking at another guy. "I don't."

"Connor."

He'd never toyed with not being here. Never experienced a moment so dark that he wanted it to be his last. But he had lost the ability to celebrate things, big or small.

He wasn't sure how to explain all of that but he tried. "I really don't. But, admittedly, that doesn't mean I've been all that thrilled about living either." When she didn't stop him, he looked for another way to say it. "Alexis's death is bound up with a whole bunch of other things. The unbearable grief. How it shredded my parents. How Hansen lost it."

"You're angry with him."

"What? No." He loved Hansen. Spent most of his life trying to *be* Hansen. Typical baby brother stuff.

She leaned against the counter just a few feet away from him. "He got to fall apart but you didn't."

"He went on a vigilante rampage and almost got thrown in jail." Those words were too strong. He wasn't sure why he said them or where they came from.

Hansen had derailed but figured it out. Now he was engaged and stable and all of that was behind him.

"And you're jealous of that," she said.

"That's not—"

"Connor." She said his name louder this time.

"It's not about being jealous. I was the responsible one." It sounded odd when he said it out loud. He was the youngest and the one least connected to the business. He actually thought about taking a different path until Hansen checked out.

"Which sucked for you. You can say it. I bet if I called your family they would all say it. Only you seem unable to admit it."

"You're not getting this."

She reached out and took his hand. Slipped her fingers through his and held on. "It's okay to be angry with him. You stayed behind and did what you had to do. You followed the rules and didn't seek revenge. You went to work and did the mundane crappy stuff to keep the family on its feet."

"All of that's true. To an extent." It would have been nice to let go, but that's how families worked. You helped each other out. One member experienced a problem and the others rushed in. "It was a joint effort."

She shook her head. "You pushed yourself. Buried your brain in work. Refused to grieve."

Alexis's face flashed in his mind and he blanked it out again. He couldn't let memories in on top of this conversation. Struggling to keep up with every comment she threw at him took all of his energy.

"I miss her every single day." It was the easiest way to express it but the words weren't big enough. They didn't convey the depth of the heartbreak.

"We're saying two different things." She squeezed his hand and then dropped it.

When she walked into the living room, away from him, the distance between them grew in more ways than one. He felt a tug on the invisible string holding them together. He wanted to reel her back in but he wasn't sure how.

"Why are you pushing this subject and insisting we explore it?" He didn't have any anger in his voice because he didn't feel anger. The emotion knocking into him right now was an overwhelming sense of loss.

With every word and unresolved piece of the argument he could feel Alexis and Maddie slip away from him.

"Because if you don't deal with her loss you'll never be able to deal with the life that comes after." She lifted her chin. "The life I want you to have with me."

That sounded like an ultimatum but she wasn't pushing or begging him for more. It was how she seemed willing to let him go forever that pricked at him. No . . . it was bigger than that. It punched through him, leaving an empty sucking hole behind.

"I've done okay for the last two years." He knew that was a lie the second he said it and rushed to clean it up. "You know what I mean."

She sat down on the arm of the couch, facing him. "Your family begged you to come here and rest."

Evan had dropped that bomb. He might not have mentioned the intervention, but there was one. They made it quite clear he wasn't welcome in the office for at least a month. After everything he did for them and their checkbooks, and how hard he worked. They abandoned him, leaving him out here without them.

An unexpected ache started in his chest and he rubbed against the spot to ease the pressure. "My job is to be the reliable one."

"Out there. Not in here." She shook her head. "Not with me."

That's what this was about. Him opening up to her and showing her . . . something. He still didn't get what it was she needed before he could tick the box and things could go back to how they were. "You want to see me lose it?"

The color drained from her face. "God, no."

"Then what?" He really needed a clue here.

"I want you to feel something."

"No." The word kept repeating in his head.

He looked at her sitting there. Slumped shoulders and sad eyes. They'd returned to the place they were that first time in Ben's office. Distrusting and circling each other, not sure what to expect.

The realization that he lost something—again—sliced through him. A raw emptiness oozed out. He wanted to lash out at her for making him deal with it. Feel it.

"Pain. Like the kind of pain that eats away at you. Where I can't look at old photos or see someone who looks like her. Or think about hiking." The memories flipped through his mind. Every mental weapon he used in the past to block them failed. He could see her and that smile . . . and that cliff. Why did he visit where she died? He could never unsee it. It haunted him every damn day. "Is that what you want me to talk about?"

She slowly stood up but didn't come closer. That was a good choice because his body felt like it was on fire from the inside out. Pain poured through him. Crashed, wave after wave. A thumping hollowness echoed in every muscle and every cell.

He wanted to stop the words, cut them off along with the feelings, and storm out. Not see her or see the welcoming in her eyes. She should shut him out and turn him away and he didn't know how to make her see that, so he kept unloading. Piled on more.

"Maybe you want to know about the guilt." The ache moved all through him now. "I couldn't look my own mother in the eye for a year. A fucking year."

His voice rose but she didn't back down. She was in front of him again. Running her palms over his chest, trying to soothe him.

"Why?" Such an innocent question.

It had an equally simple answer.

"Because I lost her baby." He choked on the words.

Maddie shook her head and tears formed in her eyes. "You didn't do it. You weren't there."

"Exactly!" He let the rage explode. All that anger and heat he'd been pressing down for so long rose to the surface and spilled over. "I messed up."

"You didn't."

"I wasn't there for my sister and she needed me." The words felt as if they were yanked out of him. Each one hurt as it scratched against his throat.

Her hands smoothed over his face and into his hair. "Babysitting her wasn't your job."

"I am her brother." Not *was*, because that part didn't end. She would also be a part of him. There, ready to give him hell.

"Right." She held his face in both of her hands now. "You're her brother. Not her guardian."

That did it. That chunk of pain that he pretended didn't exist inside him broke lose. He felt the sob inch up the back of his throat and he tried to shove it back down. "I just want her back."

"I know, baby."

He wrapped his arms around her and held on. Buried his face in her neck and let the despair wash over him. His body shook and his head pounded. It was as if his brain fought the pain until it crashed through the barriers and flooded everything.

She rubbed his shoulders and whispered his name. Rained kisses over his cheeks and in his hair. Through it all he tightened his grip. She didn't offer a lifeline.

She *was* his lifeline. The reason he could tread water instead of plunge underneath.

He wasn't sure what love felt like but he sensed this was it.

Acceptance. Forgiveness. Tenderness.

She believed in him when he didn't believe in himself. Through her he might be able to bounce back because she was seeing the worst and she didn't bolt. She'd spent years running, but she proved her staying power now.

"Don't leave me." He didn't know the words were inside him until they slipped out.

"Never."

CHAPTER 36

They spent a long night talking. Maddie knew Connor needed the emotional catharsis but she did, too. After days of feeling disconnected and worrying their spark grew out of danger and not any real feelings, she experienced a resurgence of hope. The idea that they were a temporary thing was her nightmare. It scared her more than Evan.

The darkness provided the needed backdrop to learn more about each other. A certain comfort came from lying in bed, whispering in the quiet. They talked about their lives before Whitaker, good and bad. His family stories made her double over with laughter. Her tales from Evan's imposed WITSEC training made Connor swear more than once.

Now the bright light of morning came and they tiptoed around each other. Not because they were uncomfortable but because each thought the other wanted to sleep in. At least, she originally thought that was the case. They'd showered and started their morning. Moving around each other and through the house, she noticed he didn't give her full eye contact. His gaze would graze her face, then bounce off again.

She didn't pretend not to get it. Last night he'd opened up and let her see a side he rarely exposed. She thought he might not have believed he possessed the ability for that sort of openness until the feelings came pouring out. All that hurt and pain. It vibrated in his voice and his body language.

Watching the emotions tear through him wounded her. It killed her to see him go through that pain, but she knew he needed to do it. Bottling up despair didn't make it go away. It grew until it took over so much of who he was. Impacted and chipped away at every part of his life.

He'd let her in and she wasn't going to let him shut her out. No more hiding or pretending to be okay. Not with her. She understood the temptation. She'd been doing both for so long that it became habit. It was time they both relinquished the medal and let someone else have the title.

"Good morning." She stepped in front of him, not giving him any choice but to look up or run her over.

He picked the former. "Is it?"

That question suggested some doubts still lurked under there. He smiled but the expression lacked his usual brightness. Those dark eyes held an unmistakable wariness.

Every other part of McHottiePants looked just fine.

Determined not to let him curl into an emotional ball and avoid her, she rested her hand on his chest and gave him a long, lingering morning kiss. When he made a sexy little noise at the back of his throat, she lifted her head and treated him to a smile. "You're in a mood."

The quiet ticked by for a few seconds. She was going to have to force this. Give him a gentle push. "Connor?"

He exhaled. "I'm sorry about last night. That was a lot to dump on someone. I didn't even know it was stuck in there until it tumbled out."

And there it was. He'd shown her a side she'd ached to see and finally let a piece of Alexis go, and he worried he'd upset her. Some part of him might be embarrassed. Revealing that much was not an easy thing. It could leave a hole that was tough to fill. Expose a vulnerability that wasn't easy to handle.

Only men saw that as weakness. She knew being able to process feelings like that was positive. A very human thing.

"I'm not." Her fingers curled against his soft shirt. "Sorry, I mean."

"That's a bit bloodless." But he didn't sound angry. The amusement was right there in his voice.

He no longer hid his face from her and that smile suggested he could handle a little emotional wrestling if it meant he'd find support afterward.

She lifted her arms and wound them around his neck. This close she could smell the soap on his skin. "That man from last night has a bright future. I'm betting he can get most anything he wants."

His smile brightened. "Oh, really?"

She loved this side of him. Lighter, a bit more carefree. Wearing only a pair of boxer briefs and a T-shirt she could easily slip off, and she might do so very soon.

This living together thing had a lot of side benefits.

"He's the kind of man a woman might bet on." She'd gambled everything on him last night. Bet he could maneuver his way through some heady stuff and come out better on the other side. She'd never been so happy to be right.

"I do like to think of myself as a prize," he said with his cockiness back on full display.

"Wow." She pretended the ego blast shocked her but she really loved hearing him joke.

On him, self-confidence was cute and charming. On Evan it had been pathological. She was happy that, despite everything, she could still tell the difference. He hadn't warped her or sucked away the last of her hope.

Connor's eyebrow lifted. "Too much morning bravado?"

"Just about right." Perfect, but she wouldn't tell him that just yet. There would be no stopping his ego if he knew how much she liked this side of him.

They were thrown together by threats and circumstance. They long ago could have retreated to their own homes. Even during a rocky day yesterday they stuck it out. Neither ran back home. They stayed together instead. It was too early and probably too serious, it might even put a lot of extra pressure on that a budding relationship didn't need, but she did not want their living situation to end.

To drive that point home she kissed him. He didn't know about the conversation going on in her head but the man could kiss. He put his energy behind it. Kissed her like he never wanted to stop. Whipped up the excitement in her until she forgot they were in the middle of a talk.

He lifted his head after a few minutes and rested his forehead against hers. "I spoke with Hansen this morning."

Now that sounded like progress, or at least inching toward it. "And?"

"Told him off and reminded him how much he sucked because he got to go off and lose his control and get into fights about Alexis and I didn't."

"How did he take that?"

"He agreed. It was like he'd been waiting for me to unload on him." He winked at her. "Then he told me to switch islands because there was too much death here."

Except for the last part, it was all exactly what she expected from Hansen. He was a smart man. He knew the toll his actions and all that pressure must have had on Connor. She appreciated him stepping up and being the good brother that Connor deserved.

"Are you taking your big brother's advice on the subject of geography?" If he did, she would put in a call to Hansen on her own. She had his number. Got it from Ben, just in case.

"No, because I'm actually the smarter Rye brother."

The joking tone wiped away the last of her doubts. He had no intention of running and hiding from the healing he still had in front of him. "I thought that might be the case."

"The plan is to stick around and see what happens." He lifted her up onto her tiptoes and planted a kiss on her surprised mouth.

No timetable. No details. It was as if he was drawing this out to torture her . . . and he would pay later in bed. She looked forward to that bit of revenge. "That's cryptic."

He sat down on the armrest of the couch and pulled her onto his lap. "Are you willing to take a chance on an overworked, relationship-challenged, still-grieving guy?"

She already had and it paid off big-time. "Is he hot?"

He wasn't the only one who was done running from their problems. She was ready to be in one place, plant roots. Not be looking over her shoulder.

He shrugged. "I heard someone call him McHottie-Pants."

Now that was embarrassing. It still fit. Probably even better now, but still.

"He does sound hot." She dragged her finger along the neckline of his shirt. He had the sexiest collarbone and sometimes it took all the self-control she had not to lick it. "He also sounds like he's pretty self-aware."

"He likes to pretend he is, but he's a work in progress. Good thing is, he's willing to learn." Some of the amusement left his tone. "He's also falling for you."

Her stomach flipped over. She fought to keep the giant smile from spreading across her face. Not just yet. "That's big news."

"He's terrified of that part."

He'd gone from being a no-commitment guy who didn't understand love to circling close to using the *L* word. That was a big leap. He might be scared but he wasn't letting it slow him down.

"He's not alone." He'd been honest, so she returned the same. "I had no interest in love before I met you and now . . ."

"I'm getting there, too." He dipped his head and rubbed his cheek against hers. "The love thing. It's right there. Really close."

"A few more weeks and I won't be able to let you go." She doubted she could do it now but she didn't want to scare him.

"I'm counting on that." That smile came roaring back. "Ever been to D.C.?"

"Oh, yeah. About that."

His eyes widened. "What?"

"If this—us—happens, and it's going to, by the way. Count on that."

He nodded. "Agreed."

"No more being on magazine covers that high-light your inability to leave your desk. This whole work-twenty-hours-a-day thing isn't happening." She refused to spend her days tracking him down at the office and dragging him home. It was time for a new work ethic that included downtime. "The word to learn is *balance*."

He pretended to think about her proposal. "First love, then balance. I think I can handle both."

"You've never been hotter."

"Now you're just trying for extra credit."

She let that smile show now. "Is it working?"

"Definitely."

THEY FINALLY VENTURED outside the next night. Connor was against the idea but Maddie thought they should let Whitaker know they were still alive. He doubted they cared until people cheered when they walked into the Lodge's dining room.

Nothing weird about that. On another island, maybe. Not on Whitaker.

That was only the second most interesting thing about their dinner. The first was finding Ben and Jenna sitting together at a table in the corner. Naturally, Connor invited himself to join them and gave Maddie no choice but to come along. He wasn't about to miss out on the chance to annoy Ben.

Somehow they made it through getting menus and drinks and rounds of idle chitchat. They'd just ordered when Connor looked around the room and saw a few empty tables. Not many but three or four. "I see the crowds are back to normal."

Jenna sighed. "I'm still worried that Whitaker is going to get on some sort of murder tour."

"As the owner, you can say no. Put up no-trespassing signs. Let me shoot people, only as a warning, of course," Ben said as he signaled the waiter to pour more water.

"I was waiting for you to bring up my ownership status." She smiled at him. "It took days to get around to it."

Connor looked at Maddie. She was already rolling her eyes. He could read her unspoken expression—she thought they were intruding. Connor sort of hoped so. He wouldn't mind seeing Ben in action. Turned out he gave pretty good relationship advice, especially for a guy who wasn't in one. And if the conversation with Jenna was any indication, Ben might not stay that way.

Ben continued talking to Jenna as if the other two weren't there. "Well, I've been busy with all the crime solving."

"He likes to throw that into a conversation whenever he can," Maddie said, clearly not wanting to be ignored if it meant making Ben blush. Which he did.

Connor liked her style. "It's his version of flirting."

Ben finally looked at Connor. "When do you go back to D.C.? There's a ferry tomorrow that will get you as far as Seattle."

"That's neighborly." When Ben continued to stare, Connor took pity on him. "Not to disappoint you but I'm extending my vacation on Whitaker."

"Until when?" Jenna sounded genuinely curious.

"January, at least. We'll do a quick trip home for the holidays so Maddie can meet the parents. Then we'll be back." *We* and *holiday* . . . using those words together was new. When Connor mentioned it to his mom during a call this morning she didn't say much. Three seconds later Hansen called with a million questions, insisting Mom wanted to know.

The family gossip tree worked that fast.

"More time with you. Lucky us." Ben's voice was loaded with sarcasm.

Connor guessed he was secretly excited to have him stick around. "I don't have a date set yet but keep this up and I'll be here until March."

"No, not that long. The fourteenth." Jenna dropped that little gem without any explanation.

Connor had no idea what that meant. "Excuse me?"

Ben didn't even try to hide his smile. "She has that date in the pool. January 14."

"Not you, too." Connor suddenly hated pools.

Ben smiled. "Jenna suggested this one."

"What are you talking about?" Maddie asked before Connor could stop her.

"The date people—Jenna, in particular—predict Connor will leave the island." Ben shot Connor a look that suggested he thought he'd won. "Taking you, of course. Because he's not a total dumbass, though he likes to pretend to be."

Maddie nodded. "Sounds good. Carry on and put me down for February 1."

"That's insider information," Ben pointed out.

Maddie shrugged in response.

That was the exact wrong answer. Giving Ben that sort of green light spelled disaster. "Stop betting on my love life."

Ben whistled. "Those are big words."

Well, shit. "How did this conversation become about me?"

"I wonder," Ben said in a dry tone before turning to Jenna. "What about you? You breeze in, surprise everyone by not being what we expected."

She shook her head. "You thought I'd be an old man."

Maddie jumped in with her support. Even silently toasted Jenna with her glass of water. "Of course, because only men own islands. Idiots."

Ben ignored both of them. Didn't pay attention to the rest of the room either, which Connor found interesting. He planned on giving Ben a lot of shit for that later, out of Maddie's presence. The last thing he needed was her rushing to Ben's defense.

Ben put an elbow on the table and leaned a tiny bit closer to Jenna. "Are you staying with Sylvia and maybe . . . ?"

He really sucked at this. Connor was happy he didn't know that when he went seeking advice days ago. "Subtle. As she has her own really big house on the island."

Jenna didn't seem to get it. Her eyes narrowed. "What are you really asking?"

"You and Sylvia."

"Are friends," she said, drawing the words out for emphasis. "We're not dating. She's not my type. I prefer men, actually."

"Oh." Ben sat back hard in his chair. "Interesting."

"He's truly terrible at this." Maddie didn't even try to whisper the observation.

If he hadn't been running full speed at being in love with her before then, that would have done it. She delivered the line perfectly. Connor wanted to kiss her for that . . . and other reasons.

"Shouldn't you be celebrating his continued stay on Whitaker? Maybe somewhere private that's not right here?" Ben asked.

Maddie just smiled. "We did before dinner."

"I'm ignoring you both now."

Jenna reached for her glass. "I'll be staying for a while as well."

"How long?" Ben's attention immediately returned to the woman sitting across from him.

"I'm not sure yet." She swirled the red wine in her glass.

"That's good."

Oh, Ben. "Is it?"

Ben answered Connor but kept his attention on Jenna. "Things have been out of control. Maybe having you here will calm some nerves and let people get back to normal."

"That's why you think it's a good thing?" Connor asked.

"Yes." Ben shot Connor a look that screamed *shut up* before turning back to Jenna. "And it's interesting."

Maddie smiled at Connor over the top of her glass. "I think it will be, yes."

The company and the island deserved a cheer. Connor raised his water glass in a toast. "To Whitaker."

Jenna raised her glass. "Whitaker."

"Interesting," Ben said.

Connor agreed.

ACKNOWLEDGMENTS

A huge thank you to May Chen, my marvelous editor, for supporting this series and not balking at the idea of an island of dysfunctional misfits. We had a bumpy road getting this one to production. I am eternally grateful that you gave me the time and space I needed to write it the way it deserved to be written. Mr. Higginbotham is my gift to you.

As always, thanks to Laura Bradford, my lovely agent, for pitching this project so we could both get paid. I'm a fan of getting paid.

And big thanks to my husband, James, for tolerating me during the writing of this book. Surviving this one was not easy. I wrote this during a difficult time, when my attention was pulled in 900 directions and I felt as if I were failing at everything. This truly was the "I can no longer write" book for me. I thought I'd lost it . . . but I found it again. It just took some time. I wrote a version, hated it, and then rewrote until I fixed it. Almost every last word changed from the original and I did the rewrite in less than four weeks. It wasn't the optimal way to get a book done, but we got there. I wanted to write about grief and moving on and how hard those are. Connor and Maddie let me do that.

To my readers—thank you and I hope you enjoy this one. It truly was a labor of love.